Deborah and Joel Shlian are both physicians who practiced Family Medicine for over ten years before returning to UCLA for MBAs. They have since balanced medical management consulting with writing. They often write together, producing several medical mysteries as well as non-fiction books and numerous magazine and journal articles on health-care and medical management issues. They recently moved from Los Angeles to Boca Raton, Florida.

DOUBLE ILLUSION

Every parent's worst fear is coming true
— someone is kidnapping babies. Someone with icy blue eyes who leaves behind a
blood-red trail of lipstick notes. From
Atlanta to Los Angeles, a young reporter
and the beautiful nurse he loves are
putting each deadly piece of the puzzle
into place. But still the baby snatcher
stalks . . . down a deserted hospital
corridor . . . in a darkened tenement
. . . And with every step Victor and Anne
take towards the truth, a terrifying secret
waits . . .

DEBORAH SHLIAN
AND
JOEL SHLIAN

◆

DOUBLE
ILLUSION

Complete and Unabridged

ULVERSCROFT
Leicester

First published in the
United States of America

First Large Print Edition
published 2002

British Library CIP Data

Shlian, Deborah
    Double illusion.—Large print ed.—
    Ulverscroft large print series: thriller
    1. Suspense fiction
    2. Large type books
    I. Title II. Shlian, Joel
    813.5'4 [F]

    ISBN 0–7089–4715–8

Published by
F. A. Thorpe (Publishing) Ltd.
Anstey, Leicestershire

Set by Words & Graphics Ltd.
Anstey, Leicestershire
Printed and bound in Great Britain by
T. J. International Ltd., Padstow, Cornwall

This book is printed on acid-free paper

Prologue

San Antonio
July 14, 1975

The light above labor room number two blinked. She rose and walked toward it as if in a trance, step by step. 'I don't know . . . ' She paused as if to reconsider. 'I'm not sure . . . '

The night nurse watched, disgusted. The woman was such a ninny. After all the planning, she wanted to back out.

'Please put out that cigarette,' the woman said. 'It makes my head ache.'

She's afraid, the night nurse thought. Well, she'd do it herself. She wasn't afraid of anything.

The light above number two blinked again. The night nurse went inside the sterile room carrying a pail.

Amanda Hodson, nine months pregnant, lay naked and exposed in the labor bed of the brightly lit room.

'How's the little mother coming?'

Spreading the patient's thighs, the nurse noted that the baby's head was very low, well lodged in the birth canal, the cervix dilated

1

almost the full ten centimeters. Smiling to herself, she knew it was almost time.

'I . . . the contractions . . . Every minute.' Amanda took quick, shallow breaths as the contractions began anew. Tiny beads of perspiration covered her forehead and upper lip.

Preoccupied with her pain, she never noticed the colorless liquid the nurse injected into her intravenous line. Soon she felt an overwhelming desire to close her eyes. 'Did you call Dr. Van Patten?'

'Don't worry, honey. We'll call him when we need him. Now come on. One more push and you can go to sleep.'

Amanda barely understood the words. They seemed to echo through a tunnel.

With the next contraction, a big, blood-smeared head emerged from between Amanda's swollen thighs. The nurse quickly reached for a scalpel and deftly sliced through the vagina, making a long vertical episiotomy like those she had seen performed many times before. She eased her gloved fingers inside, seconds later pulling out a healthy-looking baby girl, howling with gusto.

Massaging the woman's large, stretched-looking abdominal mound, she delivered the placenta with its white, yellow, and blue umbilical cord, thick and gelatinous in the bright light. She cut the cord, and blood spurted halfway across the room. Her heart beat with excitement. She was thoroughly enjoying this drama.

From the pail, she pulled a foul-smelling male fetus weighing less than four pounds. It had been dead at least three days, but that couldn't be helped. Tonight was the first opportunity the nurse had had to carry out her plan. She scooped the fresh placenta into the bucket, planning to discard it later and placed the dead fetus between Amanda's legs. Someone would wake this poor mother and explain that she had delivered a stillborn son. These things happened all the time. She would probably be pregnant again in no time.

Just before leaving the room, the nurse dropped a note on the pillow. A message for the little mother.

She emerged from the labor room, carrying the pink baby girl wrapped tightly in a blanket.

'Here she is — the kid you always wanted.'

The other woman cradled the baby in her arms — a dazed look in her eyes.

'It's unbelievable how easy it was,' the nurse said. 'I might just go into the baby business.' She felt triumphant. 'Oh, and don't thank me. Just forget this — and I mean

3

everything. Understand?' The tone was menacing.

The other woman nodded vaguely.

'*Everything*'

Footsteps invaded the silence.

'Damn, I'd better get out of here.' The nurse grabbed her cape. 'Hey, smile. We've just had our baby!'

Moments later, a hooded figure carrying a small bundle emerged from the side of the hospital and hurried off into the night.

Houston
July 24, 1978

Janet Evans stirred beside her husband Bill, who had just started to fall asleep. She lay on her side, long dark hair cascading over his bare chest. Kissing his ear, she snuggled closer, her warm breath caressing his face.

'Are you asleep?' she whispered.

He opened his eyes, sliding his hand over her full breasts, which almost spilled out of her silk nightie.

'Um.' One warm leg slid over his. He felt her nipples rise as he ran his fingers lightly over her breasts again.

'I've missed you,' he murmured. 'Are you sure it's okay?'

'The baby's almost three weeks old.'

'I thought the doctor said we had to wait six weeks. Don't want to damage the merchandise.'

'Doctors don't know everything. Besides, you didn't wait this long after Jason was born.'

'Two years ago we both were a whole lot younger,' he said with little conviction.

'Shut up and come here.' She silenced him with a long, lingering kiss.

A piercing wail from down the hall. Pulling away from his embrace, Janet sat up in bed. 'I'd better pick her up.'

'Can't you let her cry for a minute? You're going to spoil her.'

'She'll wake Jason.' Leaning over her husband, Janet kissed him lightly on the mouth. 'I'll just be a second. Then we'll pick up where we left off.' As much to herself as to Bill, she continued, 'I'd better check Jason first. Make sure he hasn't smothered in his Linus blanket. We've got to wean him away from that thing.'

'He's *your* son.' Bill teased. From the bed he watched appreciatively as Janet pulled on a robe and headed for Jason's room. He took the last cigarette from a crumpled pack on the nightstand, lit it, and inhaled deeply. A moment later, the baby's crying stopped

5

— probably because Janet was rocking her back to dreamland. She really spoiled that kid, he thought sleepily.

He wasn't sure how much time had passed when the night-time quiet was shattered by a blood-curdling shriek he would never forget. Janet was screaming the baby's name over and over: 'Justine! Justine!' Bill didn't bother to put on a robe. He ran naked down the hall to his daughter's room.

The coverlet was pulled back, and three-week-old Justine was not in her crib. The mattress appeared unusually large and white, and he could still make out the imprint of her tiny body on the mattress. Near the open window his wife stood, whimpering, her eyes wide, staring vacantly.

Taking her by the shoulders, Bill shook her frantically. 'Janet, where's the baby? What happened?'

It was no use. Her lips formed words, but no sound came. He noticed an envelope clutched in her hand and took it. Removing a handwritten note, he read the words scrawled in red lipstick, but didn't comprehend their meaning — 'Eye for eye.'

His mind reeled, rejecting the seeming finality of the message. He felt a ghastly hollowness deep in his gut, the sickening sensation of teetering on a high wire with only infinite darkness below. Someone had taken their baby. Why, dear God?

Turning back to Janet, now obviously in shock, he watched with a kind of bizarre fascination as her body trembled, and finally she fell in a swoon at his feet.

When she regained consciousness, Janet could not describe the figure in the hood. The room had been too dark, and she'd had only a fleeting look as she ran to the window and watched the stranger carry her baby daughter off into the night.

There was one instant when the stranger turned and stared back at her. Janet knew that as long as she lived, she would never forget the torment she saw in those eyes.

Atlanta, Georgia
June 28, 1981

Timothy Hill's rhythmic rocking back and forth on the playground's wooden pony was hypnotic, and his mother, watching the three-year-old with an expressionless gaze, soon felt her eyelids grow heavy. The child's motion, coupled with the soothing warmth of the Georgia sun overhead, was anesthetic.

Drifting off to sleep, she didn't see the hooded figure in the distance or hear the footsteps creeping nearer. Only a frightened cry from her newborn infant in the carriage beside her aroused her to a level of drowsy consciousness.

'Timothy, it's time to go home,' she called, her eyes still shut tight.

'In a minute,' replied the energetic three-year-old. 'I'm not finished playing.'

She smiled to herself, yawning and stretching languorously, savoring the feeling of relaxation. She would see to the baby — just one more minute. She didn't want the day to end, either.

'Mommy, where's Shannon?'

The young mother's heart skittered. 'What?' she cried, suddenly at full attention, her eyes wide open. Timothy was peering into the baby carriage. *My God!* It was empty!

Even as she ran frantically around the playground, she knew. It was just like the time they had called to say that her dad was dead, she had known. But she denied the reality.

Exhausted, she stopped, her mind processing the truth she couldn't accept — Shannon, her baby, was gone!

1

Los Angeles
July 7, 1981
Tuesday

The line barely moved. It coiled around the outpatient clinic like a snake, its tail lengthening every few minutes.

Here the fluid Spanish accents of the Chicanos fused musically with the rhythmic cadence of the blacks, joined occasionally by the lilting voices of the Asians and Middle Easterners among the women waiting. Most of them were in various stages of pregnancy. The others were older, postmenopausal, shoulders hunched, heads graying.

The small area could barely accommodate the number of patients who, after registering at the front desk, took seats in folding chairs lining the bare walls and began leafing distractedly through outdated issues of *Baby Life* and *Better Homes and Gardens*.

In the tiny nurses' station, two nurses watched with a kind of amused detachment as the line grew longer.

9

'Unreal today,' Stacy Gardner, a twenty-five-year-old nurse, yawned, still sleepy from last night's date. She ran her hand slowly through her thick copper-colored mane. 'You'd almost think we were having a sale.'

Florence Baxter, an unmarried forty-seven-year-old senior RN and ten-year veteran of the Ob-Gyn clinic, shrugged her broad shoulders. 'Same as every morning.'

A plain, big-breasted woman who rarely smiled, Baxter deeply resented pretty girls like Stacy. They were never serious enough about nursing. 'To these patients, L.A.U. is Mecca,' Baxter intoned with genuine reverence. The university medical center was Florence Baxter's whole life.

'Pardon me,' Stacy whispered sardonically and salaamed, but only after the senior nurse had turned her head. She refused to meet Baxter's reproachful gaze. The senior RN was quite practiced in the art of giving such looks. An exemplary nurse, she never let anything — especially her private life, if she had one — interfere with her work.

Stacy suspected that Baxter simply ceased to exist the minute she left the hospital, melting into a state of nothingness until the clinic reopened the next morning. Maybe Stacy ought to feel sorry for her, but she couldn't. She hated Baxter, and more than

10

anything, she feared becoming like her.

'Next?' a receptionist with a high-pitched voice said to the woman approaching the desk. 'What's your problem?'

The frightened-looking Hispanic woman said nothing.

'Chief complaint?' the woman snapped. 'Why are you here?' Some of these people are *so* dumb, she thought, asking impatiently.

Suddenly the young woman began to sway, destroying the uniform contour of the snake. A big-boned black woman wearing an African headdress stepped aside to give the dizzy woman more room. The receptionist stared at her in disapproval. 'What are you doing out of line? I haven't processed your forms yet.'

'Christ, this mutha's bleedin'.' The woman pointed disgustedly at blood dribbling down the trembling patient's leg and coalescing in a puddle on the floor.

'Move back. Everyone move back,' a blond nurse ordered the crowd. She grabbed the stricken woman's wrist, checking her pulse as she shot questions at her in rapid-fire Spanish. 'When was your last period?'

'It has been two months,' she responded.

'When did you start bleeding?'

'*Hoy.*'

'Today, okay. Do you feel any pain?'

'*Sí.*'

11

'*Dónde le duele?*' the nurse asked. 'Where does it hurt?'

The bleeding woman pointed frantically to her abdomen. 'Here,' she wailed in Spanish.

The nurse nodded in response. '*Sí.*'

'Who the hell is that woman?' Baxter demanded, storming out of the nurses' station. Stacy followed close at her heels.

'I forgot to tell you, Miss Baxter. The supervisor's office called earlier to say they were sending up a new part-time RN. But she's just temporary: Tuesdays and Thursdays only. Her name's Marie Fontaine. She's from Atlanta, I think.'

'Terrific,' Baxter groaned.

'I thought you'd be thrilled,' Stacy said, still shadowing her. 'Heaven knows we're overworked and understaffed.'

Baxter shook her head, annoyed. 'Seems I'm the last to know about anything around here. Dare I ask what happened to Gloria?'

'Her husband wanted her home with the kids. Made her quit. Can you believe that kind of attitude? In this day and age? Harv's a real male chauvinist pig.'

But Baxter was no longer listening to Stacy. She had elbowed her way through the gawking crowd and now stood near the new nurse who was still questioning the patient.

'*No se preocupe.* Don't worry. You'll be

fine. We'll take care of you.'

Marie grabbed a gurney and was helping the woman up when Baxter angrily interrupted. 'May I ask just what you think you're doing?'

'Probable incomplete AB. She'll need a D and C, stat,' Marie addressed the senior RN with an air of authority, momentarily putting her off.

'What the — ' Baxter's mouth gaped wide in shock and disbelief. Like the army, hospital staffs have a definite hierarchy. Everyone knows that. This new nurse was flouting that tradition with her take-charge attitude. In all her years of nursing, Florence Baxter had never seen anything like this.

For the first time, she took a good look at Marie Fontaine. It was impossible to guess her age. Marie had the kind of face that seemed ageless. She could be as young as twenty, or she could be in her thirties. Her efficient manner caused Baxter to assume that she was older.

And she was quite pretty actually, although she wore too much makeup for the senior nurse's simple taste. Her short, curly blond hair was too brassy, and her painted lips were full and sensuous. Her heavily rouged cheeks hid a clear, creamy complexion, and her powdered nose was small and straight. The cloying scent of cheap perfume hung in the air. But it was her eyes, darkly outlined and shadowed with blue-green powder, that Baxter noticed. They disturbed her; they were piercing blue-gray chips of ice.

Marie's makeup may have raised an eyebrow or two, but her demeanor defied criticism. Her coolness, her air of assumed and unquestioned superiority both irritated and intrigued Baxter.

'Don't just stand there catching flies,' Marie barked at her. 'We need a liter of half-normal saline.'

Baxter hesitated. Embarrassed by Marie's power play, she didn't want to make it worse by doing her bidding. Still, Marie was obviously adept at handling emergencies. The symptoms certainly suggested a miscarriage. No time to argue now.

She'd be damned if she'd show her true feelings in front of this crowd. No, Baxter would handle Marie later. 'Miss Gardner, get the I.V. tray.' She tried to recover her authority.

Marie called after Stacy. 'We'll need to type and crossmatch two units.'

Upstaged again, Baxter pursed her thin lips. 'And bring me a couple of syringes.' Turning to the receptionist, who was clearly enjoying the drama, she snarled, 'What are

14

you staring at? Let's get the rest of these patients checked in. We've got a clinic to run.'

Marie was now expertly inserting an intravenous line.

'Shall I page the doctor on call?' Stacy looked first at Marie and then Baxter, the priority not lost on the senior nurse.

'There's no time,' Marie snapped. 'BP's already down to ninety over fifty. She'd be in shock before he got here.'

Marie leveled her slate-blue eyes at the chief nurse. 'I'm sure Miss Baxter will want to take her patient to the emergency room for admission.'

Marie's calculated gesture of courtesy mollified Baxter. 'Miss Fontaine,' she said, 'I want you to help Stacy run the clinic while I'm gone. She'll get you started. I'll orient you later.'

'Why, thank you, ma'am.' Marie's soft southern accent became as thick as molasses. 'I'm sure I'm going to enjoy working with you.' The lightest suggestion of a smirk momentarily touched her lips, which she parted to show very white, very even teeth.

As Baxter wheeled her patient out of sight, Stacy sighed theatrically. 'Jesus, she can really be a b-i-t-c-h sometimes. The last nurse, Gloria Walker, couldn't get along with Baxter at all. She quit. I don't really know why I take

15

her crap.' Stacy paused, searching unsuccessfully for a transition. 'That was some smart move giving Baxter credit for your quick thinking. I bet she'll be eating out of your hand from now on.'

Marie winked. 'Why, Miss Melanie, ah don't know *what* you could be talkin' about.' She did a perfect Scarlett O'Hara, gesturing with long, elegantly manicured fingers.

Stacy giggled. 'Well, I was impressed. You really know your stuff.'

Marie affected a modest pose. 'Oh, that was nothing. In Texas I ran a whole obstetrics ward, and I've done more than one delivery when a resident was stuck in the sack.' She laughed to herself, enjoying some personal joke.

Stacy checked her watch. 'Speaking of tired residents, Frank — I mean, Dr. Morgan — is late for clinic. Baxter will have his ass.'

'He your boyfriend?'

'Not really. We've been out a couple times. That's all.'

'If you're smart,' Marie advised, 'you'll stay away from doctors.' The smile rippled off her face.

'How come?'

'Can't trust 'em.'

'Oh, Frank's okay.'

Marie glared at Stacy, her steel-blue eyes

narrowed to slits, her face turned to stone. 'Believe me, they're all the same. No damn good. Every last one of 'em.'

Surprised by Marie's sudden change in mood, Stacy wondered what in her past had made her so bitter.

'Let's get some of these patients in the examining rooms,' Marie spoke a moment later, her hostility quickly forgotten. 'From now on, honey, things are definitely going to be different around here.'

Los Angeles
July 7, 1981
Tuesday

Janet Evans wanted to scream, but no sound emerged. All her responses were dulled by antidepressants.

She saw her! In the rearview mirror! Janet was certain. She'd seen those eyes before. The kidnapper had had the same tormented eyes. Since the night Justine was taken, those eyes had haunted her. Now, she saw them staring everywhere. Staring at her. But she *had* really seen them this time — now.

Where was Bill? She had seen him enter the brick building, but she couldn't remember why he had brought her here. It was

17

probably another hospital. That's right, she thought — another insane asylum. Was she crazy? Bill thought so. The child had been gone three years now. That's how long it had taken her to finally fall apart.

Janet's personality had always comprised some elements of insanity, but for most of her thirty-two years she had been able to maintain madness and sanity in a very delicate balance. In fact, it had been this vulnerable sensitivity that many young men, including her husband Bill, had once found so attractive.

Bill left her in the car to register her. She was getting used to the routine; it was like checking into a hotel. The only difference was that in every city, there was another doctor. When would she get well? Maybe never. It was so much safer inside her self-made cocoon.

How much more could she take? Her tragedy was God's punishment, she knew. Just as the kidnapper's note had said: 'Eye for eye.' She was paying for her sins. First Justine had been kidnapped. Then Jason had died of pneumonia eighteen months ago.

She would never replace them. Bill wanted to try for more babies. He thought it might snap her out of her depression. What did men know?

Bill opened the car door and reached in for her. 'Come on, Janet. I want you to meet Dr. Westbourne. She's the psychiatrist I was telling you about. She's going to help you get well.'

Janet appraised the woman standing on the sidewalk with Bill. In her horn-rimmed glasses and conservative tweed suit, Dr. Olivia Westbourne did not appear clinical and distant, like most psychiatrists. She was around forty, but she appeared younger. She had a nice figure, generous mouth, short auburn hair, and kind hazel eyes. The eyes were very important.

Janet's tongue felt like marshmallow, and the tranquilizers she had taken made her speech slurred. Never mind. She had to tell them. 'I saw the eyes again. Here. In the mirror.'

Bill peered in as his wife frantically pointed to the rearview mirror. Except for his own reflection, he saw nothing. Bill tried not to appear annoyed, but he'd been through this so many times before. 'Of course, Jan. It's okay now. Nobody's there.'

Why didn't he believe her? 'We've got to tell Gus.' The words tumbled out in slow motion.

'Gus is dead, honey. Don't you remember? He died two months ago.'

19

Exasperated, Bill turned to Dr. Westbourne. 'I'm sorry, Doctor, but this is what I was telling you. She's obsessed. She thinks she'll find the person who took Justine.' He clenched his fists in frustration. 'She saw only the woman's eyes that night. The woman was cloaked and hooded, and it was dark. We're not even sure it *was* a woman.'

'Who was Gus?' the psychiatrist asked.

'Gus Larsen. One of the police detectives. He stayed on the case long after everybody else gave up.'

Dr. Westbourne sensed reproof in Bill's voice. 'You wanted Gus to give up, too?'

Bill's face tightened. 'I know Gus meant well, but he kept encouraging Janet, telling her he would find Justine safe and sound. They called each other at least once a day for three years.'

'You said Gus died?'

'Yes, in May he had a sudden heart attack. After his death, Janet retreated even deeper inside herself. She hardly says one word now except when she thinks she sees that damned woman's eyes.'

The psychiatrist noted the anxious expression on Bill's handsome face. 'This tragedy has really taken its toll on you, hasn't it, Mr. Evans?'

'Yes, it has. I feel worn out. I can't

communicate with Janet anymore. She doesn't talk to me . . . '

Bill felt a growing sense of detachment, as though he were talking about two other people instead of himself and his wife. 'You're really our last hope, Dr. Westbourne. Janet doesn't seem to be getting any better.'

'Mr. Evans, has it occurred to you that maybe therapy could help you too?'

'What do you mean?'

Olivia spoke with studied neutrality. 'Often when one member of a family is having emotional problems, others are affected as well — if for no other reason than that it's difficult to live with someone who's disturbed.'

Bill was surprised to hear the psychiatrist speak so freely in front of Janet. 'And you think *I'm* developing problems?' he asked, incredulous.

'Are you?' She tossed the question back to him.

'Look, Doctor. I'm a very busy man. I don't have time to spend on this' — he searched for a better word than *nonsense* — 'this therapy. If you can help Janet, I'll be very grateful.'

Dr. Westbourne didn't press further. 'I believe I can help your wife. I've successfully treated several patients with similar problems.

Now,' she said, leaning inside the car where Janet still sat, stiff and silent, staring blankly ahead, 'let's get you settled in, Mrs. Evans.'

'I think you'll need a wheelchair,' Bill explained. 'She doesn't walk.'

'Don't worry,' the psychiatrist said. 'Janet, I'm going to take your hand, and I want you to come inside with me.'

Bill was surprised to see his wife follow the command. Her movements were stiff and puppetlike. Still, the doctor had persuaded her to walk. My God, how far we have come, he thought bitterly, to be grateful that Janet would follow such a simple direction.

It had rained earlier — unusual for July — but now the sky was clear, the air clean. White-coated interns and residents walked briskly in and out of the imposing brick edifice. Like the Mad Hatter, Janet thought — late for a very important date.

Dr. Westbourne pushed open the heavy glass door and led her into a huge foyer not unlike the entrance to an elegant estate. Janet was oblivious to the Impressionist paintings on the walls and the obviously expensive Persian rugs scattered haphazardly around the large open area. Still, Dr. Westbourne insisted on giving her the full tour. She explained that the Institute had a worldwide reputation. Consequently, it attracted the best staff and the wealthiest patients who often gave large donations after they were discharged.

'Here, on the first floor, and upstairs on two, is inpatient service. Our care is very personal, and we never have more than twenty-four full-time patients.'

Bill and Janet followed the psychiatrist down a long corridor to a ward. 'This is much more informal than I had imagined,' Bill observed. 'There don't seem to be many guards or locked doors.'

'No, there aren't. We think it's important for our patients not to feel closed in or shut away. And every activity here teaches patients new skills that will help them cope with life on the outside. That's why we try to give them a maximum of responsibility — commensurate with their mental and physical condition, of course.'

Bill interrupted the well-rehearsed introductory speech. 'Doctor, how long do you think Janet will have to stay here?'

'That will depend entirely on Janet,' the psychiatrist replied. 'The shortest possible hospitalization is not really what we're after. We want to see a permanent change in her behavior, Mr. Evans. You can't rush this process.' Her voice was firm.

'I didn't mean to imply — ' Bill started,

23

feeling like a child being chastised.

'I understand what you meant. We all want what's best for your wife. Now, Janet,' Dr. Westbourne said, turning her attention to her new patient, 'this is where you'll live.' She selected a bed at the end of a row of similar beds. 'Naturally, we have certain rules here, but I don't think you'll find them too restrictive. You'll get your own orientation program this afternoon.'

As Bill and the doctor continued to talk, Janet stared vacantly at a set of double doors on the opposite side of the ward. Suddenly, she saw a pair of eyes looking back at her through the glass. They were *her* eyes! The hysteria Janet had been holding back now swept over her. Her mouth opened, and the scream that had been struggling in her throat burst forth.

The sound seemed to ricochet off the walls of the empty ward as it tore out of the terrified woman.

Bill and the psychiatrist rushed over. Pointing to the doors, Janet kept repeating, 'The eyes, the eyes,' over and over. Was her mind playing tricks on her? The eyes seemed to grow larger as she watched. Then, suddenly, they disappeared.

Her anguished cries rose to a hysterical pitch. Within seconds, two white-coated attendants grabbed her arms and held her down on the bed.

'Get me fifty milligrams of Thorazine, stat!' Dr. Westbourne said to a nurse.

The injection had an instantaneous effect. Janet lay like a rag doll, arms and legs at odd angles. Her eyes, once deep indigo pools, were now dull and empty. Her long dark hair fell across her face, but she was too sedated to brush it away.

'She'll be all right,' Dr. Westbourne reassured Bill. 'It's probably just the excitement and the unfamiliar environment.'

'What's on the other side of those double doors?' Bill asked, wondering if there was something behind them that could have set Janet off.

'The obstetrics clinic. The general hospital building is connected to the Institute. Those doors are always locked, though. We wouldn't want our patients to wander off. It's easy to get lost around here.'

After Janet was settled in, sleeping peacefully, Bill still felt uneasy. Janet was going to be safe here, wasn't she? Of course she was. Perhaps Dr. Westbourne was right; it *was* all getting to him. He felt an overwhelming urge to get out of this claustrophobic place and back to normalcy.

Not more than fifteen minutes after

excusing himself abruptly, Bill Evans was speeding south on the San Diego Freeway toward the Los Angeles airport, leaving Janet to the ministrations of Dr. Westbourne and her staff.

July 7, 1981
Tuesday

Inside the Ob-Gyn clinic, just beyond the double doors, Marie took one last puff of her cigarette before dropping the butt on the floor and crushing it under her foot.

'Sometimes I think they put the loony ward right next door so we won't have far to go when we crack up.'

Marie wheeled around, unaware that Stacy had come up behind her. 'What?'

Stacy laughed. 'Working here can drive you nuts,' she said.

'Oh, it's not so bad,' Marie said a little too sweetly.

Stacy rolled her eyes. 'You've only been here a few hours. Give yourself time.'

'Hey, could someone give me a hand with a pelvic?' A tall, white-coated young man stood in the doorway of an examining room.

Stacy sighed. 'See what I mean? If it's not Baxter, it's some resident on your back. It never stops around here.'

'Hey, I need some help.'

'Coming, Doctor.' Stacy smiled at Marie. 'At least this one's cute. See you later.'

'Sure, honey.' Stupid cunt, Marie thought as she watched Stacy walk away.

At the front desk, the receptionist was talking to Juanita Hernandez about her appointment.

'I'm sorry, miss.' The receptionist did not seem sorry at all, but then, Juanita did not understand the subtle nuances of English. The convent school in Mexico had taught only the basics.

'Dr. Van Patten can't see you today. There's a question about your eligibility for MediCal. Why don't you go over to the business office and show them your identification? When your forms are approved, come back. We'll reschedule you.'

The Mexican girl only nodded, turning away quickly. She didn't want the receptionist to see her tears. It was no use, she knew. Without a green card, she'd never get the care she needed for her baby.

Patting her oversized belly, she whispered, 'It's okay, *mi amorcito*,' and started down the corridor toward the exit. At almost eight months, her pregnancy made her gait unsteady.

A simple girl from Pitiquito, Mexico, Juanita was barely eighteen years old, the child of a laborer and a seamstress. Until her untimely pregnancy, her horizons had extended only from her parents' tiny adobe home to the church down the street where she dutifully went to mass and confession. An unwed mother did not fit into her parents' strict Catholic view of life, and so she'd had no choice but to leave home in disgrace. Like so many before her, she had come to Los Angeles looking for a better life.

Now, living in a dirty efficiency apartment in East Los Angeles, paid for with the last few pesos she had stolen from her father, she was desperate. She hoped the hospital would take care of her, but even they wanted money. If only she had money. Tears fell slowly from her eyes, wetting her cheeks as she walked out of the clinic. What was she going to do?

She was only vaguely aware of someone following her until a blond nurse fell into stride beside her.

'A little bad luck, huh?'

Juanita wasn't eager to start a conversation, but the woman persisted.

'My name's Marie Fontaine. Fontaine's French, like my father.'

Juanita nodded indifferently.

'I see you're in the family way.' Marie pointed to the girl's protruding abdomen. 'Makes it kinda hard to walk like normal people.' Her laughter had a certain infectious quality, and Juanita found herself laughing, too.

'What's your name, honey?' Marie asked, smiling, her voice a soft, sensuous purr.

'Juanita Hernandez.'

'Juanita.' The syllables rolled off Marie's tongue. 'That's a beautiful name. You know, I think we're going to be great friends.'

Marie didn't tell Juanita that theirs was no chance meeting, that she had watched the Mexican girl standing alone, nervously waiting her turn in line. Juanita had short, mousy brown hair, a complexion marred by acne scars, and large brown eyes that revealed a sadness and vulnerability that were especially intriguing to Marie.

'I heard the receptionist say you didn't have insurance. You just came from Mexico, didn't you?'

Juanita didn't answer.

'I'll bet you don't have a green card, either. Am I right?'

Silence. Suddenly the girl was frightened. What did this woman want from her?

Sensing her fear, Marie reassured her. 'Don't worry, honey. I won't make any

29

trouble with Immigration. I said I was your friend, didn't I?'

Juanita felt her defenses weaken. 'You can help me?'

'Maybe. Do you have a job?'

Juanita shook her head. 'No more. I worked in a factory downtown, sewing dresses. The heat made me sick. My boss sent me home. He says I can't work there anymore.'

'Jesus, they'd let a poor girl starve, wouldn't they?' Marie eyed the gold cross that hung between Juanita's swollen breasts. 'You're not one of those religious freaks, are you?'

'*Sí*. Catholic.'

Marie appraised her for a long moment. 'Well, never mind. First let's find you some work. There must be something on campus that pays well but isn't too strenuous.'

Farther down the corridor a bulletin board listed available jobs.

'Hey, here's something for a nurse.' Marie pointed to an ad for a part-time position.

'A nurse?'

Marie stared blankly for a second, then, struck by the absurdity of her suggestion, threw back her head and laughed. 'Well, we'll just have to find something else, won't we?'

Marie looked over the board again, finding

nothing suitable for someone like Juanita.

'Look, I've got an idea,' Marie said. 'I'll ask around for a job for you. It'll take a couple of days. Then we'll meet for dinner. Say Thursday.'

Juanita demurred, unaccustomed to such impulsive behavior.

'Come on,' Marie pleaded. 'I want to help you. You need a friend in this town. It's too big for a little thing like you.' She laughed again. 'Now here's where we'll meet.' She hurriedly wrote down the name of Gusty's and an address on Sixth Street. 'I'll see you there Thursday at five o'clock sharp. We'll have a long chat and a bite to eat. Okay?'

Juanita looked worried. She had very little money — too little to squander on restaurant food.

Marie saw her hesitation. 'Honey, it'll be my treat,' she said, patting Juanita's arm. 'Now go home and get some rest. You've got to start taking better care of your baby. I'll see you soon.'

'Okay.' Juanita began to relax for the first time since they had started talking. Marie was certainly a hard woman to turn down. The nurse was so enthusiastic and persuasive that the Mexican girl found herself almost mesmerized. Besides, she rationalized, she had to trust *someone*.

31

2

July 8, 1981
Wednesday

Anne Midlands was uncomfortable under Dr. Westbourne's penetrating gaze. She knew she had no reason to feel self-conscious in front of the kind psychiatrist, but she did.

'Tell me, why do you want to work in a psychiatric hospital?' the doctor asked.

That's odd, Anne thought. Why, indeed? She really was becoming scatterbrained lately. She wasn't even sure how she'd found out about this position. Maybe the psychiatrist wouldn't ask.

Not that she didn't have good reason for being a little disconnected — a new city, new faces, and so many job interviews. They all melded together in her mind.

Besides, today had started off all wrong. She'd overslept and had to run all the way from the bus stop to L.A. University. When she arrived, she was told that the job in the main hospital had just been filled.

With nothing to do, she had wandered around campus, enjoying the air left crisp and

32

crystalline after the morning's rain. It reminded her of home — the East Texas desert. She loved Texas best after the rains. The sharp, pungent odor of wet greasewood plants. It was oddly exciting.

As she thought back to her walk around the campus, she remembered how she'd found out about the opening at the Institute. The ad for the job had fallen from her purse when she pulled out a handkerchief. A collector of sorts, Anne often saved clippings from newspapers and magazines. She must have clipped out the classified ad for this job and then forgotten about it.

Anne wasn't sure she wanted to work on a psychiatric ward, but she certainly needed a job. After all, she had to eat, and the rent on her apartment was due next week. Everything was so expensive in Los Angeles. Besides, this job had to be more challenging than those temporary positions. Dr. Westbourne certainly seemed nice enough. So why was Anne so nervous?

Sitting rigid and tense in the high-backed chair facing the psychiatrist, Anne looked like a fragile china doll, although she was a willowy brunette and stood about five feet six. She had a creamy complexion and a straight nose that neatly balanced a pair of dainty plastic-rimmed eyeglasses. She looked vulnerable and much younger than her twenty-eight years.

Shy, formally dressed in a conservative cotton skirt and blouse, Anne sat with her feet close together and cleared her throat, trying desperately to think of a good answer to the doctor's question. Why *did* she want to work there? She focused on the brocade-curtained window behind the psychiatrist's desk.

'Well, I, uh, feel I work well with people, and uh . . . ' How stupid she must sound, Anne thought hopelessly. Her head began to throb. She wanted to change her position in the chair, but, meticulous to a fault, she was afraid of wrinkling her skirt.

She removed her glasses and rubbed her eyes. Opening them again, she thought she saw something in the window; it was the reflection of someone staring at her. She blinked, and the image was gone. I must be tired, she thought, pushing the plastic frames back on her nose.

'Have you had any experience in psychiatry?' the doctor asked, bringing her back to reality.

'I have my RN license and I rotated through almost every department in the general hospital back home.' She frowned, struggling with a thought. 'Years ago I did work in a small mental hospital in Texas.'

Suddenly, Anne looked at Dr. Westbourne, deciding this was all pointless.

'I'm sorry, Doctor. I haven't been entirely honest with you.'

'Oh? How so?'

Anne explained that she was new in town and had been hoping to find a job in the general hospital. This position at the Institute was really her second choice. 'I'm afraid I'm quite desperate,' she confessed. 'If I don't find a job this week, I don't know how I'm going to pay my rent.'

Listening to Anne's soft, well-modulated voice, Dr. Westbourne was taken with this pretty, unassuming young woman. She had an air of quiet dignity, and her face was intriguing, with its expression of contained sadness. What kind of unhappiness had painted that look in her eyes?

'May I call you Anne?' Olivia asked.

'Yes, of course.'

'I appreciate your honesty, Anne. That's a rare quality in anyone these days. And I'll be frank with you; we lost one of our best nurses this week. I'm really desperate for a replacement. You sound like a godsend.' She smiled as Anne wiped her forehead gingerly with a freshly laundered handkerchief. 'Could you start on Friday?'

Surprised, Anne exhaled a long-held rush of air. 'Of course.'

Olivia was touched. This young woman must really want the job.

'Ordinarily we would require references right away, but I have a good feeling about you. Have them sent in the next few weeks. I'll waive the rules in your case.'

The trace of a smile softened Anne's normally sad expression. 'That's wonderful.'

The psychiatrist stood up and extended her hand. 'Okay, Anne, welcome to the Institute. One of our senior RNs will give you a proper tour of the facility and introduce you to your patients. You'll work on ward number one.'

'Thank you, Dr. Westbourne. I'll try to do a good job.'

'I'm sure you will, my dear.'

As Anne got up to leave, she thought she caught a glimpse of that same fleeting image in the window. It was crazy. Yet, she couldn't shake the feeling that someone was watching her.

3

July 9, 1981
Thursday

Everything about Mark Van Patten was serious, from the deep worry lines on his chiseled face and the slow, deliberate way he spoke, to the conservative cut of his Brooks Brothers clothes. He'd put all his energies for the past fifteen years into medicine, leaving nothing over for personality or charm. At thirty-seven, he was a rather dull human being, but a brilliant doctor.

Another routine morning with a full load of clinic patients. This one was his last, thank God. Then he'd have to hightail it over to the operating room. He had to perform two hysterectomies before grand rounds at six. He wouldn't have time for lunch.

Marie studied his face as he examined the young girl, probing and palpating as she lay on the examining table, her heels in the stirrups, her pregnant body modestly draped with a sheet.

'When was your last period?'

The girl's voice was shaky. She looked no

more than sixteen, with dark hair, small bones, and large doe eyes swollen from crying. 'Around the middle of March, I guess. I'm not exactly sure.'

Van Patten shook his head. 'I think your dates are off. You seem much farther along than four months.'

'Would you like a real-time B scan, Doctor?'

The obstetrician looked up. 'I beg your pardon?'

Marie smiled. 'Real time ultrasound. To assess gestational age.'

He looked at Marie closely for a second. There was something oddly familiar about her. He wondered where he had seen her before. He was about to ask, then dismissed the subject with a shrug. He had never been good at remembering faces.

'Shall I order the test?' she asked, interrupting his thoughts.

'What? Oh, yes, thank you.'

'What are you going to do?' the girl moaned. 'Will it hurt?'

Van Patten was exasperated. Sixteen-year-old babies having babies.

'You're late for the O.R., Doctor. I'll explain everything to her. When the test is completed, I'll reschedule her with you.'

Grateful, Van Patten peeled off his latex

gloves, quickly washed his hands, and left the room, reminding himself to compliment Miss Baxter on her efficient staff.

Alone with the patient, Marie flipped open her chart. 'Glynnis McCombie. That's pretty name.'

'Are you a doctor?' the girl asked anxiously. 'I'm glad you're a woman.'

Marie figured the girl's flat 'a' to be from somewhere in the Midwest, probably Kansas.

'I'm a nurse. My name's Marie Fontaine.'

Glynnis offered a thin smile. 'Hi.'

Fixing her eyes on the girl's swollen belly, Marie asked, 'Six months, right?'

The girl nodded, her face dissolving into silent tears. 'I thought it might be too late for an abortion if I told the truth.'

'You're a long way from home, aren't you?'

'Yeah, Ypsilanti, Michigan. Until a couple weeks ago you couldn't tell I was pregnant. Everyone just thought I was getting fat. My parents would kill me if they knew I got knocked up.' Her eyes glistened. 'I only did it once. Honest. My boy-friend said the first time was safe.' She was crying openly now. 'Why does everything always happen to me? I can't do anything right.' She looked at Marie, pleading, 'You won't tell anyone, will you?'

Marie smiled sympathetically. 'Of course not. Do you have a place to live?'

'Friend of a friend has a small apartment in Hollywood. He's out of town for a few months. Said I could stay as long as I wanted. I figured I'd come to L.A.U., have the abortion, and go home.'

Marie patted the girl's abdomen maternally. 'You wouldn't want to lose this baby. It's going to be beautiful.'

'What makes you so sure?' Glynnis sniffled, her mouth trembling slightly.

'I know.'

'I'm so afraid. What am I going to do?'

'Now, don't you worry, honey. I'm going to take care of you. From now on, you just depend on me.'

July 9, 1981
Thursday

He was not handsome in the classic sense, but he was good-looking in his own way. His face was definitely attractive, and his violet eyes, well-formed mouth, strong jawline, and thick waves of sandy hair all added to his appeal.

Victor Larsen was appealing, he was also single-minded. He never doubted that someday — someday soon — he would become a famous investigative reporter, maybe even as

40

famous as Woodward and Bernstein. He just needed the Big Story. Never mind that at twenty-eight, with only two years of news-writing experience, he was still a relative newcomer to the business. Since coming to work for the *L.A. Tribune* he'd done little more than a few feature pieces — celebrity profiles, charity drive stories, movie premiere coverage. But that didn't matter.

Two months ago he had arrived in L.A., fresh from the *Houston Journal* full of bright hopes and ambitions. He had rented a small apartment in West Hollywood near the Strip and awaited his destiny. Others in his position might have been less self-assured, but not Victor Larsen. Lack of confidence wasn't his style. He knew his big break was just around the corner; all he had to do was grab it.

Sitting in the busy newsroom, papers strewn across his desk, he checked the assignment sheet for the day. Shit, *another* feature — this time about slum landlords. Jesus, when was McFadden going to give him something he could really sink his teeth into?

He was about to ask the news editor for another story when his eye caught something just coming over the wire service: 'The mother of two-week-old Shannon Hill, kidnapped last week from an Atlanta playground, received a strange note . . . ' He read farther. ' 'Tooth for tooth,' written in red lipstick. Police have discounted any connection to the kidnapper . . . ' Victor's pulse quickened. Oh, God, he thought, that's not true. There is a connection. Dad. Janet Evans. Only her note had said, 'Eye for eye.' This wasn't a coincidence; it couldn't be.

Striding over to the editor's desk, he cleared his throat to get McFadden's attention. 'Harmon, I'd like to talk to you.'

'Yeah, what is it?' McFadden returned dryly, flicking an ash from his cigar into his half-empty coffee cup without looking up from the notes he was making.

'I think I may have an angle on the Shannon Hill kidnapping.'

'Yeah?' McFadden's tone was patronizing.

'The story on the wire service says Mrs. Hill received a crazy note.'

'What'd it say?' McFadden asked impatiently.

'Only three words: 'Tooth for tooth.' '

'So?'

'Well, about three years ago a baby was kidnapped in Houston. Her name was Justine Evans, and her mother also got a note like that, only it said 'Eye for eye.' '

'And . . . ?'

'And that's it. I think the kidnapper could be the same person.'

McFadden looked up at Victor, annoyed. 'You've got to be kidding. That's pure speculation. How can you relate two separate kidnappings in two different cities three years apart?'

'But it'll be a hell of a story if it's true, won't it?'

'*If* it's true. But we don't invent news around here; we report it.' McFadden began reading over his notes, indicating that the audience was over, but Victor continued to hover. Finally the editor looked up. He put on his best sardonic smile.

'Look, Larsen, children get kidnapped every day. Do you think the same person is responsible for all of those as well?'

'Of course not.' Victor was angry. 'Listen, my father, Gus Larsen, was the police detective assigned to the Evans case. He spent practically every free moment of the last three years of his life looking for that little girl. He never even found a trace.'

'That's all the more reason to believe you're not dealing with the same perpetrator.'

'I don't understand.'

'*Because*, my boy, if it's the same person, why'd he wait three years to do it again?'

'Maybe he didn't.'

'What?'

'Maybe there were other kidnappings in

between that we just don't know about.'

'Larsen, give it up.' McFadden waved his cigar in the air like a conductor's baton. 'There is no connection and there will never be a connection.'

'That's what I'm trying to explain; there *is* a connection.' Victor looked exasperated. 'The wire service report said that the note Mrs. Hill received was handwritten in red lipstick — just like the one the kidnapper left Mrs. Evans.'

'Doesn't mean a thing. Haven't you ever heard of copycat crimes? Even nuts read the newspapers and — '

Victor interrupted McFadden. 'Suppose I get copies of the notes and prove that the same person wrote both of them?'

'I told you, forget about it. It's too much of a long shot. Why don't you get to work on the story I assigned you today?'

'Slum landlords! What kind of story is that?'

'An important one. Kids die every day because some schmuck in Beverly Hills who owns a rat trap in East Los Angeles didn't bother to keep his building up to code. There's supposed to be a tenants' demonstration at one of the properties' — he checked his notebook — 'on Alvarado this afternoon at five. I want you to be there.'

'Okay, but can I follow up on this lead?'

McFadden shook his head. 'How long you been working on the *Trib*?'

'Two months.'

'And before that?'

'Two years on the *Houston Journal*.' Victor didn't mention the three years he'd spent in New York trying to write the great American novel.

'So what's your hurry?' McFadden assumed an avuncular tone. 'Leave this kidnapping alone, kid. It's not the great story you're hungering after. I've been where you are, Larsen. We all have. But listen to me. Your story will come; give yourself time. Trust me; I know what I'm talking about.'

'Okay,' Victor muttered and slunk back to his desk looking, McFadden thought, defeated. The editor was sorry he'd spoken so harshly to the boy, but he had to set him straight. He'd meant what he said. He'd been an ambitious young reporter once, too. He didn't remember, however, that ambitious young reporters like to go their own way, and he couldn't have known that Victor was thinking out his plan as he sat at his desk.

Oh, Victor would do the landlord story all right, but the first thing tomorrow afternoon he'd hop a plane to Atlanta and have a talk with Mrs. Hill about that note. Victor didn't

45

care if he spent twice what his modest expense account permitted. He'd follow his hunch wherever it led, whatever it cost.

July 9, 1981
Thursday Evening

Gusty's was a typical bar. Its clientele was mixed, like the neighborhood. It drew its share of gays, show business hopefuls and hangers-on, singles, off-duty cops, students, and even bored housewives who stopped in for a drink before their husbands came home from work. Its simplicity was part of its appeal. It had no pizzazz, no gimmicks. Aside from the PacMan game in the corner, it offered nothing more than comfortable booths, pleasant low lighting, a small selection of plain sandwiches chalked on a blackboard in the corner, and good drinks at reasonable prices. It was also a place where nobody asked questions. The philosophy seemed to be, You mind your business, and we'll mind ours.

Juanita slid into a booth facing Marie who was already on her second margarita.

'Glad you found the place.' Marie sat slumped in the seat, affecting a relaxed and casual pose. When two off-duty hard hats

46

walked by, she flashed them a smile, at the same time crossing her legs provocatively so that her short dress edged even farther up over her knees. She hummed a seductive tune, eyes closed, shoulders swaying to the rhythm.

'Can we join you, ladies?' one of the men asked.

Juanita panicked and shot Marie a pleading look that begged her to refuse. Marie shrugged indifferently. It was all the same to her.

'Sorry, boys, we're spoken for. Maybe next time.'

The men left, and Juanita breathed a sigh of relief. She didn't need any more trouble. Marie's suddenly flirtatious manner made her uncomfortable, but she didn't want to offend this strange woman who had befriended her. Besides, it *was* nice to see someone who obviously enjoyed life, she thought, watching Marie move to the beat of the tune she was humming.

'They need a jukebox in this joint,' Marie complained, red lips pouting. She took a long sip of her drink. 'Listen, don't worry about making me miss out with those guys. To tell you the truth, they weren't my type. No class.' She giggled and held up her drink. 'You should have seen the one I tied on a few weeks ago in a little bar on Santa Monica. And no headache the next day,' she boasted.

'That night, I almost picked up this one guy,' she went on. 'He was standing at the bar, see, and I thought he was making goo-goo eyes at me.' Tears of laughter streamed down her rouged cheeks. 'Well, honey, it wasn't *me* this dude wanted. It was the *guy* standing behind me!' Marie was almost hysterical with laughter. 'Can you believe it? The fuckin' guy was a fag!'

Juanita couldn't translate.

'Gay, honey. He was fuckin' gay!' Pulling a pack of cigarettes from her pocket, Marie lit one and took a long drag. 'Can you believe it?' She started to laugh again.

'Isn't that bad for you?' Juanita asked, nodding toward Marie's cigarette.

'What?'

Dr. Van Patten kept saying the same thing over and over: 'Smoking. No smoking, no alcohol, no drugs.'

Marie suddenly lashed out. 'Who the hell asked you?' She gave Juanita a murderous look. 'You're the one who's pregnant, not me. I'll do whatever I damn well please.'

Juanita was caught off guard. A moment ago, Marie had been lighthearted and joking. Her sudden burst of anger frightened the Mexican girl.

'I'm sorry, Marie. I didn't mean to upset you.'

Marie's anger disappeared as quickly as it had erupted. She smiled again.

Juanita tried to change the subject. 'You have a husband?'

'Husband?' Marie laughed. 'No, I'm *Miss* Fontaine, sweetheart. I don't plan to ever settle down and waste my time on just one man. Life's too short, and there are too many fish in the sea.'

Unbidden tears appeared at the corners of the Mexican girl's sad eyes, and a blush of shame crept over her face. 'Like you, I have no husband,' she said. She told Marie how she had had to leave home after discovering her pregnancy. 'José didn't want me. My parents are very religious. They were so ashamed.'

'That's terrible,' Marie sympathized.

'Maybe my child will have a better life.'

A sallow-looking, gum-chewing waitress stopped at their table. 'What can I get you, ladies?'

Juanita looked sheepishly at Marie. 'Just a glass of milk.'

'Nonsense,' Marie declared. 'Two margaritas and a couple of thick jack cheese sandwiches. Oh, and bring the check to me.'

'Sure thing.' The waitress loudly cracked her gum.

'*Gracias*, Marie.'

'I told you this would be my treat. Besides, you look as if you haven't been eating right. If you're gonna have a healthy baby, we've got to see that you keep up your strength. Right?'

Teary-eyed, Juanita whispered, 'No one's ever cared about me before.'

Marie leaned over and patted Juanita's arm affectionately. 'Now that you've met Marie Fontaine, you have nothing to worry about.'

'But what am I going to do without insurance? No doctor will take care of me, not even Dr. Van Patten.'

'Look, I've got this all figured out. Just leave it to me.'

'But *how?*' Juanita persisted. 'I like Dr. Van Patten. He knows me now.'

'I'm going to help you from now on. When you're ready to deliver, we'll call an ambulance and take you to L.A.U. Dr. Van Patten will have to take you as an emergency patient. That's the law.'

'Really?' Juanita tried to digest what Marie had just said.

'Sure.' Marie grinned.

The waitress put their drinks and sandwiches on the table. 'Anything else, ladies?' she asked. Then she blew a huge bubble with her chewing gum.

'No, thank you,' Juanita replied absent-mindedly. When the waitress disappeared again, she looked at Marie. 'Are you sure everything will be all right?'

'Stop worrying. I've had lots of experience. I'm an obstetrics nurse, remember? Don't you believe me?'

'It's not that,' Juanita stammered. What could she say? She had just met this woman. Could she really trust her with the baby's life? What else could she do?

Sensing her uneasiness, Marie reassured Juanita. 'Don't look so worried; I'll take care of you. I thought about you today, and I decided it's silly for you to bother looking for a job at this stage in your pregnancy. You're too far along to be working.'

'But how will I pay the rent?'

'I said not to worry. Just relax. I'll take care of everything.'

Juanita smiled wanly. 'Okay, I guess I'm just afraid.'

'You don't have to think any more about the baby right now, honey. We can talk again later. Now go ahead, eat your sandwich.'

4

As soon as he turned his MG onto Alvarado Street, Victor noticed the fire. From a block away he could see smoke billowing out of the eight-story brick tenement on the corner. He even heard the crackle of flames erupting wildly from the upper floors. Black flecks of soot filled the air, settling on his windshield like a swarm of strange insects, nearly obstructing his vision.

He pulled over to the curb and sat watching for a moment, unbelieving, as an old woman, encouraged by the crowd below, leaped to safety from a third-story ledge. Sirens screamed in the distance. So far only one police car had arrived at the scene.

Jumping out of his car, Victor ran up the block and tapped a young woman on the shoulder. 'I'm from the *L.A. Tribune*, ma'am. What happened?' he asked. His heart was pounding as much from exhilaration as from fear.

She looked at him, not understanding, and

replied in Spanish, *'No entiendo.'*

A clean-cut young man with curly black hair stepped over to Victor. 'You a reporter?'

Victor nodded.

'I'm Sy Goldblatt from the ACLU. I represent these tenants.'

Victor thought Goldblatt looked about a month out of law school. He wore a corduroy jacket over a green turtleneck, loose-fitting slacks, and a pair of Nikes. Only his leather attaché case was new — probably, Victor guessed, a graduation gift from his proud parents.

'How did the fire start?' He took out his notebook and began to write down what Goldblatt said.

'I heard that someone was cooking dinner on a hot plate in one of the efficiency apartments. It's really illegal to allow cooking in those tiny units, but the landlord gets more rent if he lets tenants use hot plates.' He shook his head disgustedly. 'Anyway, there must have been some loose wiring. There always is in these hellholes. A few sparks, and the whole place went up like matchsticks. Fortunately, most of the people were outside getting ready for our demonstration.'

'You think anything can be salvaged?' Victor asked as he watched the flames consuming the structure.

'I doubt it. But maybe it's for the best.'

'Why do you say that?'

'Because at least this is one building that will have to be rebuilt.' He pointed to a row of similar tenements all in varying states of disrepair. 'Look at this block. Those buildings are death traps.'

'Why don't the tenants complain?'

Goldblatt smirked. 'You're either awfully naive or new in town. These tenants are almost all Mexican, and most of them are illegal aliens. One word from them and Immigration would get on their case. They'd be south of the border again before you could say *hasta luego*. The landlords know this, so they don't worry about keeping buildings up to code. I tell you, it's a disgrace.'

A few people overcome by smoke lay moaning on the ground nearby. One old man whose face was badly burned was staring back at the building, obviously dazed.

'*Mi nieta, mi nieta,*' he sobbed.

'What did he say?' Victor asked Goldblatt.

'Something about his granddaughter.'

The old man pointed frantically toward the building. Victor stared in horror as a little girl appeared at a fourth-floor window. He knew if she didn't get out fast, she'd be cremated alive. Pushing his way through the crowd, he ran up to the fire truck that had just arrived.

Goldblatt followed.

'There's a child on the fourth floor,' Victor shouted above the engine's noise.

The fire chief looked over. 'What's that?'

'A little girl is still inside the building.'

By this time everyone else had seen the child. The window was shut, but from the expression on her face and the soundless scream from her mouth, it was obvious she was terror-stricken.

'If she can open the window, maybe we can get her to jump,' one of the firemen suggested.

'She'll never hear us. Besides, the window's probably stuck,' Goldblatt shouted. Then he turned to Victor. 'I told you these buildings are firetraps.' He said to the fire chief, 'There's a fire escape on the other side of the building. Get someone up to the fourth floor. He can walk along the ledge, open the window from the outside or just break it, and get the kid out.'

'We'll never get to her in time. The fire's practically gutted the entire structure already. It's too risky.' The fire chief shook his head. 'I'm sorry.'

'Look, could I at least give it a try?' Victor volunteered.

'You're crazy, kid. The whole thing's going to collapse any minute.'

Refusing to argue, Victor ran around the back of the building. As he started up the rickety fire escape, small tongues of flame licked around him. He felt his heart beat at a frantic pace and the exhilarating rush of adrenaline as he confronted the danger. The heat from the inferno was almost suffocating. Sweat pasted his shirt to his chest.

Carefully, he pulled himself onto the fourth-floor ledge, using the tiny spaces between the bricks as footholds. Flattening his body against the building, he edged his way slowly along the ledge, afraid to look down. When he reached the window where the little girl waited in terror, he could clearly hear her pitiful screams. 'Grandpa, help me!'

'What's your name?' Victor yelled.

'Angela.'

'Okay, Angela, stand away from the window. Move back,' he shouted.

The little girl obeyed. Balancing himself carefully, Victor slammed his elbow hard against the glass near the latch. It shattered, falling into the smoke-filled room. He pushed a large shard out of the way, reached in, unlatched the window, and opened it as far as it would go.

'Come on, sweetheart.' He held his arms out to the child who ran to him tearfully. 'I'm going to move over a little. Then I'll help you out onto the ledge. Okay?'

Angela nodded. Victor helped her squeeze through the window, then held her with one arm, at the same time hugging the side of the building. They were standing side by side, their backs to the wall. Victor urged her toward the fire escape.

The seconds seemed like hours until Victor reached the safety of the fire escape. Grabbing the youngster in his arms, he descended the stairs two at a time, almost collapsing at the bottom. Two firemen pulled them away from the burning structure.

'Well done, kid!' The fire chief slapped Victor on the back. 'You know you're a lunatic, don't you?' He pointed up at the building, which was now engulfed in flames. One wall buckled as the roof collapsed, and the ledge he had been standing on only moments before toppled to the ground with a thundering crash.

'Are you all right?' Goldblatt gasped in awe. 'Angela's grandfather wants to thank you. You're certainly the hero of this neighborhood today.'

Victor couldn't respond. He was trembling with delayed terror and appalled that a child had nearly died in that hellhole. McFadden was right. This *was* an important story.

'I'm fine,' he said finally, trying distractedly

to brush the soot from his clothes. 'Sy, how would you like some front-page publicity for your cause?'

Goldblatt eagerly snapped to attention. 'Fantastic!'

'You've got it.' Victor grinned. 'But I'm going to need your help in interviewing some of these people. I don't speak Spanish.'

'No problem.' The young lawyer led Victor to a group of tenants gathered on the sidewalk. After he promised not to print their names, they reluctantly described their plight. In broken English, each giving variations on the same theme, they corroborated the lawyer's story.

Finally, satisfied that he had enough details, Victor thanked Goldblatt and handed him his card. 'Where will these people stay now?' he asked.

'I've already called my boss. He's found temporary housing for them. Of course, once your story appears, I expect the landlord will be only too happy to pick up the bill.' Goldblatt chuckled.

Victor recognized several reporters from other papers just arriving and was eager to reach the *Trib* office in time to scoop the others. After giving little Angela a hug, he loped toward his car. Several photographers, including one from the *Trib*, were busy shooting the still chaotic scene.

Stepping into his MG, he noticed two women walking arm in arm. As they passed him, the *Trib* photographer snapped a picture. The flash illuminated the women, capturing their startled faces in its iridescent blue light.

As they hurried away to enter one of the tenements farther down the street, Victor noted the contrast in their appearances. The brunette, plain and pregnant, looked like many of the Mexican women he had just interviewed. But the blonde looked oddly out of place in the run-down neighborhood.

5

Anne Midlands dressed carefully for her first day at the Institute. She wanted to look perfect. There were no uniforms; Dr. Westbourne said they were too formal. Anne had agreed that this policy made good sense.

The previous night she had carefully laid out the clothes she planned to wear: a beige polyester blouse that felt like silk and tied in a bow at the neck, an A-line cotton skirt, nylon pantyhose, cotton bra and panties, and a pair of low-heeled brown pumps.

Adjusting the hem of her skirt, she had a sudden impulse to check her reflection in the mirror . . . but Mama would never approve of such vanity. Anne had had the dream again last night. What was it about? She couldn't remember all of it. Only Mama quoting Proverbs as if she were right here in the tiny apartment: 'He who pursues vain things lacks sense.' *I'm not vain.* 'The reward of humility and the fear of the Lord are riches, honor and life.' *Yes, Mama, I know.*

Anne knew she was being silly. After all, it was just a dream.

Her temples were throbbing. Why was she getting these headaches again? Probably the excitement of moving to a new city and starting a new job. Smoothing her silky hair with her hand, she picked up her purse, locked the apartment, and headed toward the bus stop.

Yesterday's rain had left the air crisp and clean. Everything appeared flawless, like a movie set. Puffy white clouds floated aimlessly across the azure sky. The sun was so bright that Anne had to lift a hand to shield her eyes when she left the shade of her building. It was a spectacular morning. She hoped the weather was a good omen. After all, wasn't Los Angeles the place where dreamers came to forget the past? To start out fresh?

The bus dropped her at Westwood and LaConte, a block from the Institute. She enjoyed the walk. It gave her a chance to look into the shop windows along the street. Maybe, once she saved a little money, she'd buy herself a dress like that one in the Lanz window. The simple navy jumper looked good on the mannequin, which had Anne's coloring. The pink taffeta gown in the corner was much too bright and frilly for her taste.

Anyone could see she preferred colors that let her blend into her surroundings. She wasn't one to call attention to herself.

She admired the display for another second. Then her heart stopped. There it was: that face again. This time she was certain. There *was* someone watching her. All the anxieties she'd been holding in check now overwhelmed her. She was too frightened to look around. Instead, terrified, she ran the rest of the way and breathlessly entered the foyer of the Institute.

A huge woman with a jowly face sat like a sentinel at the receptionist's desk in the middle of the room. She eyed Anne with suspicion. 'May I help you?'

Profoundly shaken and disturbed by what had just happened, Anne could hardly think straight. Her head began to throb again. 'No — I mean, yes. I'm Anne Midlands. I'm starting today as an RN on ward number one. Dr. Westbourne hired me.'

The receptionist looked her over with renewed interest. 'Dr. Westbourne. I see,' she said, inspecting Anne through Ben Franklin half-frames. 'She's the best. You're lucky to be working for such a fine doctor.'

'I know,' Anne replied, afraid she'd already made a bad impression.

Dr. Westbourne seemed to materialize out

of nowhere. 'Why, hello, Anne. I'm glad to see you. Looks as if you've met Mrs. Milsap, our receptionist.'

The receptionist grinned, pleased that the psychiatrist remembered her name. So many of the doctors thought they were better than everybody else. Not Olivia Westbourne, though. She was different.

'Well, Anne,' Dr. Westbourne said, 'it looks as if I'm going to be your tour guide this morning. The senior RN is busy with a group therapy session,' she explained. 'Everyone on our staff takes part in patient treatment.'

The psychiatrist took Anne by the arm and gently led her to the elevator. A middle-aged woman carrying a mop and pail was just stepping out. Anne saw that she wore a blue smock over what looked like a flannel nightgown, and she had a red bandanna over her carefully coiffed hair.

'I've finished upstairs, Doctor. Should I start down here?'

'If you like, Mrs. Winchester, but first I want you to meet Anne Midlands. She's the new nurse on your ward.'

Carlotta Winchester smiled. 'Pleased to meet you.'

Anne was surprised. Surely this cheerful woman wasn't a patient. She seemed too . . . normal.

'I know what you're thinking,' Dr. Westbourne said when they had boarded the elevator and the doors had closed. 'She seems fine now, but you should have seen her when she first came.'

'Really?'

'A month ago Carlotta was so depressed that she swallowed a whole bottle of sleeping pills. Apparently her husband told her the pot roast wasn't up to par. It's difficult to believe, I know.' Olivia shook her head. 'She was in a coma for a week, and when she came out of it she told me everyone would be better off if she were dead. She wouldn't eat, and she couldn't sleep. She just lay in bed staring at the ceiling. After I put her on an antidepressant, though, she started to come around. In fact, she'll probably go home soon.'

Anne sifted through her fragmented thoughts. *Better off if she were dead . . .* How sad. She followed Dr. Westbourne out of the elevator on the third floor and walked with her toward the kitchen.

'We encourage everyone to participate. Some of the patients like to help out with the cooking.' Olivia approached a short stocky woman who was kneading dough. Her ruddy cheeks were flushed, and her breath was coming in short bursts as she pushed and pulled on the dough like a masseuse.

'Sarah, I'd like you to meet Nurse Midlands. She'll be working on your ward.'

Surprise. This woman was a patient, too. 'How do you do,' Anne said formally.

'Don't have time to waste on idle chatter. There's work to be done,' Sarah replied, eyes glued to her task.

'All right, then, Mrs. Lungren, we'll talk to you later.'

'I can't believe she's sick,' Anne said when they were back on the elevator.

'Sarah killed her husband,' Olivia stated simply, waiting for the shock to register on Anne's face — just as it did on the face of everyone who met Sarah and then heard what she had done. 'Sarah was a battered wife. Her husband beat her unmercifully, and the years of abuse took their toll on her. She'd suppressed a lot of anger. One night her husband threatened her with a gun, but she grabbed it and squeezed the trigger. Just like that, she snapped, and everything she had held in careful check came spilling out. Now she takes out her hostility on bread dough,' the psychiatrist added as an afterthought.

'Why is she in a hospital? I mean, instead of a prison?'

'For observation. Her lawyers want to enter a plea of temporary insanity, and we have just three weeks to make a diagnosis. *Three weeks* to get inside the head of an obviously frustrated and hostile woman.' Olivia didn't hide her own frustration. There was never enough time.

What did Dr. Westbourne say? Sarah's husband used to beat her. Anne could almost feel Sarah's pain. But she killed him, didn't she? Self-defense? Wasn't murder a sin? Anne's head began to throb again.

They toured the inpatient service on the second floor. There were two wards, each with six narrow beds, three along each wall. It was clean and antiseptic. There were no decorations, no rugs on the cold tile floors. The place was sterile, like most hospitals — and most prisons, Anne thought. 'This ward is much more formal and sterile than the area downstairs,' Anne commented.

'You know,' Olivia explained, 'a hospital is a kind of sanctuary, a place where patients can escape from life's responsibilities and stress. We want our patients to feel secure and protected here, but we don't want them to get too comfortable. They'd never want to leave.'

A sanctuary, Anne thought. Yes. *From life.*

A loud, authoritative voice came from behind a closed door: 'Thatcher calls rioting a spree of naked greed.'

Anne was startled.

'That's Deborah Fortune,' the psychiatrist

66

explained. 'She's a schizophrenic.'

'Where is she?'

'In the bathroom.' Dr. Westbourne pointed to the closed door. 'Every morning she spends an hour or two in there reading the newspaper out loud. She thinks she's a T.V. news commentator. The bathroom is her studio.'

'With the controversy still raging over his decision to ban aerial spraying, the governor launched his ground attack on the Mediterranean fruit fly Thursday . . . '

'Deborah is harmless. Besides, you can sleep a little later in the mornings and get the news from her.' The doctor laughed lightly.

An old woman dressed in an expensive silk dress and mukluks shuffled by. 'I want to get a good seat,' she said. 'Alan is going to make the marriage work this time. I'm sure of it. He's still in love with Hope.'

'Aggie, this is Anne Midlands, the new nurse on your ward.'

' 'Guiding Light' or 'General Hospital'?'

'Beg your pardon?'

'Come on, dearie, we haven't got all day. Which is it?'

'I'm afraid I don't understand.' Anne looked helplessly at Dr. Westbourne.

'Mrs. Barlow is a soap opera fan. She tests all the new staff. If you make the proper choice, you're okay.'

Aggie nodded. 'So which is it, dearie?'

'But I don't watch T.V. I wouldn't know which to choose.'

'Don't worry,' Dr. Westbourne whispered conspiratorially, 'you can't lose.'

Anne was totally confused by the game, but finally said she preferred 'The Guiding Light.'

Aggie beamed. 'That's the girl. I could tell you knew your business. You'll do.' She turned and shuffled off down the corridor toward the elevator.

'Aggie's senile,' Dr. Westbourne said gently. 'Except for her soap operas, she can't remember much of what goes on from minute to minute.'

'I see.' Anne felt sorry for the old woman. *Can't remember. Too bad.*

'Well, here's ward one, where you'll be working.' Olivia indicated a room that looked exactly like the male wards on the second floor. The only difference was the vase of fresh mums on one bed table and a beautiful hooked rug on the floor in front of another bed.

'The flowers are Sarah Lungren's,' Dr. Westbourne said. 'She goes out into the garden and picks fresh ones every day. The rug is Tanya's work. Her real name is Evelyn Tuckman, but she prefers to be known as

Tanya, so that's what we call her. Only eighteen and she's already been the route. She ran away from home at thirteen, and she became a prostitute and a heroin addict soon thereafter. She's in our rehab program now. So far so good.'

So young. Anne shuddered. *So young*.

As Anne continued to survey the ward, she noticed the woman in the last bed. Something about her attracted Anne. She wasn't like the other patients. This woman seemed more alone . . . more vulnerable somehow. Maybe it was the way she lay on her side, in the fetal position, as if trying to protect herself from the outside world. Anne felt pulled toward her as surely as iron is pulled to a magnet. She wanted to hold her, comfort her, tell her everything would be all right.

Dr. Westbourne interrupted her thoughts. 'That's Janet Evans. She just had an injection, so I don't think we ought to disturb her. I'll tell you about her; let's go to my office where we can talk.'

Anne followed Olivia back along the corridor to the small office where she had been interviewed the other day.

'Coffee?' the doctor offered, pouring herself a cup from a small coffee machine perched precariously on the window ledge.

Temples pounding, Anne noted gratefully

that the curtains were drawn. She wouldn't see the staring face today. 'No, thank you,' she said.

Dr. Westbourne sat down behind her desk. 'Well, now you've met all the women on ward one except Tanya,' she began. 'And although you'll be running the group therapy sessions, I think the most important part of your job is to observe. Try to get as close to the patients as possible. Encourage them to talk, especially Mrs. Evans. She's very depressed. She has suffered several extreme shocks in the past few years.'

'What happened?'

'Her newborn baby was kidnapped three years ago. Then eighteen months ago her young son died of pneumonia.'

'My God, how awful!'

'Yes,' Dr. Westbourne agreed. 'She's become completely withdrawn recently. And paranoid, according to her husband. In fact, yesterday she swore she saw the person who took her little girl. She became so hysterical I had to sedate her.'

'Do you think she really saw someone?'

The psychiatrist shook her head. 'No, I don't think she did. I suspect that she's delusional. If she is, she may be having a psychotic breakdown. I certainly hope not, but it is a possibility.'

Anne felt another headache coming on and gently massaged her forehead to relieve the pain. 'I hope not, too,' she managed. She was thinking about the face she saw in the window that morning, the face of the person she had fled from on her way to work. Was *she* going crazy? How can I help Mrs. Evans, she wondered, if I can't even help myself?

Atlanta
July 10, 1981
Friday

Victor unfastened his seat belt as the Lockheed L1011 slowly taxied along the runway toward the Atlanta terminal. He hardly remembered the flight. After filing his story about the fire, Victor had almost missed his plane and was the last passenger to board. Although he'd slept most of the way, he still felt exhausted.

Struggling to pull his thoughts together, Victor remembered McFadden's response to the fire story. 'A hell of a job, Larsen. Hope you do a follow-up.'

'Of course I will. This really is an important story.' Victor had produced his best conciliatory smile. He went on to tell the editor about the tenant interviews and his plan to expand

71

the story into a lengthy feature.

'That's the stuff,' McFadden said. 'And feel free to make use of *Trib* resources; that's what they're there for.'

Monday, Victor would call Sy Goldblatt to try to get more background material. Meanwhile, he'd spend this weekend tracking down his hunch about the kidnapped children.

'We're here.'

He was startled out of his reverie by an attractive redhead in a Delta Airlines uniform leaning over him.

'I'm sorry?'

'I hope you have a better place to sleep tonight than this,' the flight attendant teased.

The overhead light illuminated her emerald-green eyes. Victor was conscious of her closeness, the smell of her perfume. He also realized the plane was nearly empty.

Jumping up from his seat, he grabbed his jacket from the overhead storage. 'Sorry. Guess I was daydreaming.'

The stewardess followed him to the front of the plane. 'This your first trip to Atlanta?'

'First in many years,' he confessed.

'Perhaps you'll need a tour guide, then?'

The suggestive tone in her voice was not lost on Victor. He hesitated, weighing conflicting claims, then reluctantly shook his head. 'I wish I did, but I'll only be here for a few hours — on business,' he added by way of explanation.

'Too bad. Maybe next time.'

As he left the plane, Victor wondered if he'd made the right decision. It might have been an interesting evening of obligatory sexual sparring — verbal and perhaps physical — but he knew that's all it would have been.

He was not unaware that women found him attractive, but he didn't let his success go to his head. He was tired of superficial relationships. They were like appetizers; they were tasty, but never completely satisfying. Yet he couldn't seem to find what he was looking for. It was easier not to get involved at all. That way he wouldn't be disappointed.

He never wanted to fall in love again. Once was enough. Suzanne had spoiled it for him. He'd loved her more than he thought he could love anyone. They'd met three years ago when he was living in Manhattan, hacking away at his unpublished novel. She was marvelous — gorgeous, charming, witty, bright. At least that was how she had seemed to him at first. Gradually, he'd discovered her other qualities: spoiled, bitchy, selfish, deceitful.

At the first opportunity, she'd left him for a

more successful man, someone who could help her fledgling acting career. He'd been taken in by her surface beauty. Next time — if there ever was a next time — he'd fall in love with someone who had more substance.

He was still thinking about Suzanne when he reached the car rental desk. He opted for a Toyota Corolla and drove straight to the address he'd found in the airport phone directory.

The drive took him out Interstate 85 toward the Buckhead area of Atlanta. It was dusk when he pulled up in front of the Hill house, a modest place on Acorn Street. A tall, thin man with dark circles under puffy eyes answered the doorbell.

'Mr. Hill?' Victor asked.

'Yes?'

'I'm Victor Larsen from the *Los Angeles Tribune*. I wonder if I might talk with you and your wife?'

'Please, can't you people leave us alone? We've had enough of your badgering.' He started to close the door.

Victor wedged his foot in the doorway to stop him. 'Look, I'm not here to badger you. Believe me. I want to help you. I've got some information.'

'Information?' Mr. Hill paused, peering through the half-closed door.

'About the kidnapper. I think it's important.'

A soft voice came from somewhere inside the house. 'It's okay, Ross. Let's hear what Mr. Larsen has to say.'

Reluctantly, Ross Hill opened the door again. 'All right, come on in. But just remember, my wife isn't well.'

'I won't take too much of your time,' Victor promised.

Mrs. Hill stood in the foyer, wearing a flannel robe over her nightgown. Like her husband's, her face was gray and withdrawn. Seeing her made her tragedy all too heartbreakingly real.

'I want you both to know how sorry I am about your daughter's disappearance,' Victor said quietly.

'Would you like to sit down, Mr. Larsen?' Mrs. Hill offered, turning her head slightly to hide tears forming at the corners of her eyes.

Her husband put a hand on her arm to steady her. 'Laura, dear, do you really think you're up to this?'

She waved his concern away. 'I'm fine, Ross. Really I am.'

She led them into a dimly lit living room, furnished in Early American. Victor couldn't help noticing the tricycle and baby carriage in the corner. When they were seated, Mrs. Hill looked anxiously at him.

'All right, young man,' her husband prompted, 'you have some information about our daughter?'

'Well, not exactly.' Victor hesitated. 'I understand you received a letter just after the kidnapping. Is that right?'

'No, the papers had it mixed up. I got the letter when I was still in the hospital,' Mrs. Hill replied.

'Hospital?'

'Grady Memorial. I had my baby there a month ago.'

Victor was confused. 'I see. So you got this letter while you were at Grady.' He wondered about the significance of this fact.

Mrs. Hill nodded.

'Do you have any idea who might have sent it?'

'No. The nurses brought all my cards and letters to my room. To be honest, at the time, I just thought it was a mistake or' — her voice cracked — 'a sick joke. I never even mentioned it to Dr. Van Patten, my obstetrician.'

Ross Hill interrupted. 'Mr. Larsen, you said you were here to help us. It sounds as though you don't have anything at all.'

'I'll be honest, Mr. Hill. I really don't have anything definite, but I do have a hunch

76

about the kidnapper.'

Mrs. Hill leaned forward, her eyes just a little brighter. 'What is it?'

'May I see the letter?'

From the pocket of her robe, Mrs. Hill produced a folded piece of paper with ragged edges, obviously from repeated readings. 'The police don't think this is important. Why do you?'

Victor unfolded the note and read it carefully. The words were scribbled in bright red lipstick: 'Tooth for tooth.' That was all. 'I think it could be a link to the kidnapper,' he told them.

'How?' Ross Hill asked skeptically.

'Three years ago a child was kidnapped in Houston. My father was the police detective on the case. Anyway, the kidnapper left a letter behind after taking the baby from her bedroom. The message was very similar — 'Eye for eye' — and in both cases there was no ransom note, no demand for money.'

'That's exactly why the police think the note is a red herring,' Ross Hill interjected.

'I think they're wrong,' Victor insisted. 'I'd like to make a copy of your note if you don't mind.'

'Take this,' Mrs. Hill offered tearfully. 'The police don't have any use for it, and I want you to have it if it will help.'

'Thank you. I'll make a copy and send this back. It's probably best if you keep the original. I plan to compare it with the Houston letter. If the handwriting is the same, at least we'll have a start in breaking both cases.'

'You mean that child is still missing?' Mrs. Hill's eyes widened with fear. 'Ross, oh, my God — ' She began sobbing uncontrollably. 'You don't think she's dead, do you?'

Her question shocked Victor. Dead? He'd never really considered that.

Ross Hill put his arm around his wife. 'Mr. Larsen, as you can see, this talk of the kidnapping is upsetting my wife. I think you'd better leave now.'

He escorted Victor to the door, speaking softly so that Laura didn't hear. 'I hope this pans out, Mr. Larsen. My wife can't take much more. She's ready to fall apart. Thank God for our son, Timmy. He's what keeps her going.'

Victor read the sorrow in the man's eyes. Such a sad face. Now that he looked carefully, he realized Ross Hill was more likely in his late twenties than his thirties as he had guessed earlier. The disappearance of his baby daughter had obviously aged him beyond his years.

He hoped he wasn't chasing shadows.

McFadden would boil if he learned that Victor had left town on his own. Unless, of course, he struck pay dirt. Then he'd be a hero again.

Before turning to go, Victor asked one more question. 'Did you or your wife have any enemies? Anyone with reason to . . . ' His words trailed off as he watched Ross Hill's expression change from sad to thoughtful.

'No, not that I know of. We're both active members of this community. I can't think of anyone who would harm my family or me in any way. If you come up with anything, you'll let us know, won't you?'

Victor nodded and headed for the Toyota. He had just enough time to catch the 10:00 P.M. flight to Houston. Fingering the crumpled paper in his pocket, he reviewed his plan. He needed the Evanses' letter from his father's file. If his hunch was right, this might just be one of the missing pieces of the puzzle. He had a feeling, though, as he buckled his seat belt, that he still had a long way to go before he would solve this mystery.

6

Los Angeles
July 11, 1981
Saturday

Juanita turned around clumsily in the shower, lathering soap over her protuberant belly. She loved being pregnant. Because she had always believed that having children was her primary function, the fact that her body was stretched and misshapen didn't bother her. It rather pleased her. She was a real woman now. Her only regret was that the baby wouldn't have a father.

She lifted her face into the spray, smiling as the growing fetus somersaulted in her womb.

'Soon, *mi amorcito*, just a few more weeks and then you will be born.'

As if to answer, a tiny leg pushed outward from deep within her abdomen. She smiled again. Sweet pain.

As the stream of warm water rinsed the soap from her skin, she closed her eyes, luxuriating in the pleasure of the shower. It was so relaxing; it invited drowsiness. She'd lie down for an afternoon nap.

Shutting off the water, she stepped languorously from the stall and stood naked, dripping on the terry mat she'd bought at J. C. Penney's. It was wonderful to be in America — even in this shabby apartment. She was very happy, especially now that she had a friend.

The bitter lesson was still fresh. It wasn't easy to find someone she could trust. Certainly not José. He refused to acknowledge that he was the father of the baby when she confronted him with her pregnancy — even though he had forced himself on her. Not her parents. They sent her packing. Not even the church. Father Valdez had shaken his head, offering platitudes but no real solace. In the end there was no one. Except Marie. How lucky Juanita was to have met her.

Just as Juanita reached for the towel, she heard the front door open and then quietly close. Sweet Jesus! She'd forgotten to lock it!

Time seemed to stop for her. As if in slow motion, she moved toward the bathroom door, seconds ticking away in her head. Thank God the door was shut. She turned the latch, locking herself in. She was trapped — but perhaps she'd be safe if she kept quiet.

From the other side she heard footsteps creaking around the tiny apartment. Someone was in the kitchen area, opening and closing drawers. What could anyone possibly want? She had nothing to steal.

Juanita felt her frantic heartbeat in her temples; her breath came in ragged bursts. Maybe if she kept very still, the intruder would just go away.

The stillness was shattered by the radio being turned on full blast, blaring a rock tune. Oh, my God! They'd kill her, and no one would hear her scream! She crossed her arms over her naked breasts. Help me, Jesus! Her knees buckled, and the room began to sway. Feeling faint, she slid to the floor, resting her head against the door.

Houston
July 11, 1981
Saturday

Victor opened his eyes. The luminous numbers on the clock radio by the bed blinked 4:00 P.M.

Jeez, he'd slept most of the day away. Stretching, he sat up and looked around the room in which he'd spent so much of his childhood. He had come home when his father died two months before, but he hadn't slept in his old room since he left Houston five years ago to try his hand at writing. When

82

he had returned to town to work on the *Houston Journal*, he had rented an apartment in town.

The room was exactly as he'd left it, not unlike the bedrooms of thousands of other young boys; the walls were covered with posters of football heroes and rock stars. There were tubes of glue, bottles of colored enamel and a variety of crafting tools stacked neatly on a desk beside several model airplanes. Seeing them now, he recalled the pleasant hours of solitude he had spent working at his hobby.

Pulling on a robe, he went to the closet and slid open the door. They were all there. His mother hadn't thrown any of his memories away — not the green Astros baseball cap, not the skateboard, not even the blue suit he wore to his high school graduation ceremony.

Deep in a musty corner was a carton of books, the collected works of his favorite authors. He tugged at the box, pushing it out onto the middle of the room. Victor thought of the rainy days he had spent reading the works of authors who had inspired him to become a writer himself, men like Hemingway, Faulkner, T. S. Eliot, and Fitzgerald. Dad had said he shouldn't shut himself up in his room like that. *Real* men weren't writers. A flood of memories engulfed him as he picked up the books and studied each one lovingly, reverently.

'I'm glad you're up.' Nora Larsen stood in the doorway.

'Mother, I missed you last night. My plane was late. I didn't want to wake you.' He went over and gave her buxom frame a bear hug. As she squeezed him back, he could smell the fresh, clean scent of her skin. For a moment, he was a little boy again.

'You're too thin. What do they feed you in Los Angeles?'

'No one feeds me, Mom. I live in an apartment and if I do say so myself, I'm a pretty fair cook.'

As he stepped back, he gave his mother an appraising look. She was a ruddy woman with rough, square features except for two bright blue eyes sparkling like tiny jewels in her round face. Victor loved her dearly.

Her long flaxen hair had turned gray, though she still wore it in a braid wound around her head. His father had gone back to the old country to find a wife. Bergen, Norway, not far from where Edvard Grieg was born, Nora used to tell her children.

'Well, never mind. I've made all your favorite dishes, so you're going to come with me, sit in the kitchen, and eat.'

Victor smiled as he followed her downstairs

past the living room where he got a fleeting look at his parents' wedding picture on the old upright piano: Gustav, the tall, gaunt groom towering over his pretty bride. The aroma of baking bread assailed Victor's nostrils reminding him he hadn't eaten in over twenty-four hours. He was famished.

In the kitchen, Nora busied herself at the stove, stirring something with a long wooden spoon. 'I made you faar-i-kaal.'

Victor knew she only made the heavily peppered cabbage and mutton stew, the Norwegian national dish, on special occasions. He was touched by her gesture. 'It smells wonderful.'

'Just a few more minutes and it will be ready.' She put the spoon aside, clapped a lid on the pot, and wiped her hands on the apron she wore over her plain dress. Then she sat down at the table facing him.

'So, how have you been?' Her wonderfully blue eyes probed his face for unspoken answers.

It was a familiar scene for Victor. As the youngest, he always had more of his mother's time than his three brothers, often spending the hours after school sitting with her at the kitchen table, recounting his day.

Now he told her about his illegal alien

story, even boasted about saving Angela from the fire.

'Your father would be very proud.'

'The only thing that would have made Father proud is if I'd become a cop like my brothers,' Victor said bitterly. 'He never understood how I could run off to New York to write. Maybe if my novel had been published . . . '

'Gustav loved all his boys,' she said wistfully, twisting the plain gold wedding band around and around on her finger.

Victor saw her eyes glisten, though no tears fell. His mother had always been so strong, always there when he needed her. Somehow he hadn't realized how difficult things must have been for her since his father's death. 'You miss him very much, don't you?'

She nodded. Then, as if ashamed of her admission, she jumped up and began ladling the stew onto a plate. 'Here's some fresh baked bread to soak up the gravy.'

'Delicious,' Victor pronounced between bites.

'It wouldn't hurt if you had a nice girl to look after you,' she said, watching him eat. 'Have you thought about getting married? It's time you settled down.'

'No nagging, Mom. Remember, you promised.'

'I'm getting old. I forget.'

'Not you. You're always the same. Every time I see you.' He gave her cheek an affectionate tweak.

'Stop with the flattery and eat your stew. It's getting cold.'

They talked as Victor ate several helpings of stew. Then he pushed away the plate and said he was full. 'Besides, I'm going to miss my plane back to L.A.'

'You mean you're not staying over?'

'I'm sorry, Mom. Not this time. I've got to get back to L.A. In fact, I'm really here working on a story. Listen, is it okay if I look through Dad's papers?'

'What do you need?'

'You know the Evans case?'

A faint, twisted smile crossed her face. 'Yes,' she stated simply. 'I'm more and more sure that's what killed your father.'

Her words shocked Victor.

'It broke his heart,' she explained. 'Looking for that baby everywhere for almost three years and never finding a trace. Every day he'd call the mother and have to tell her he had no news. It just broke his heart.' Her lower lip trembled.

'What did he do with the note Mrs. Evans received the night her baby was kidnapped?'

'He kept it in his file until he died.'

87

'And then?'

'Then last month Mr. Evans came to see me and asked if he could have it back.'

'Why, I wonder?' Victor thought aloud.

'I don't know. I just assumed he would continue the search for his daughter on his own now.'

'I guess I'd better give him a call.'

'I don't understand how you're involved, son.'

Victor told his mother about the Hill kidnapping in Atlanta and said that Mrs. Hill had received a handwritten note very much like the one the Evanses had found.

'I'd like to put those notes side by side to compare the handwriting. Somehow I have a feeling about this case. Do you have the Evanses' telephone number, Mom? Maybe if I call, I can drop by on my way to the airport.'

Mrs. Larsen walked to the counter, pulled out a pocket-sized phone directory, and handed it to him. 'It's the first number on top. Of course, your father knew it by heart.'

Watching her son eagerly dialing the number, Mrs. Larsen shook her head and smiled. 'You remind me so much of your father when you get excited like this.'

What she didn't say was that, like Gus,

Victor was persistent and single-minded even with all the odds stacked against him.

Los Angeles
July 11, 1981
Saturday

Juanita didn't know how long she had been lying half conscious on the bathroom floor. Through a kind of fog, she heard the doorknob jiggle, suddenly rekindling her terror. Her mind whirled.

Silence.

Why wasn't the radio playing? The intruder must have turned it off. She tried to look under the door. No one was standing there, just empty space.

More silence, and then someone jiggled the knob again. Frantic now. Pulling herself up to the keyhole, she peeked through. In shocked relief, she saw *Marie* on the other side of the door.

'Marie?' she whispered, not trusting her voice.

'Are you in there, Juanita?'

'Yes.' Her reply was barely audible.

'Well, I declare, honey. I thought you were out shopping or something. Good thing I had to pee. You okay?'

With trembling fingers, Juanita wrapped a towel around herself and unlocked the door. She opened it shakily and stepped out. Marie was wearing the same short dress she had worn the other night, and her reddened lips were spread in a wide smile.

'Why, honey, you surely are a sight for sore eyes.'

Juanita felt tears scald her cheeks. 'My God, Marie, you scared me to death.'

Instantly, Marie's smile vanished, her mouth hardened in anger. 'This is how you show your appreciation for a friend? Why the hell didn't you let me know you were home?' she lashed out. 'I made a special trip to see you.'

Marie's reaction caught Juanita off balance. 'I'm sorry. I'm kind of jumpy lately — you know, with the baby almost due and being all alone in this apartment. I hear noises and I get scared.'

Marie's features softened again as she smiled, the peak of her anger passing quickly. 'Sure, I understand. This really is a dump. It would give me the willies, too.'

Embarrassed, Juanita looked around her tiny efficiency — at the chipped paint and the ground-in dirt. In the corner that served as the kitchen area, there was a stained sink and a hot plate, two rickety chairs from Pic and

Save and a small wooden table, the top scarred with cigarette burns. A few feet away in the bedroom-living room was a battered sofa bed. After spending nearly two days on her hands and knees scrubbing the place, Juanita had realized that any real change was impossible. 'It's all I can afford,' she said apologetically.

'Well, once this baby is born, we'll find you a better place. In the meantime, I'll give you my phone number. Call me if you need me,' Marie said, searching in her purse for a pen. She finally gave up, grabbed her red lipstick, and scribbled the number on a paper napkin.

'*Gracias.*'

'I bet you're starved. While you get dressed, I'll fix you something to eat. Listen, what are you doing tonight? How about going out for a few drinks?'

'No, thanks, Marie. I think I'll just stay in.'

She shrugged. 'Suit yourself. But you're gonna miss a wild Saturday night. I plan to really whoop it up this weekend.' Marie smiled wickedly.

Juanita relaxed as she watched her friend putter in the kitchen. She was feeling calmer than before. After all, hadn't Marie been helping her all this time? So Marie had wandered in and made herself at home. What was wrong with that? That was Marie. It was as much Juanita's fault for not locking the door. She'd just have to be more careful in the future.

July 11, 1981
Saturday

Bill Evans picked up the phone on the seventh ring. 'Hello,' he said gruffly.

'Mr. Evans?'

'Yes, yes, what is it?'

'My name is Victor Larsen. I'm Gus Larsen's son.'

There was a brief silence.

'What do you want?'

'I'm a reporter for the *L.A. Tribune*. I'm investigating a kidnapping case very similar to your daughter's.' Victor quickly told him about Shannon Hill's disappearance in Atlanta, his meeting yesterday with her parents, and the connection he suspected between the two cases.

Evans listened without comment.

'My father showed me that note you got three years ago — 'Eye for eye' scribbled in red lipstick. He always hoped it might lead him to the kidnapper. Now I have a

92

feeling the same person has taken the Hill baby — '

'Impossible.'

Victor wasn't sure he understood. 'What?'

'You heard me. I don't think there's any connection between the two cases,' Evans said flatly.

'But your daughter . . . Maybe we can find her now if we prove the two notes were written by the same person.'

'She's *dead*, Mr. Larsen. It's taken me three long years to accept that fact. I only wish my wife could do the same. It's partly because your father wouldn't let her hope die that she's sitting in the L.A. Psychiatric Institute like a goddamned vegetable right this minute.' His voice was bitter.

'I'm sorry to hear that.' Victor couldn't help wondering if Mrs. Hill was headed for a breakdown, too. He *had* to find those babies. 'Could I at least take a look at the note? My mother said you took the file back.'

'I destroyed it.'

'What?' Victor was incredulous. The one thing he had been pinning his hopes on was gone. Just like that. Unbelievable. 'But why?'

'I told you. My daughter is dead. I want to go on with my life now. I only hope the doctors in Los Angeles can help Janet. Maybe

93

someday we can be a family again.' His voice cracked with emotion.

'I'm sorry to have bothered you, sir,' Victor said. There was no answer on the other end. Bill Evans had hung up.

7

'What's your name, little girl?' The clown hopped about the cardboard stage looking here and there. 'Cat got your tongue?' the puppet taunted, its painted lips curled in a smirk.

Anne felt her face flush. Surely this . . . this creature wasn't addressing her — a grown woman. Her heart began to pound.

Sometimes an event from the past seems to occur again, if for only a fraction of a second: déjà vu. Both the present occurrence and the remembered incident tumble and collide in the minds, confusing the real and the imagined. For a moment she imagined her mother's voice, mocking her — 'Cat got your tongue?' — and she caught herself watching the remembered scene, detached, as if from the vantage point of a separate person.

'My name's Anne,' she whispered.

'Anne what?' her mother demanded.

'Anne Midlands.'

Her mother slapped her face hard and laughed. 'Little girls should be seen and not heard.'

Anne willed the tears not to fall, though her left cheek grew hot and started to sting. No matter what, she'd never let Mama see her cry.

'I hate you,' she yelled at her mother.

'What's wrong with that lady?' The sound of the child's voice propelled Anne back to reality.

'Shh.'

Slowly Anne opened her eyes. Was she dreaming again? A crowd of children and their parents were staring at her.

'Time to go. Everybody back on the bus.' A tall man in a cap with 'tour guide' stenciled on the crown was clapping his hands.

Time was passing ineluctably. You could never hold it in your hand. She imagined spaces between raindrops, shadows on a moonlit night, whispers in the wind.

Sometimes, especially lately, everything around her seemed to move too quickly while she felt as though she were drifting through Jell-O in a crazy slow-motion ballet. Sleep-walking through life. That's what Mama would say.

Anne blinked in the noonday sun. Some-times she had only a misty recollection of time. Like now . . . The bus. Sun Tours. That's right. She wanted to see Los Angeles as the brochure promised: 'See where the movie stars play.' Beverly Hills, Santa Monica, Malibu, Fisherman's Village, now Venice Beach. A puppet show! Of course. Not a dream at all.

'Miss, we're ready to go.'

Anne looked up. The tour guide was waiting impatiently beside the already filled bus. She could see the faces pressed against the glass, staring at her, distorted, disgusted. She looked away. 'I think I'll stay here.'

'I beg your pardon?' It was obvious from his tone he thought she was crazy.

'I'm not going on. You can leave without me. I'll find my own way back.'

'Suit yourself.' He shrugged. 'Just remember Sun Tours is not responsible once you leave the group.'

She nodded.

As the bus pulled out of the parking lot, Anne looked around her, it seemed, for the first time. It was a Sunday in Venice, California — alive as always, with frenetic activity, a dazzling chaos. Old and young mingled along the crowded boardwalk, boats and surfers challenged the cresting waves, kites and gulls soared on currents generated by soft ocean breezes.

The puppeteer had packed up his peripatetic show and was moving on down Ocean Front Walk, looking for a new audience. Taking a tentative step, Anne nearly collided with a young black boy on roller skates, a huge portable stereo tape deck on one shoulder.

'This lane ain't for walkin', lady,' he called from halfway up the bike path, his voice barely carrying over the roller disco music.

Two bikers wearing headphones squealed past her before she could heed the boy's warning. Terrified, Anne stumbled onto the grass.

A bikini-clad teenager laughed at her obvious distress. The stoned girl took a drag on her homemade cigarette as she strolled languidly past Anne, indifferent to the T-shirted L.A.P.D. officer staring in her direction.

Trembling, Anne moved away from the girl, who was leering at her now. She wanted safety, anonymity. She wished only to melt into the Sunday parade. Yet the press of humanity was almost suffocating.

On the boardwalk, bums and shopping cart people rummaged through trash cans. A few students carrying signs demonstrated peaceably against nuclear power. Some had painted the slogan 'No Nukes' on their foreheads.

Anne stopped for a moment to watch them, and a gray-haired woman pressed a picture postcard of Jesus into her hand, murmured, 'God bless you,' and disappeared in the opposite direction.

Turning to thank her, Anne looked up at the red face of a man looming over her, shouting, 'Repent, sinner.' The bearded old man stood on a bench, arms raised in supplication. 'There is no sanctuary against evil.'

The sound of his voice was like a drum, booming, shaking her insides. She stared at him for a moment, puzzled, uneasy.

'Are you a sinner, young lady?' The man had drawn quite a crowd now. They were waiting for an answer.

Anne said nothing, afraid.

'Of course you are. We are all sinners.'

Anne shuddered. 'No, please. I'm a good girl. Can't you see? I *am* good.' She backed away, trying to dissolve into the crowd.

'Why so upset? Life is just an illusion,' said a voice behind her.

Anne whirled around. The woman who had spoken looked about forty. She had thick sable-colored hair and piercing ebony eyes whose expression was amused and slightly patronizing. She wore gold hoop earrings.

'What?'

The Gypsy woman winked at her. 'Life is just an illusion. We see what we want to see. Now, show me your hand. I'll tell your fortune.'

Obediently, Anne surrendered her palm to the Gypsy.

'Ah, very interesting. You are a long way from home. I see.'

'Texas,' Anne offered, impressed.

'Hmm, this is most unusual. Two separate lifelines running parallel and yet . . . ' The woman traced the creases in Anne's palm, frowning. 'Here the lines mingle. I don't understand . . . '

Anne pulled back her hand as though she'd been burned. She wanted to scream. 'You don't even know me . . . You can't — ' She broke off abruptly and began to run. God, her head was pounding.

'You can't run away,' the Gypsy called after her 'There's no place to hide.'

8

The moment Victor walked into the newsroom Monday morning, he was bombarded with questions and congratulations from fellow reporters who'd heard about his heroism on Alvarado Street.

'Nice going, Viking.' A *Trib* photographer slapped him on the back, giving him a new nickname befitting his Scandinavian coloring and background and now his act of bravery.

'What's going on?' McFadden demanded, walking over to Victor's desk. 'Doesn't anybody around here plan to work today?'

The crowd dispersed quickly, and McFadden returned to his own desk.

'What's his problem?' Victor asked the reporter at the next desk.

'McFadden's just a sore loser.'

'What do you mean?'

'He lost the office pool. Bet fifty bucks that the baseball strike would be over by this morning, and the wire service just reported that negotiations in Washington are stalled.

101

Those guys won't be playing for weeks.'

Victor smiled, thinking of his old Astros baseball cap. He'd been so busy lately, he hadn't even followed the strike.

'Hey, Larsen, call for you on line three.'

The cacophony of word processors and telephones combined with people yelling back and forth was even louder than usual.

'Yeah?' Victor shouted into the receiver.

'Sy Goldblatt here. Victor, I tried to reach you all weekend.'

Victor lowered his voice, at the same time looking in McFadden's direction. The chief was muttering to himself — probably complaining about someone's writing style — and scattering cigar ashes all over the story he was reading.

'I was, uh, out of town.' He didn't want the reporters on either side of him to know he was working on the kidnapping story.

'Can't hear you.'

'I was out of town working on something, Sy,' he repeated.

'I called to tell you my tenants' group is in trouble.'

'What do you mean?'

'I mean the landlord claims the fire was caused by tenant negligence. Can you believe that man's chutzpah?'

'What about the tenant interviews?'

102

'No good,' Sy explained. 'Without proof to the contrary, it's the word of an upright taxpaying American citizen against that of a bunch of illegal aliens.'

'But isn't there any evidence to prove he was responsible for that fire?' Victor persisted. 'You said it's illegal for him to let tenants have hot plates in those efficiency units. Isn't there some way to connect the hot plates with the fire?'

'No, the building was totally destroyed. There's no way to reconstruct what happened. And get this' — Victor could picture the young lawyer's earnest face — 'the landlord insured the building for twice what it was worth. He's actually going to *make* money on the fire.'

'I don't understand,' Victor said, unwilling to believe what he had heard.

'It means, my friend, that not only does the landlord get rich, but we can't prosecute. We have no evidence, no case.'

'So where does that leave us?'

Goldblatt laughed. 'I knew I liked you as soon as I saw you the other day. *Us.* I like that.' Then his tone changed to one of bitterness and frustration as he turned back to the subject of the fire. 'It leaves us behind the goddamned eight ball, that's where it leaves us.'

'Wait a second,' Victor shouted. 'Don't give up so fast. Let's talk things through. Does the landlord own any other buildings in the area?'

'Several, as a matter of fact. He owns another one on the same block, and two more farther east.'

'Terrific. I'll meet you in two hours. Give me the street number of the other building he owns on Alvarado.'

'Can't you tell me what this is all about?'

'I'll tell you when I see you,' Victor replied, writing down the number. 'I've got another stop to make first.'

July 13, 1981
Monday

Anne woke on Monday with a blinding headache and a sour taste in her mouth. She knew she'd been dreaming again, but she didn't want to remember, even if she could. She would just push the dream back into the dark space of her mind, as she always did.

She had spent most of the weekend looking forward to her first full week at the Institute. Her first day, Friday, had been mostly orientation, and she couldn't wait to get started on the real work with the patients. Before leaving the apartment, she grabbed the letter she had written to the mental hospital in Texas where she had once worked. Eager to please Dr. Westbourne, she hoped the hospital would send good references to the Institute.

Today Mrs. Milsap, the lobby sentinel, recognized her. 'Good morning, Miss Midlands. Dr. Westbourne said to have you go right up to group.'

'Group?'

'Group therapy. The session for ward one begins at nine. You'll just be sitting in today.'

'Oh . . . okay, thank you.' For the moment Anne feared that the familiar disorientation might engulf her again, but the feeling passed.

'It's on three,' the receptionist said.

'Yes, I remember.'

Anne took the elevator to the third floor and found the group therapy room at the far end of the corridor opposite the dining room. She walked in just as the session was about to begin. Dr. Westbourne motioned for her to take a seat beside her before introducing her to the patients.

'Ladies, I want you all to meet Anne Midlands. She's the new nurse on ward one.'

Enthusiastic applause came from Aggie Barlow at the far end of the room. Nothing from the rest. Anne felt uncomfortable.

'Tanya, do you want to join the group?' The psychiatrist directed her question to a beautiful young girl with long, straight brown hair, wearing blue jeans and a red T-shirt. She had assumed a yoga position on the floor and gave no sign of having noticed anyone. She remained motionless, expressionless, and silent.

'All right, then, since this is Miss Midlands's first session with us, perhaps we'd better go over the ground rules for group therapy.'

'I won't miss 'General Hospital' today, will I?' Aggie whined.

'No, Aggie,' the psychiatrist promised.

Anne thought she remembered that 'The Guiding Light' was the old woman's favorite soap. Oh, well . . .

'The most important reason for group, of course, is to help you get well so that you can go home. We focus on individual problems and then share our feelings about them.'

'It's all bullshit.' Tanya spoke so softly that the psychiatrist didn't hear, but Anne did, and she turned to study the girl. The serene expression on Tanya's face gave no indication that she was deeply troubled.

'We should all feel comfortable here,' Dr. Westbourne continued. 'We're all friends. Most of us had a little stage fright at first, but

106

we know we're here to help one another.'

Sarah Lungren nodded.

'There should be no fear of ridicule or rejection.'

'Day thirty-one of the baseball strike, and the players have rejected management's most recent proposals. No new talks are scheduled.'

It was the first time Anne had seen Deborah Fortune, the woman who spent most of her mornings in the bathroom reporting the news. She was about forty, with a wiry frame and carrot-colored hair that stood out at odd angles from her head.

'Everybody gets a turn in group,' said the psychiatrist, going on with her explanation in spite of Deborah's interruption. 'We try not to leave anyone out. After all, the success of this kind of therapy depends to a large extent on the degree to which the members get involved in the discussion.'

No one seemed to have anything to add.

'All right, then, let's get started.'

Anne looked at the faces of the women sitting in the circle. Only Tanya remained detached. Janet Evans was present, but seemed to be staring past everyone, in her own world. On Friday Dr. Westbourne had suggested to Anne that Janet was hovering on the brink of irreversible madness. Anne could almost feel the poor woman hanging there now, and she wanted desperately to reach out, to give the woman someone to hold on to.

'At the close of Friday's meeting we were discussing Carlotta's problems with her husband. She told us of her feelings of ambivalence toward him. On the one hand she appreciates the fact that he is a strong man, but on the other, she resents his complete domination of her.' Although Dr. Westbourne was reading from her notes, she skipped her own psychiatric diagnosis: 'Passive, insecure person with strong feelings of inadequacy.'

Carlotta sat very still, shredding a Kleenex into smaller and smaller pieces.

'Why do you think you let your husband bully you?' Dr. Westbourne asked.

Carlotta shrugged. 'I just don't like to argue with people. It's better to get along with everyone.'

Tanya snorted contemptuously.

'Do you feel guilty and upset if you get angry?' The psychiatrist continued.

'Yes.'

'How about if somebody gets mad at you?'

'I don't think people should fight and argue with one another,' Carlotta persisted.

'So you let your husband walk all over you,'

108

Sarah Lungren interjected.

Tanya unwound from a full lotus position, stood up, and took a seat opposite Carlotta. 'I don't believe you. Why the hell don't you just leave your old man?' she challenged.

'Where would I go?' the older woman whined.

'She can't stay, and she can't go.' Aggie sounded like a parrot.

'What about your children? They're grown up and independent now. Couldn't you stay with them?' Sarah asked more gently.

Carlotta shook her head sadly. 'They don't want me. I'd just be in the way. They have their own lives to live.'

'I really don't believe this.' Tanya rolled her eyes in disbelief. 'Why can't you just leave and live on your own?'

'Like *you*?' Sarah sneered. 'I've noticed how you treasure *your* independence.'

Anne watched this verbal tennis match with a mixture of shock and frustration. The ball was back in Tanya's court.

'I take care of myself. I don't depend on nobody but me. Not like Mrs. Milquestoast over here.' She pointed to Carlotta who was dabbing at her eyes with the shredded Kleenex.

'You're one to talk about independence,' Sarah taunted. 'You didn't depend on a husband; you just gave all that hard-earned money you made lying on your back to a no-good pimp.'

'That's different,' Tanya sputtered.

'Really? How so?'

'He helped me when I was sick.'

'What was wrong with you?'

There was an uncomfortable silence before Tanya answered, 'I had an infection.'

'You mean you had V.D.' Sarah pronounced both letters precisely.

'So what of it? It's no big deal.'

'A woman I knew once had V.D.,' one of the other women announced, almost proudly. 'After that, she couldn't have babies.'

Anne was becoming uncomfortable with the direction of the session. Her head had begun to throb. Pulling off her glasses, she massaged her aching temples.

'What about after you got well?' Sarah was relentless in her attack on Tanya. 'Why did you stay with your pimp then? Why did you give him all the money you made?'

'He took care of me, bought me clothes, gave me anything I needed.'

'Didn't he also get you hooked on dope? Why didn't you leave him before he started you on drugs, Tanya?' she persisted.

The young girl's shoulders began to tremble and her voice shook. 'Because,' she sobbed, 'he would have killed me.'

Sarah leaned back in her chair, weary from the discussion, and closed her eyes. Anne remembered that Sarah had killed her husband. She shuddered at the idea of murder. Killing was a sin, no matter what the reason.

'It's almost ten, ladies,' Dr. Westbourne broke in. 'I think we'll stop now and pick up again tomorrow.'

★ ★ ★

Near the end of the therapy session, Dr. Westbourne had noticed Anne rubbing her temples. She was clearly suffering from a severe headache. She also recalled that Anne seemed to have had a headache on Friday, when they were talking in her office. The psychiatrist wondered if this was a recurring problem for her new associate.

'Do you get those headaches often?' she asked.

'Why, uh, they're nothing, really.'

'Anne, as well as being your employer, I'm also a doctor, and I hope your friend. I saw you in there and you were obviously in pain.'

A moment ago the pain had almost been gone. But now the throbbing had started again, harder, pounding at her temples like a

111

thousand tiny hammers. She tried not to show it, but the darts of agony she felt behind her eyes were so acute that the muscles in her face tensed.

Dr. Westbourne put a comforting hand on her shoulder. While they didn't know each other very well yet, Olivia had sensed Anne's shyness and vulnerability from the start, and she wanted to ease it if she could. 'I'd like you to come to my office this afternoon. I've had a lot of experience treating people with migraines. Perhaps we can find out what's causing yours.'

Somehow Anne managed a smile. 'It's really not necessary, I'm fine now.' Her head *was* hurting. She felt as if a vise had tightened around her skull.

'Nonsense. I have a free hour at three o'clock. I'll see you then.' She turned and was halfway down the corridor before Anne could reply.

July 13, 1981
Monday

His mother was right. He was single-minded, like his father. Victor was not going to give up just because Bill Evans had destroyed the kidnapper's note.

112

After talking on the telephone with Goldblatt, he hurried out of the newsroom before McFadden could ask where he was going. His MG was in its usual spot, a no parking zone on a side street. Victor removed his press card from the dashboard.

Another clear July day. Santa Ana winds had blown the smog out to sea leaving the sky the color of lapis lazuli, interrupted only here and there by cottony white clouds.

Victor followed Sunset Boulevard west, enjoying the purr of the sporty car as it hugged the road. At Hilgard he turned left entering the L.A. University campus. It took three tries to get correct directions to the Psychiatric Institute. Evidently, few people knew exactly where it was.

He parked in the doctors-only lot and propped his press card up on the dashboard. He knew he wouldn't get a ticket; he still had his Texas license plates.

Entering the impressive foyer of the Institute, Victor spotted a woman guarding the entrance like a sentinel. He hadn't expected to have trouble getting in. Well, he'd just have to turn on his southern charm.

'Good morning, ma'am,' he said, approaching the receptionist's desk. He smiled down into her wary eyes and handed her a card that bore the logo of the *L.A. Tribune*. 'I'm here to do a story on the Psychiatric Institute.'

'Pardon?' Mrs. Milsap asked warily.

'It's going to be a *big* series of articles,' Victor said, emphasizing the word *big*. 'At least three or four stories. I'm here to interview the staff. I thought I'd begin with you, since new patients meet you first.'

The receptionist perked up. 'You mean *I'm* going to be in the paper?'

'That's right.' Victor beamed, opening his spiral notebook. 'Now, how do you spell your name, Mrs . . . ?'

'Milsap,' she purred. 'M-i-l-s-a-p, as in Paul.'

'About how many patients do you have here at the Institute, Mrs. Milsap?' Victor continued his charade.

'Twenty-five. Mr. Reynolds was discharged today. We'll probably get another admission, though. We're always filled. You know, with our wonderful reputation.' Her wariness had vanished, and she had become eager to talk.

'Of course,' Victor agreed. 'You seem to attract patients from all over the country.'

Her head bobbed up and down, reminding Victor of a dashboard ornament. 'The world, even. Why, we've had all kinds of famous people and their relatives here. The daughter of an Arab sheikh was our patient last year. Catatonic. Poor thing. But we cured her.'

114

'You know, I'm from Texas,' Victor said innocently. 'Anyone recently admitted from Texas?'

'As a matter of fact, yes. Just last week a woman was admitted to ward one. Janet Evans. She seemed awfully depressed. I do hope Dr. Westbourne can help her.'

Bingo. On the first try, no less. Not bad, Larsen. So Janet Evans was in ward one, and Westbourne was her psychiatrist. He checked his watch. 'I don't want to be late for my appointment with Dr. Westbourne. Why don't I talk with her now and then check back here? I'll want a complete profile on you. You know, how you came to be working here et cetera. It'll take more time to get all that information.' He flashed an ingratiating smile.

'Of course,' the receptionist cooed, obviously enjoying her newfound status. 'Shall I tell Dr. Westbourne you're here?'

'No need, ma'am. I'll go right to her office. She's expecting me.' Victor hurried down the corridor.

Mrs. Milsap considered buzzing the doctor anyway, because it struck her as a bit odd that Dr. Westbourne hadn't told her about a reporter coming to the Institute. But then she decided that he'd looked so nice. He wasn't the type to cause trouble.

A woman dressed in a smock directed

Victor to ward one. 'But don't mess anything up,' she warned him. 'I just cleaned in there.'

Victor promised Carlotta Winchester he'd be careful.

The ward was empty except for a woman lying on one of the narrow beds in the corner of the room facing him. Victor recognized Janet Evans immediately from her picture in his father's files. Of course, back then she had looked less gaunt, prettier. Uncertain if she was sleeping, he approached her quietly.

'Mrs. Evans?'

Janet opened her eyes, but they didn't seem to focus. It was almost as though she were looking through him.

'Mrs. Evans, I'm Victor Larsen — Gus Larsen's son.' Nothing in Janet's face indicated that she recognized the name.

He took out the note he had brought from Atlanta and unfolded it. 'Mrs. Evans, I want to help find your daughter. My father told me about the note you got the night Justine was kidnapped.'

Still no response.

'Two weeks ago a baby was kidnapped from a playground in Atlanta. I talked with the mother after I learned that she had received a note very much like yours. Mrs. Evans, I think it's possible that both babies were stolen by the same person. I hope you'll

116

look at this note and confirm my suspicions.'

Victor held the paper up to Janet's face so she could read it: 'Tooth for tooth,' scribbled in red lipstick.

Janet's body began to tremble, like a volcano about to erupt. Her lips moved as she tried to speak. Finally she let out a shriek that Victor would never forget: like an injured animal. He froze. The sound grew louder and louder, bouncing off the walls, filling the ward. He didn't know what to do. She seemed to be having some kind of seizure.

July 13, 1981
Monday

Entering Dr. Westbourne's office, Anne was nervous. She hoped the psychiatrist could help her, but she was also frightened of what Olivia Westbourne might find out about her.

'Please sit down.' The doctor gestured toward the upholstered chair opposite her desk. She shut the door, making Anne feel suddenly claustrophobic. Why was she so afraid?

With a slightly awkward smile, Anne said, 'I shouldn't be wasting your valuable time, Dr. Westbourne. I feel fine now. Really.'

The psychiatrist smiled back, trying to put

this anxious young woman at ease. 'I thought we'd just have a friendly chat today. I want you to know that my staff is as important to me as my patients are. I want to help with any problems.' She leaned forward, palms pressed flat on her desk. 'That is, if I can.'

Anne breathed deeply, willing her body to relax. She had nothing to fear. Dr. Westbourne wanted to help her.

'So,' the psychiatrist continued, 'you seem to get pretty bad headaches. Do they come often?'

'I don't know.' Anne shrugged. 'Off and on, I guess.'

'Tell me about them.'

'What do you mean?'

'Well, how do they feel?'

Anne pressed her lips together, trying to remember. 'First I get this pain here.' She pointed to the back of her head. 'And then it moves to my temples. After a while it seems to pound behind my eyes.'

Taking a freshly laundered handkerchief from her skirt pocket, she began to roll, twist, and crumple it nervously. Olivia noted her slightly bitten, unpolished fingernails. Why was the girl so afraid?

'What exactly seems to bring them on?'

'I don't know,' Anne replied, looking down at her hands and twisting her handkerchief.

Mama, I'm scared . . .

'These headaches worry you, don't they, Anne?'

She was silent. *Help me* . . .

'Are you afraid?'

Anne lifted her head and eyed the doctor steadily, her hands for the moment motionless. *Yes, I'm so frightened* . . .

Dr. Westbourne smiled encouragingly. 'Do I seem to be reading your mind just a little?'

Anne gave an abrupt, muted laugh, her expression a mixture of anxiety and relief. 'Yes, I suppose so.'

'I don't really read people's minds. I'm not that good. However, after spending many years listening to people talk, I am able to make educated guesses about their problems.'

Anne said nothing. *Please don't* . . .

Dr. Westbourne studied her face. What secrets hid behind that troubled look?

'As I told you, I've helped many people who had severe headaches like yours. Usually they improve with therapy. What do you think? Should we give it a try? I'd be more than happy to talk with you like this in my office a few times a week.'

So afraid. 'All right,' Anne said reluctantly, not really sure this was such a good idea.

Dr. Westbourne's secretary suddenly burst into the room, breathless. 'Sorry to disturb you, Doctor. It's one of your patients.'

'What is it?'

'Janet Evans. She's — she's gone berserk.'

'Call the techs. I'm on my way.' Olivia quickly rose and hurried from the room, Anne close at her heels.

9

Dr. Westbourne rushed into the ward just as the screams abated. 'What's going on?' she demanded.

Janet was huddled on the bed, her back against the wall, knees drawn up under her chin, arms wrapped around herself like a cocoon. Her eyes, unnaturally wide, stared vacantly, and she whimpered to herself.

Anne ran over to Janet and held her. 'There, there,' she soothed in a reassuring, maternal tone. Rocking, like a mother with her child, she calmed the older woman. 'It's all right.'

By the time the techs arrived seconds later, Janet's whimpering had ceased, and she lay quietly against Anne.

'Do you want me to give her a shot?' one of the techs asked.

'No, it's not necessary now,' Dr. Westbourne replied, surprised that Anne had been able to comfort this frightened woman so easily.

121

Turning to Victor, who was standing a few feet away, stunned by Janet's outburst, she snapped, 'Who are you and what are you doing here?'

Victor stood up now and faced the psychiatrist. 'I'm a reporter.' He whipped out his press card as if somehow it might justify his actions. 'I work for the *L.A. Tribune*. My name is Victor Larsen. I wanted to ask Mrs. Evans a few questions about her daughter's kidnapping. I'm sorry. Really, I never meant to — '

Dr. Westbourne cut him off. 'Young man, don't you realize that this is a hospital? Our patients are very disturbed. You had no business being on the ward.'

He nodded sheepishly. 'You're right, of course, and I'm truly sorry I upset Mrs. Evans, but I came here because I thought I could help her.'

'Help her?' The psychiatrist's tone was skeptical. 'How?'

'I thought if she could remember some details about the kidnapper, it might provide a clue.' He was careful not to mention the note, which he'd already pocketed.

Dr. Westbourne's lower lip quivered with annoyance, but she kept her voice under control. 'I'm not naive enough to believe that.

122

You didn't come to help Janet Evans. You came to get a story. The woman is here to recover from the tragedies of her past. I won't allow an insensitive reporter to stir up bitter memories.'

Victor looked over at Janet, who was quiet now. 'I didn't mean to upset her.'

'You're leaving,' Dr. Westbourne told him, her voice tense. 'The techs will show you out.'

'It's okay. I know the way.' Victor turned and walked down the corridor to the elevators.

'Hey, aren't you going to interview me now?' Mrs. Milsap called after him as he passed her.

Victor wasn't listening. He was thinking about what had just happened, playing the scene over and over in his mind. Obviously Mrs. Evans had recognized the note. The handwriting; the red lipstick. Hers had said, 'Eye for eye,' but otherwise the two notes were identical. No wonder she had screamed. Seeing it again was a shock.

Victor allowed himself a self-satisfied smile. He'd been right all along. The notes *were* written by the same person. He was sure of it now.

Anne was perplexed. Why had Janet Evans reacted so violently to the reporter? She held the woman close until she quieted down.

'You certainly have a way with her,' Dr. Westbourne had acknowledged. The psychiatrist had suggested that Anne stay with Janet. Then she had ordered everyone else out of the room. 'Maybe when you're alone together, she'll tell you what happened,' she had said before she left.

Now Anne cradled Janet's head in her lap, stroking her hair as she lay with vacant eyes, staring into space. Janet's body was rigid and motionless. She seemed so frail. Anne's heart went out to her. What had she seen?

'Mrs. Evans?' Anne whispered.

No response.

'Mrs. Evans, my name is Anne Midlands. I'm a nurse, and I want to help you.'

Janet's lips parted. Her mouth moved ineffectually as she tried to speak, but no sound emerged. Anne bent over, her ear near Janet's mouth.

'Do you want to say something?'

Janet moved her lips again, but only a gurgling moan emerged from deep within her throat. Tears appeared at the corners of her eyes and began their slow descent down over her hollow cheeks. 'I . . . saw . . . her. She's here.'

Anne barely understood the garbled words. 'What did you say?' She wanted Janet to repeat them, but suddenly, as if exhausted from the effort of that speech, Janet closed her eyes and fell into a deep, dreamless sleep.

Anne watched her for a few minutes then leaned her head against the wall, feeling weak and tired and frightened.

She closed her eyes, rubbing her throbbing forehead with one hand. Somehow Anne knew that Janet was not having delusions as Dr. Westbourne suspected. No. This time Dr. Westbourne was wrong. Janet *had* seen someone. And knowing that made Anne more frightened than ever.

July 13, 1981
Monday

This time Victor paid more attention to the passing scene as he headed east on Beverly Boulevard toward Alvarado.

The drive from the Institute took him from Westwood through Beverly Hills with its opulent homes and wide, tree-lined avenues. The neighborhood was too perfect — like a

125

residential Disneyland.

West Hollywood was more in keeping with his image of L.A.: men in too-tight jeans, strutting arm in arm past the Design Center, referred to disdainfully as the Blue Whale. Women were probably right, Victor thought. A *real* man was a rare commodity in this town.

At Beverly and Fairfax, he slowed to let two old bearded men in long black coats and fur hats cross the street.

He always thought it remarkable how each neighborhood seemed to have its own distinct flavor.

Farther east he passed weatherbeaten bungalows, then cheap markets and fleabag hotels. A couple of kids were playing ball in the street between cars, enjoying the warm summer day. The work of spray-can Picassos began to appear on the sides of buildings; unintelligible words written in broad, colorful slashes. Litter cluttered the sidewalks.

Deadbeats and unemployed laborers ambled down the street, gathering in aimless groups to discuss whatever men without hope find to discuss. They drank cheap red wine from bottles hidden in paper bags. Victor could see it spilling over their stubbled chins. Old, ragged men stinking of decay huddled on benches in parks where years before prominent L.A. families had strolled. Pregnant women, with little ones still in diapers close at their heels, pushed baby carriages up and down the dirty sidewalks. All this was a chilling contrast to the drive uptown.

Goldblatt was waiting when Victor finally pulled up in front of the tenement. The building was two doors down but identical to the burned structure on the corner.

'Where have you been?' Goldblatt demanded. 'I've been waiting almost twenty minutes. I thought something happened to you.'

'Sorry, I was delayed.'

Goldblatt's sharply planed features softened. 'Guess I sound like a Jewish mother, huh? It's in the genes, you know. My people are born worriers.'

'I see.' Victor laughed.

'So what's the great idea you dragged me all this way to hear?' Goldblatt asked.

'We're going to stage a demonstration.'

Goldblatt was nonplussed. '*That's* your great idea? What did you think we were planning the night of the fire?'

'No — listen. *This* is going to be a different kind of demonstration.'

'All right. I'm listening.'

'We're not going to march around in this neighborhood. It's not effective. Who's going

127

to see it besides the other neighbors? And you've already said they have no clout. Even if it's on the news, no one pays attention to the plight of illegal aliens.'

'Okay, go on,' Goldblatt urged.

'Well, I suggest we take this demonstration right to the landlord's neighborhood. We rent a bus and bring thirty or forty tenants along with their children and relatives. Then we all march around in front of his posh Beverly Hills home. We might even bring specimens of some of the bugs and rats that live in his buildings.' Victor gave Goldblatt a conspiratorial grin. 'I'll bet that will get a rise out of him.'

'Not bad, Larsen,' the lawyer conceded grudgingly.

'I knew you'd approve. Now we've got a lot of work to do. We've got to go from door to door and talk with the tenants in all of the landlord's buildings. We'll explain our plan and see how many will participate.'

'When do we get started?' Goldblatt asked.

'Right now.'

10

Juanita felt uneasy as the cramped service elevator creaked its way slowly to the basement. In the closed car the biting stench of urine saturating the stale air made her dizzy. She stepped back, leaning against the cold wall for support.

The elevator bulb was out, and in the dim light she imagined unseen terror in the eerie shadows. Ever since Saturday her nerves had been jagged, on edge. Maybe she *should* have waited for Marie. Her new friend said she'd stop by later. But then Juanita couldn't depend on her for everything. That wouldn't be fair to Marie.

The tiny wire cage made a sudden thud as it hit bottom. Slowly, Juanita pushed open the door with one hand, balancing her yellow plastic laundry basket on her hip. The hallway to the laundry room was also dark, littered with chunks of fallen plaster and shards of glass. What kind of people would let a place get so dirty? She shuddered.

The laundry room was nothing more than a large, open, unheated area. Half a dozen coin-operated washers and dryers stood along one wall, two deep double sinks along the other.

A dark-haired older-looking Mexican woman wearing a soiled housedress and slippers was taking her laundry out of a dryer. She acknowledged Juanita with a nod and a smile that revealed a wide space where her two front teeth should have been.

The woman stacked her clothes in two neat piles, then gathered them in her arms and carried them silently out of the room. Juanita heard the elevator begin its slow, creaking ascent.

Now she was completely alone. The silence was disquieting. She was anxious to finish her laundry and leave. This place frightened her.

Taking two quarters from her purse, she loaded her laundry into the washer. Should she go back to her apartment until the wash was done? That would probably be silly. By the time she got upstairs in the creaking elevator, her washer would have turned itself off.

She settled down on the splintered plywood bench in the corner, leaned back against the wall, and closed her eyes. Lately, because of the size of her growing belly, she hadn't been able to find a comfortable sleeping position. The drone of the churning clothes was almost hypnotic. She started to nod off.

The sound of breaking glass jolted her awake. She looked around, trying to identify the source. A tall black boy with skin as dark and smooth as hand-rubbed ebony stepped out of the shadows. Judging by his acne-covered face, he was fourteen or fifteen. His blue jeans were at least one size too small, and his black T-shirt bore a drawing of an ominous skull, identifying him as a member of a local street gang.

'Hey, mutha.' He grinned, his teeth very white in his dark face.

'Hello,' Juanita replied, her voice trembling.

'Got a quarter?' he asked. 'Ain't got no change.'

She opened her purse and foraged for the few loose coins that remained.

When she looked up again, there were two other similarly dressed black teenagers in the room. Her heart stopped. Sweet Jesus, help me, she prayed silently.

The boys came toward her. One of them picked up a broken beer bottle lying on the floor near the washer.

Juanita backed away. 'Please don't hurt me.

I'm pregnant. Don't hurt my baby.' Her voice was edged with hysteria.

'We ain't gonna hurt you, mutha. We just need some bread.'

Juanita couldn't understand them very well. She trembled with raw fear.

'Hand it over, lady,' the pimply-faced boy demanded.

Still she didn't understand, clutching her purse to her breast. With a rough gesture, the boy grabbed the cheap cloth bag and turned it upside down, spilling its contents over the stained concrete floor. Juanita could hear her few remaining coins clink as they landed and rolled underneath the washers.

'You don't have much in this bag, but I bet I know where you keep the bankroll.' The boy leered at her swollen breasts.

'Help me, somebody!' Juanita screamed before a strong hand clamped itself over her mouth. They dragged her into a corner and started pulling at the buttons of her blouse. There were three sets of hands on her body at once, pawing, fondling. She wanted to die with humiliation and revulsion. Only the thought that they might hurt her baby kept her from struggling.

She felt a rough hand groping between her naked breasts. Thank God she hadn't worn her gold cross. At least they couldn't take that.

'Shit, muthafucker. Where's the money?' One of the thugs held the broken bottle to her face. 'You'd better tell me or I'm gonna make your ugly face even uglier.'

'I have no more money. Please,' she whimpered, eyes closed, trembling.

'I'd like to believe you, but I'm gonna have to check it out for myself, since you ain't gonna cooperate.'

Juanita's heart stopped as he pulled up her skirt. She could smell his foul breath, feel the heat of his sweaty face. Fear made her legs rubbery and turned her insides to water. She wanted to vomit.

'No!' she screamed. The hand covered her mouth again, tighter now. She began to struggle, writhing and twisting, while the pimply-faced boy pulled her cotton panties down to her knees. His two companions laughed.

'Why don't you fuck her, Leroy? C'mon, man, do it.'

Hearing this, Juanita was overwhelmed by surging waves of emotion — fear, anger, terror, hate. She could feel Leroy's hands between her legs. She managed to free her mouth just enough to take a healthy bite out of the boy's palm.

'Bitch!' he yelped, slapping her face until blood trickled from her mouth. He raised the broken glass above her head, drawing small rapid circles in the air with the point, as if to tease. The boy's crooked smile had been replaced by an expression of murderous fury. 'You asked for it,' he hissed. Juanita's eyes were wide with panic. She knew he would kill her.

Suddenly the high-pitched voices of two women chattering together reached Juanita's ears. Their words echoed off the walls of the elevator shaft. The elevator! She prayed it was coming down to the basement. She wanted to cry out, but the hand across her mouth tightened. *Please! Help me!*

'Hey, man, someone's coming. We'd better split.'

The women were clearly on their way to the laundry room. Juanita could hear the clicking of their high heels on the concrete.

Thank God! Juanita's last thought before passing out was that she had been spared.

July 13, 1981
Monday

On the fourth floor, Victor and Goldblatt were trying to convince Carmen Gonzalez to

134

participate in their demonstration.

'I got five kids and a no-good husband,' she said in broken English. 'What happens if the landlord gets mad and throws me out on the street? You boys gonna take me in?'

'Mrs. Gonzalez, there's absolutely nothing to worry about.' Victor spoke in his most reassuring tone. 'My friend here is a lawyer. He'll protect the legal rights of all the tenants.'

The harried woman looked from Victor to Goldblatt, still unconvinced. 'You sure?'

Goldblatt nodded.

'I don't know. Lemme think about it.'

'That's all right. We understand, Mrs. Gonzalez. We'll let you know the exact day of the demonstration. We hope you decide to come. Thanks for your time. *Adios*.'

She watched them walk down the dimly lit hallway to the next apartment. Only after Victor had knocked several times did she tell them the occupant was out. 'She's in the laundry room. Came in just as I was leaving. Poor little thing's so pregnant, looks like she's ready to pop!'

'Well, I guess we'll have to talk to her sometime later this week.'

'Suit yourself.' Mrs. Gonzalez shrugged and shut the door to her apartment.

July 13, 1981
Monday

When Juanita opened her eyes again she was fully dressed. Someone pressed a cold cloth to her forehead.

'Estella, she's waking up,' the woman said in Spanish.

Juanita looked into the face of the young Mexican woman who was gazing down at her. 'You were unconscious. How do you feel now, honey?'

'Okay, I guess.' She wasn't really sure. Had the boys raped her? Probably not. The women must have scared them off. Still, she had been violated, and the thought of it filled her with despair.

Unexpectedly her vision blurred with hot tears. She couldn't hold them back any longer. Her body shook with sobs. The women didn't try to stop her crying, but waited until it subsided into occasional shuddering gasps.

'I'm sorry,' she sputtered. 'I feel so . . . ashamed.'

'Ashamed? *You*? You got no reason. It's that damn black gang from Clinton Street. They call themselves the Pirates. They been coming around looking for a fight with our boys. Every other kid's in a gang around here.

136

It's not safe for a woman alone anymore. You gotta be more careful next time. Okay?'

Juanita nodded.

'You think you need a doctor?' the other woman asked.

'No, please.' Juanita tried to sit up, but a wave of dizziness overcame her. 'I'm fine. Really.'

Her act was unconvincing. Estella smiled sympathetically. 'No green card, right?'

'You won't tell?' Juanita pleaded.

The woman laughed. 'Of course not. How do you think my brother made it to this country? If he waited for papers, he'd still be in Juárez. Don't worry, little one. We won't tell.'

'*Gracias*.' Then, remembering Marie, she said, 'I do have a friend I'd like to call.' She pointed to a folded paper napkin that had fallen from her purse when the boy turned it upside down. 'My friend's telephone number.'

Estella picked up the napkin and went to the pay phone on the wall.

'My money fell under the washer,' Juanita explained.

'I have money.' Estella inserted a dime from her pocket and dialed the scribbled number.

Please be there, Marie, Juanita prayed

silently. I need you.

After several rings, Estella hung up. 'Sorry, your friend's not home. Maybe you can try later.'

'Yes. Thank you for trying.'

'Do you think you can make it to your apartment? You should get into bed. That baby may decide to come early after all this excitement.'

Juanita nodded. The two women helped her up and guided her down the hall and into the elevator.

11

McFadden was livid.

'I told you to forget it, and now you tell me you've been flying all over the country following some cockamamy hunch! I hope you don't think these expenses are coming out of the *Trib* budget. You were working on your own time, kid.' He puffed furiously on his cigar, sending out thick clouds of smoke.

'Harmon, will you just hear me out?'

McFadden sat on the edge of his desk. 'I'm all ears,' he said sarcastically.

Victor filled him in on the details of his trip to Atlanta, then pulled Mrs. Hill's crumpled note from his pocket.

'Where's the other note?' the editor asked after a quick examination. 'You were going to match them up. Wasn't that the purpose of your wild-goose chase?'

'True . . . ' Victor hesitated. He didn't want to lose McFadden just when he had his ear. 'But . . . well, after my father died, my mother returned the note to Mr. Evans.'

139

'So? Did you ask Mr. Evans for a copy?'

'He destroyed the note,' Victor muttered, avoiding McFadden's disdainful glance.

'He *what?*'

'Wait, here's the clincher.' The words rushed out, tumbling over one another. 'I went to see Mrs. Evans. She's a patient at the L.A.U. Psychiatric Institute. After her baby was kidnapped, she sort of went mad and — '

'And how did you get into the Institute? Visitors usually need special clearance,' McFadden broke in.

Victor shrugged sheepishly. 'I just sort of walked onto the ward.'

'Oh, great. Now you're breaking into hospitals. What next, Larsen?'

'Uh, well, I showed her Mrs. Hill's note and she recognized the handwriting.'

'You mean she actually *said* it was the same?' McFadden was suspicious.

'Well, not exactly.'

'What *did* she say?'

'She didn't actually *say* anything. She took one look at this note and started screaming as if she'd seen a ghost.'

McFadden looked incredulous. He lowered his necktie to half staff and began to sputter. 'I must be hearing things. Now, let me get this straight. Some crazy woman in an insane asylum has a screaming fit, and you're saying it proves that the person who wrote this note in Atlanta last week is the same one who wrote the note in Houston three years ago? I think you're the one who ought to be locked up. Tell me I'm dreaming, God. This guy's not serious.'

'I *am* serious,' Victor said defiantly.

McFadden took a long, slow puff on his Havana. He lowered his voice. 'I'm gonna tell it to you like it is just one more time, kid. You need *facts* to be a good newspaperman. Cold, hard facts. Not whims or hunches and certainly not hysterical testimonials from insane people. And definitely *not* feelings,' he added.

'You're right, Chief, but just the same, I have a feeling about this case. What do you suggest I do?'

'*Now* you're asking my advice?' The editor used his most derisive tone. 'I already told you what to do: Give it *up*. Unless of course you've got any *good* leads?'

Victor did have one idea, but it was a long shot. Better not say anything right now. 'No, I don't.'

'Then do me a favor, son. As I told you the other day — leave it alone. Now, if you don't mind, some of us have work to do.'

Victor strode away from the editor's desk without mentioning the plans for a Beverly

Hills demonstration. This probably wasn't the proper time. He'd tell McFadden about it later.

July 13, 1981
Monday Evening

Anne didn't notice the young man standing just outside the Institute as she emerged that evening; she was too absorbed in her own thoughts.

'May I talk with you?'

Startled, she looked up, staring directly into Victor's violet eyes. They held hers for a moment before she recovered. 'I beg your pardon?'

'I'm Victor Larsen. I saw you today on the ward.' He offered his most appealing smile.

'Oh, yes,' she said, surprised he remembered her.

'You're the nurse working with Janet Evans.'

Anne nodded.

'Guess I caused a bit of an uproar. I didn't mean to upset her. Hope she's okay now.'

'She finally calmed down.' Anne spoke more sharply than she intended.

'Do you think Dr. Westbourne will ever forgive me?'

'I don't know.'

Victor suddenly laughed. 'Are you always so serious, Miss . . . ?'

'Midlands.'

'Well, Miss Midlands, do you have a first name?'

A warning stab of fear shot through her. What did this man want?

Sensing her shyness, Victor tried to reassure her. 'I don't mean to be pushy, but I'm new in Los Angeles. It's so hard to meet people in this town. I guess I sometimes come on too strong.' He grinned.

Anne took a good look at him. The fact that he was handsome didn't impress her, but his eyes were kind, she thought, and his smile was warm.

'My name is Anne Midlands,' she stated formally.

'Pleased to meet you, Anne Midlands,' Victor replied, equally formally. 'Would you care to join me for a cup of coffee?'

'Now?' Her heart fluttered in panic at the question. Part of her wanted to, but she wasn't sure. Mama would never approve. She'd just met this man.

'There's a nice place just down the street. They serve great burgers if you're hungry.'

Anne shook her head slowly. 'I don't think I should.'

'Why do I get the feeling you don't like me?'

'That's ridiculous. I don't even know you.' Anne was uncomfortable in the face of his self-confidence.

'There. You see? You haven't even given me a chance.'

Just a shadow of a smile crossed her face as she realized he was teasing.

'Do you have something else to do?' he persisted.

'Well, no.' She regretted the words as soon as they escaped her lips. She wished she had said that she was busy, that she had an appointment, that she was expected somewhere.

'Terrific, then let's go.' He took her gently by the arm and led her down Westwood Boulevard.

At six o'clock the sun was still bright in the summer sky. It was the best part of the day for Victor. As they walked, he furtively appraised her slender figure, lovely skin, pretty mouth. She was a very attractive young woman, though it was obvious from the way she dressed and carried herself that she didn't think so. She was hiding behind prim spectacles and a reserved pose. He wondered how she'd look with some makeup, perhaps a new hairdo.

Still, there was a certain vulnerability about her now that made him want to reach out and protect her. She looked so fragile, like a china doll. He couldn't explain the effect she had on him. They'd just met, but already he felt a stirring within him unlike anything he had felt before. This is silly, he thought, to feel so attracted to a wisp of a girl like Anne Midlands.

The waitress at the Old World Restaurant seated them at a corner table in the No Smoking section.

'You see, we already have something in common,' Victor commented.

Confused, Anne wrinkled her brow.

'Neither of us smokes,' Victor explained.

She looked at him thoughtfully, offering no reply. There was an awkward silence, and Anne wished she hadn't come. Victor wondered what he could say next that wouldn't upset her. The waitress, returning to take their order, saved him for the moment.

'Try the peasant burger. It's one of their specials.'

'I'm not really very hungry,' Anne protested.

'Please, I insist.' To the waitress he said, 'Make that two peasant burgers.' When they were alone again, he turned to Anne. 'I hope you won't be offended, but your accent — it's delightful. There's a touch of Texas in it, right?'

Her face flushed. 'East Texas.'

'I don't think anyone is native born out here. I'm from Houston myself.'

'That's nice.'

She answered his questions woodenly asking none in return. Was she always so quiet? Victor wondered. Maybe she was just shy, the type who took a while to warm up. He intended to give her every chance. 'East Texas. The only place I know in that area is Longview. You aren't from Longview, are you?'

Surprised that he had guessed correctly, Anne nodded.

'I bet your father was in oil,' Victor surmised.

'Yes.'

'A lot of men made their fortune in those oil fields. I used to hear stories about Texans striking oil. I hope your dad was one of the fortunate ones.'

'Until his luck ran out.' Luck, luck. She didn't want to remember, not any of it. She wanted to forget Luke Midlands, always saying how lucky he was. 'Anything will do for brains,' he'd told Mama, 'if you've got luck.' Poor mama . . .

'Did you stay in Longview after his luck

ran out?' Victor interrupted her reminiscence.

'No, we moved around a lot.' Before she was eleven, Anne had lived in every godforsaken town between San Antonio and Laredo.

'What kind of work did your dad do?'

'He was a rancher.' She wanted to laugh at the sound of it. A rancher! He was more like a field hand. *Oh, God, don't make me remember . . .*

'That must have been nice, growing up on a ranch. Wide open spaces, clean air. Not like the city.'

'No, that's true.' Even now, after all these years, Anne could still smell the stench in their 'home' in Catulla — the unpainted one-room shanty — no heat and no plumbing.

The waitress brought their food. Anne wasn't hungry. Instead of hamburger, she saw cabrito, potatoes, corn, and greens being ladled out of a filthy pot.

'Did you keep moving all your life?'

Why was he asking all these questions? Anne's head began to ache. 'No, we finally settled in San Antonio. I was thirteen.' *Don't make me remember. Please . . .*

'San Antonio — the pearl city of our great state.' Victor smiled at her.

Anne could think of nothing to smile

about. She'd lived on the poor side of town in a house made of scrap lumber — four tiny rooms, walls warped and splintered, tar-paper roof held in place with stones, privy in the back. Why was she remembering this now? What was the point? Besides, it was all so muddled in her head.

'Anne?' Victor startled her from her memories.

She looked up, distracted. 'What? I'm sorry. I was day-dreaming.'

Such sad eyes. What was she thinking? Somehow Victor had the feeling she was more than she seemed. Her cool veneer was just a facade, a kind of protection. She was not worldly. No, quite the opposite, and for some reason, he assumed that her life had not been happy. Suddenly he wanted to know everything about her.

'Tell me, why did a little East Texas girl come all the way to Los Angeles? I'll bet your father didn't want to let you go.'

Anne's face clouded over. 'My father's dead,' she said.

'Oh, I'm sorry.' He'd blown it again.

'That's all right. You didn't know.'

'Just the same, I shouldn't be so nosy, especially when I first meet people. It's the reporter in me. Sometimes I can't help myself.'

Anne said nothing.

Victor shifted uncomfortably in his seat. He changed the subject. 'You were amazing today.'

'What do you mean?'

'I saw you handle Janet Evans. It was fantastic the way you quieted her down. I could tell that even Dr. Westbourne was impressed.'

Perking up for the first time, Anne said, 'Really? Do you think so?'

Victor nodded. 'Absolutely. Have you worked with her long?'

'Just a few days.'

'Psychiatric nursing must be difficult. I can't imagine dealing with so many depressed people.'

Anne shook her head. 'Actually, it's very interesting.'

'I guess patients tell you things . . . I mean about their personal lives.'

'Sometimes.'

'Has Janet Evans said anything to you about her baby's kidnapper?'

'Like what?' Anne asked wanly, afraid of the answer he might give.

'Well, I understand she got a pretty good look at the woman who did it, and since Mrs. Evans seems to feel most at ease around you, I thought maybe she'd told you about that night.'

So that was it, Anne thought bitterly. He only wanted to use her. Just like all men. Anne gave him a piercing look. 'Is that the real reason you invited me here tonight? To get a story?' she snapped.

Her response took Victor by surprise. 'No, I — uh, well, really, Anne, it doesn't matter anymore. Yes, that was my intention at first, but not now. I want to be here because of you, not some story.' Victor hoped she believed him; he really meant what he'd said. When she didn't say anything, Victor looked at her intently, 'You've hardly touched your food,' he commented in a low voice.

'I'm not hungry.'

'Are you all right?'

'I've got a headache,' she whispered. A thousand tiny ice picks were chipping away at her temples.

'I'll drive you home.'

'That's not necessary. I can take the bus. I don't live far from the bus stop.'

'That's ridiculous. I insist.'

'Please, Mr. Larsen, don't press me.'

'I'd hoped you'd be calling me Victor by now.'

She pushed back her chair. 'Thank you for dinner. It was lovely.'

'Thank *you*.' Victor gently touched her

shoulder. 'I'd like to take you out for a real dinner sometime soon. Next week, maybe?'

Anne panicked. 'No,' she replied, too quickly.

'Don't you like me even a little bit?'

'You seem nice enough.' What else could she say?

'Well, then, why can't we have dinner sometime?'

'I don't want to date anybody right now,' she answered firmly. 'Now, if you'll excuse me, I have to be up early tomorrow. Good night.'

Victor watched helplessly as Anne escaped from the crowded restaurant. He began to feel like the prince who'd just lost Cinderella as the clock struck midnight. There was one difference, though: He didn't need to worry about a glass slipper. He knew exactly where to find his mystery woman again.

July 13, 1981
Monday Evening

As soon as Juanita closed the door to her apartment, she collapsed in a heap on the floor, hands to her face, crying. Her whole body shook with sobs, and the hiccups that followed. Never had she felt so dreadfully alone, and while the tears eventually subsided, the feeling of desperate loneliness did not.

As she sat on the floor, miserable, it occurred to Juanita that there was one place that had always offered her solace throughout her whole life: the church. She got to her feet, retrieved her gold crucifix from its special place in a drawer of her dresser, and put it around her neck. Although she hadn't been to church since she left home, Juanita now felt compelled to pray. She hoped that somehow she could find comfort in the house of God.

Impulsively, she rose to her feet, straightened her wrinkled dress and started out the door. There was an old chapel two blocks from the apartment. She had seen it on the walk back from Gusty's the other night. Thank God it was still light outside. No one would bother her at this hour on a busy street — at least she hoped not. Still, she walked quickly, looking over her shoulder every now and then.

Pushing open the squeaking front door of the Church of Our Holy Mother, Juanita entered the vestibule. To the left was a marble font half filled with holy water; above was a statue of the Virgin Mary.

'Hail Mary, full of grace,' she murmured, staring at the cracked statue. 'The Lord is

152

with thee. Blessed art thou among women and blessed is the fruit of thy womb, Jesus.' The words came easily, even after all these months. 'Holy Mary, Mother of God, pray for us sinners, now and at the hour of our death. Amen.'

Trembling, she dipped two fingers into the holy water, crossed herself, and walked on into the chapel.

July 13, 1981
Monday Evening

After Anne departed, Victor paid the check and left the restaurant. He drove aimlessly through the city for a while. Although he was not given to romantic fancies, he could not deny that Anne's effect on him was unlike that of any other woman he'd known.

Later, in his apartment he tried to read, but his mind wandered back to Anne. The way he was feeling — it was really extraordinary, he thought, getting up to pour himself some brandy.

Was it love at first sight? Come on, Larsen, he chided himself. That happened in the movies, but not in real life — not to him. But if not that, then what *was* happening here? He stared into his drink, looking for answers.

How did she do it? She was a total stranger. Really, what did he know about her? He knew her name and a few facts about her childhood — not much. Still, there was no denying it. She had touched a place in him — a place he had not known existed. From out of nowhere Anne Midlands had sudenly entered his life.

He tried to picture her now as he sat alone. She wasn't a knockout — at least not like Suzanne. But she had a natural kind of beauty. Besides, her appeal went beyond looks. Something in Anne's manner attracted him; she seemed remote, preoccupied. And he was more than a little intrigued by her elaborate defenses. What was she protecting herself from?

He finished his brandy. One thing was certain: He'd be damned if he'd let her slip away from him. Tonight he'd almost scared her off; he'd just have to go more slowly next time.

It hadn't occurred to Victor that Anne might not like him. Self-confidence was one of Victor Larsen's salient characteristics. And he had every intention of seeing Anne Midlands again — soon.

12

Marie felt restless and bored. It was still too early to visit Juanita. She didn't want to get there until well after dark. Maybe she'd take a walk along Sunset first; it was such a beautiful night.

After a quick shower, she threw on a low-cut sapphire shirt of raw silk and seductive cotton slacks that clung to the curve of her hips. She chose high-heeled sandals to accentuate her slim ankles.

'Not bad, if I do say so myself,' she exclaimed, applying a bit more blusher to her cheekbones. She dabbed just a hint of perfume behind her ears and slipped several brightly colored bracelets over each wrist.

Finally, Marie searched through a bureau drawer and found a small box containing a set of plastic fingernails. She curled up on the sofa and carefully glued the false nails over her own shorter ones. It took only a moment to select the nail polish she would use: a dark, sultry red. She painted her nails and let them

155

dry, holding her hands out to admire her work.

As she dimmed the lamp near the sofa, Marie smeared the polish on one fingernail. 'Fucking lamp,' she cursed as she repaired the nail. 'Never liked that damn thing.'

Moments later, after a last puff of her cigarette and a final admiring peek at herself in the bedroom mirror, she hurried out the door into the balmy night air.

The bus dropped her off on Sunset near Vermont Avenue. She walked aimlessly along the brightly lit boulevard. The neon signs of bars and discos flashed above her, a constantly changing kaleidoscope of colored patterns.

'Hey, sweetheart,' a man called from a passing car. 'Want a ride?'

'Not with you, buddy,' Marie replied flippantly. With her looks she could afford to be choosy. Besides, she was busy tonight.

She smiled flirtatiously at two young men who returned her frankly admiring glance as she passed. She was a young single woman, full of life. L.A. was her kind of town.

Outside Sunset's Body Shoppe Burlesque, a short, skinny man with a megaphone delivered his pitch in the style of a carny barker: 'Step right up, folks. See the amazing Helena shake her heavenly orbs.'

He tossed Marie a leer. 'Come on in, honey. Monday's amateur night. There's a striptease contest later. Fifty bucks if you win.' He reached out and clamped a skinny hand around her wrist.

'Get your filthy paws off me, you son of a bitch, or I'll call a cop.'

As though he'd been burned, he released her wrist. 'Sorry, honey. I thought you were out for a good time.'

With an imperious toss of her head, Marie turned and hurried on her way. Men! They were all alike.

July 13, 1981
Monday Evening

It was dark inside the small chapel, except for the flickering light from dozens of votive candles burning in front of the small altars along the side walls.

An elderly couple prayed silently in one pew. Juanita walked down the aisle, the sound of her heels echoing off the tile floors. She genuflected, entered the pew, and knelt. She hadn't felt religious in so long. A tear coursed down her cheek as she folded her hands and bowed her head in prayer.

After a few minutes she rose and left the

church, walking toward the rectory. Juanita hoped the priest would be in and available to hear her confession. The past few months had been so lonely and full of guilt. Now, after the incident in the laundry room, she felt especially in need of absolution, of the comfort of confessing.

The priest was in and he agreed to hear her, guiding her back into the chapel to the confessionals. How bleak it seemed, the worn wood paneling and frayed velvet kneeler. In the tiny space it was difficult to ease her pregnant body into a kneeling position, but she managed it, then folded her hands and whispered softly, 'Bless me, Father, for I have sinned.'

'Go on.' The priest's voice was authoritative but kind.

'It's been a long time since my last confession,' she said, 'almost eight months. I — ' She choked on her tears. 'I have committed a terrible sin, Father.'

'Don't be frightened. I'm here to listen to you.'

'I'm pregnant and not married.' Her heart pounded as she told him about how José had forced himself on her and how he had refused to acknowledge his child when she'd told him about it.

'Is there anything else?' he asked, sensing

there was more she wanted to tell him.

She wiped her wet cheeks and rested her head wearily against the screen. The image of the three gang members came before her — almost raped again. She told him everything and when she finished, the catharsis was complete. Exhausted, she finally felt rid of the guilt and self-doubt.

'I cannot absolve you as you have committed no sin,' the priest said. 'It is not a sin to be raped, my child. You were a victim; you have done no wrong.' He paused. 'God loves you, remember that. And he will give you the inner strength to fight the evils around you.'

Juanita felt a rush of relief as the burden of her shame lifted. 'Oh, thank you, Father. Thank you so much.'

'You're welcome, my child. Now take care of that baby and come back whenever you like. I'm usually here.'

Juanita stood up and left the chapel, feeling lighter than she had in months.

July 13, 1981
Monday Evening

Carmen Gonzalez kept the guard chain on as she watched the woman approach the apartment next door. Carmen had seen the woman with Juanita the other night, so they must be friends.

'She's not home,' Carmen called out after Marie had knocked several times.

'What?'

'Your friend. I saw her on my way home from the market. She went inside the church.'

'What church? Where is it?' Marie demanded.

'Not far.' Carmen gave directions.

'I have to find her,' Marie mumbled to herself as she hurried down the hall. 'It better not be too late . . . or she'll be sorry.'

Carmen didn't hear the last comment. She had already shut her apartment door and returned to her television show.

July 13, 1981
Monday Evening

By the time Juanita emerged from the old church, darkness had enveloped the deserted street. She knew she shouldn't have stayed so long. Thank God her apartment was only two blocks away.

She hadn't walked far before she heard footsteps behind her and the sound of heavy breathing. She felt the blood rush from her body. Please, God, she prayed, no more.

Turning slowly, she peered into the darkness. No one was there, and yet she knew someone was watching her. She could feel a presence. Terrified, she began a walk-run down the street. Perspiration poured down her face. The footsteps moved faster now in time to the clicking of her own heels.

After she had gone less than a block, she had to stop. Her pregnant body was just too big to keep up the fast pace. She felt like a huge lumbering animal. Again she turned to confront the darkness. This time she saw someone staring back at her.

Juanita's expression constricted into one of terror. A gasp escaped from her throat. She wanted to cry out or to run, but her muscles were frozen in place, her body numb with fear. In the moonless night she could see nothing but a pair of eyes — terrible and cold, like chips of ice. Sweet Jesus, she wanted to scream.

'Scared you, didn't I?'

The sight of Marie nearly stopped her heart. 'I thought you were — ' Juanita's voice shook. 'Oh, Marie, I'm so glad to see you.'

In the darkness, the eyes seemed to flash with an angry fire. 'What were you doing?' Marie demanded. 'Don't you know better than to go out alone in your condition?'

161

Juanita was surprised by the intensity of Marie's anger.

'I wanted to go to church,' she explained. She told Marie about the attack in the laundry room. 'I asked someone to call you at home, but no one answered. I had to tell someone. That was why I went to church,' Juanita explained.

'I see.' Marie's voice softened. 'They didn't hurt the baby, did they?'

Juanita shook her head.

'Okay, then, honey, let's get you home. I'm gonna have to take better care of you from now on.' She put her arm around Juanita, who was still trembling. 'Don't you worry. It's all right now.'

July 13, 1981
Monday Evening

As Anne lay in bed that night, she couldn't stop thinking about Victor Larsen. Why did he frighten her? What was it about him that made her so uneasy? He was nice enough — a little too self-confident, maybe, but he seemed sincere. He also seemed to care about her, about what *she* thought. Hadn't he asked about her past, her family, and her childhood? No man had ever shown that

162

much interest in her.

So what was wrong with her? Why had she refused his dinner date? What was she afraid of?

Because . . . one thing might lead to another . . . *Yes, Mama. I'll be good . . .*

Everything was going so well now. She was happy at the Institute in a way that she'd never been happy in her life. She was starting to settle into a comfortable routine. She had a new job and new responsibilities. She was fitting in. Why spoil it by letting this young man into her life?

13

July 14, 1981
Tuesday

Marie adjusted the counterweight, sliding it across the top of the scale until it reached a delicate balance. Then she looked up at Glynnis McCombie. 'Gained three pounds this week,' she told the girl. 'Not bad. Are you following the nutrition plan I gave you?'

Glynnis nodded. 'I even drank the milk, and I *hate* milk.' She made a face.

'Good girl. We've got to take care of our baby, don't we?'

'You're the boss.'

'Okay, young lady, lie down on the table. I want to examine you.'

'Isn't Dr. Van Patten here?'

'He's busy in the operating room. I'll handle today's visit. It's just routine.'

Glynnis smiled. 'I don't know what I'd do without you.'

'Why, honey, I'm just doing my job.' Her voice was smooth and syrupy as she expertly palpated the girl's abdomen.

'Fundal height is consistent with twenty-six

164

weeks. Let's auscultate the fetal heartbeat.'

'Huh?'

Marie positioned the Doppler device over Glynnis's belly. Soon a soft lubdub-lubdub echoed rhythmically through the room.

'What's that?'

'The baby's heartbeat. A perfect one hundred forty beats per minute.'

Glynnis was fascinated. 'I'm glad I decided to have the baby.'

'Okay. We're all through. Get dressed. I want you back here next week, same time.'

'So soon?'

Marie gave her an odd look. 'Don't you trust me?'

'Sure. It's just that my friend said his sister only went to the doctor once a month. Is something wrong with the baby?'

Marie smiled. 'Honey, that baby's going to be just perfect. You're both in tip-top shape. But my patients get special attention. Okay?'

Relieved, Glynnis pulled on her T-shirt and jeans.

Leaving the examining room, Marie almost bumped into Stacy.

'It's a goddamned zoo around here, for a change,' the young nurse complained. 'Every woman in L.A. must be pregnant. I haven't stopped running since this morning.'

'Miss Gardner, I hope you're not giving

165

Miss Fontaine the impression that we usually have time to chat all day.' Baxter's voice boomed like that of a drill sergeant. 'Dr. Morgan needs help with an endometrial biopsy in room A.'

'Bitch,' Stacy muttered through clenched teeth.

'Did you say something?'

'I'm on my way, Miss B.' To Marie she whispered, 'Talk to you later.'

'Miss Fontaine, I'd like a word with you.' The senior RN summoned Marie to the nurses' station.

Marie looked concerned. 'Something wrong, Miss Baxter? I hope my work is satisfactory.' Her smile was wide and charming.

Caught off guard, Baxter broke one of her cardinal rules: Never give too much praise. 'Why, no. As a matter of fact, you're one of the best nurses we've ever had. That's why I hate to lose you.'

'What?' Marie asked, slightly confused.

'I heard from the supervisor's office that you had applied for a temporary position.'

'I did that only because I wasn't sure I'd be staying in L.A. Later on, though, I decided to stay here permanently, but things have been so hectic that I just never got the chance to tell you. I hope you have no objections.'

Florence Baxter couldn't have been more pleased. Having someone as capable as Marie around left her time to catch up on her administrative duties. Marie reminded Baxter of herself when she was young. Bright, responsive, eager to please, Marie was a gem — someone she'd like to have around for a long time.

'As long as you're happy here, I'm delighted to have you working with us.' Baxter honored Marie with one of her rare smiles.

'Why, thank you, ma'am. You're very kind. Now, if you'll excuse me, I'd better get moving. We've still got a clinic full of patients.'

'Of course,' Baxter nodded as Marie disappeared down the hall.

July 15, 1981
Wednesday

Anne ran her eyes over the assembled faces, trying to conceal her anxiety. She had never led group before, and she wanted to do well.

'All right, ladies. Let's get started.' She cleared her throat nervously.

Dr. Westbourne was watching, smiling encouragingly.

167

'Does anyone remember where we left off last time?'

There was silence, even from Aggie Barlow and Deborah Fortune. Janet Evans, of course, said nothing.

'Tanya?' Anne prompted.

The beautiful face remained an unreadable mask.

Finally Sarah Lungren spoke. 'Tanya was giving Mrs. Winchester a hard time.'

Tanya's mask tightened. 'Jesus H. Christ, the fuck I was. I was the one getting hassled.'

'Someone should wash your dirty mouth out with soap, young lady,' Carlotta Winchester observed primly.

'Who asked for your opinion?'

'I think everyone is entitled to an opinion in group,' Anne reminded her gently.

'Bullshit,' Tanya said clearly.

'Carlotta's right.' Sarah shook her head, looking disgustedly at Tanya. 'Your parents didn't do a very good job of bringing you up. You're a spoiled brat.'

'Fuck you!'

Anne smiled apologetically toward Dr. Westbourne as though she had spoken the words herself.

'Oh, dear, I hate it when you fight like this,' Carlotta whined.

Sarah and Tanya exchanged silent, hostile glances.

Like a sailboat suddenly becalmed, the group drifted into motionless quietude. Minutes passed.

Somebody talk, Anne thought helplessly. Group therapy was supposed to proceed on its own momentum. What should she do? What would Dr. Westbourne have done?

Finally, Anne took a deep breath. 'What about your parents, Tanya? Do you think they did a good job of raising you?'

Dr. Westbourne nodded very slightly in approval.

'They're okay,' the girl said defensively. 'I had everything I could want — big house, nice clothes, my own car.'

'Well, then,' Sarah challenged, 'if everything was so terrific at home, why did you run away?'

'I got tired of the scene, that's all. No big deal.'

'Did your parents try to contact you after you left?' Anne asked confidently. Now she was starting to feel in charge.

Tanya shrugged, affecting indifference. 'They were really cool about it. They said it was my life, I could do what I wanted.'

'Terrific parents,' Sarah snorted.

Even Janet Evans seemed to be paying

169

attention to this verbal tennis match; her eyes moving back and forth followed the conversation. Anne wondered what Janet was thinking.

'My parents gave me everything.' Tanya was petulant and still defensive.

'Except love,' Sarah retorted. 'They didn't care enough to come after you.'

'I don't believe this!' Tanya cried, outraged. 'Who are *you* all of a sudden — *Doctor* Lungren, hip psychiatrist? What do *you* know?' In spite of her bravado, Tanya's mask had cracked a little.

Sarah smiled sadly. 'Don't you see? That's what all your running is about, Tanya. You're looking for someone to love you.'

'I don't need anyone.' The tough words emerged from trembling lips.

'You probably need a good spanking. Someone should knock some sense into that thick head of yours,' Sarah stated.

'You're not my mother.'

There was a pause. 'True, but if I had a daughter, I'd never let her go so easily.' Sarah's face quivered as she struggled with her own feelings. 'I would love her with all my heart,' she said, almost to herself.

Like a bullet hitting its mark, the words stopped Tanya cold. Suddenly her tightly controlled expression dissolved, and she burst into tears.

Another moment of terrible silence hung over the therapy room. Then Sarah went over to Tanya and threw her arms around the girl, folding her into a tight embrace and rocking her back and forth.

Anne watched them with an odd sense of something missing, something she had missed as a child. *Don't think about it now.*

'Miss Midlands, is it time for 'As the World Turns?' I want to get a good seat.'

Anne checked the clock. It was almost ten. 'All right. Why don't we stop here?'

The women filed out, Tanya and Sarah together. Only Janet Evans remained seated, her head bowed.

'Mrs. Evans, are you okay?'

Janet lifted her head to look at Anne. Her face was wet with tears. 'I didn't let my daughter go. She took her.'

'I know.' Anne held her hand, trying to soothe her. 'Come. Let me take you back to the ward.'

At the door, Dr. Westbourne stopped them. 'You did a good job today, Anne. I was very pleased.'

'I'm afraid the session upset Mrs. Evans.'

Janet gripped Anne's hand tightly, like a frightened child.

'You finally made her react,' the psychiatrist said, smiling. 'That's a very good beginning.'

171

July 15, 1981
Wednesday

Juanita became increasingly dependent on Marie toward the end of her pregnancy. She was no longer able to maneuver up and down the stairs easily, and after being attacked in the laundry room, she was afraid to ride the elevator alone. She looked forward to Marie's visits each evening. Her friend seemed kind, always bringing food and cheering her up with funny stories or showing Juanita the latest disco steps. She usually brought a stethoscope with her.

'We have to keep track of our baby's heartbeat,' she explained, 'so we know when it's time to induce labor.'

Juanita didn't understand the technical language, but Marie seemed competent. She always checked her belly just the way Dr. Van Patten had in the clinic.

'Everything's fine,' her friend assured her. With each visit, Juanita's fears had diminished so that by now she had complete trust in Marie.

July 15, 1981
Wednesday

At three o'clock, Dr. Westbourne led Anne into her office and motioned her into her usual seat across from the desk.

Today she hoped to learn more about Anne Midlands. Observing the tense, bespectacled girl sitting before her, she wondered for a few silent moments about the young woman who hid behind that chilly mask of efficiency. Olivia, in her earlier talks with Anne, had been fascinated by her complex personality. Anne had allowed her only a few brief glimpses into her intricate past — just enough to reveal the extent of her pain and the psychological scars she bore as a result of it.

'Anne, we touched a little bit on your headaches during our first session, and I'll want to hear more about them later, but today I want to review in detail your current life situation, a little of your background, and some of your past relationships.'

Anne was suddenly terrified. What would this woman discover? She wanted to run from the room, scream, hide, anything. Dr. Westbourne waited patiently for her to reply.

'Now, let me see,' the doctor started, looking at her notes from her previous session with Anne, 'you're twenty-eight?'

Anne looked into the psychiatrist's face, finding comfort in her kind eyes. 'Yes.'

'And you're not married?'

'No.'

'Children?'

'Excuse me?'

'Do you have children?'

'Uh, no.'

'It's not unusual these days for single women to be parents,' Dr. Westbourne observed. 'As a doctor, I have to be open-minded.'

'I understand.'

During the next fifteen minutes, Anne and the doctor sketched the barest outline of her childhood. Although she revealed more to the psychiatrist than she had to Victor, Anne was still very reluctant to expose herself to the psychiatrist's gentle probing. She answered all the questions put to her, but stiffened when the doctor asked her to discuss her feelings.

Seeing her reluctance to reveal her emotions, Dr. Westbourne returned to factual questions. 'You're an only child?'

'Yes. My parents were always good to me,' she added — a little too quickly, Dr. Westbourne thought.

'Are they both living?'

'No, my stepfather died when I was fifteen.'

'And your biological father?'

174

'I never knew him. He died around the time I was born.'

'What about your mother?'

Mama? What should I say? Help me . . .

'Is your mother living?' The doctor gently repeated the question.

'Yes.'

'Where does she live?'

'In Texas.' Anne spoke so softly that Dr. Westbourne wasn't sure she heard correctly.

'In Texas?'

'Yes.' Anne hesitated for a moment. 'Near the Mexican border, not too far from Laredo and only about a hundred and twenty miles from San Antonio, where we lived when I was a teenager. Sometimes, when Mama gets sick she has to go to the hospital in Laredo.'

'Your mother isn't well?'

Anne sat silently, looking down at her feet. Dr. Westbourne repeated her question while Anne continued nervously gazing at the floor. The psychiatrist wondered if Anne was so reluctant to answer because of the nature of her mother's illness.

'Is your mother mentally ill, Anne?'

The young woman nodded, afraid to speak.

'I see. How long has she been sick?'

'On and off since I was little. But she wasn't hospitalized until I was thirteen.' Anne's head began to throb.

Several moments passed in silence.

Dr. Westbourne was aware that she was touching a painful area for Anne.

'Your mother's illness has bothered you a great deal at times, hasn't it? That sort of thing can be traumatic for a child. Perhaps we can talk more about your mother in future sessions.'

No, I can't. Don't make me . . .

The psychiatrist checked her watch; their hour was over. 'I realize some of this is upsetting to you, Anne, but I think I can help relieve your headaches if you'll work with me.'

The doctor's look was kind, but somehow Anne felt almost naked under her gaze. Getting up from her seat now, she was glad to escape from those probing eyes.

14

The girl lay on the examining table with her feet in the stirrups, her shiny black leather boots striking an incongruous note. Stacy could see the fear in her eyes. She was obviously trying to act tough, but the look on her face betrayed her pain. Moreover, the hardness of her features couldn't hide the fact that she was just a child. Probably no more than sixteen or seventeen, Stacy figured. Poor kid. The nurse gently pushed the girl's thighs farther apart.

'Who came with you today?' Dr. Van Patten asked.

'Nobody.'

Damn, what kind of fucking world was this anyway? Mark Van Patten swore under his breath as he palpated the girl's swollen fallopian tubes. Just a kid and already a veteran two-bit hooker for some son-of-a-bitch pimp who couldn't even be bothered to bring his damaged property to the hospital.

'Ouch, that hurts.'

177

'What's her temperature, Nurse?'

'One-oh-three, Doctor,' Stacy reported.

Van Patten turned away from the examining table, shaking his head. 'It doesn't look too good, young lady.'

The girl began to shiver, although her face was flushed with fever.

And she's supporting a habit, too, the gynecologist thought bitterly, noting the fresh tracks on her thin arms.

'What's wrong with me?'

'You've got badly infected tubes. This isn't the first time you've had V.D., is it?'

She shook her head.

'Your abdomen is rigid. Peritonitis. That means the infection has spread.'

'Will I die?' she asked in the dull, matter-of-fact tone of someone who was used to hearing bad news.

'No, the antibiotics will probably control the infection. If they don't, we may have to operate.'

'Operate?' The girl looked at Stacy, her fear now showing openly on her face.

'A complete hysterectomy,' he said. 'I'm sorry, but we may have no choice.'

The girl shut her eyes against Van Patten's words, but even so, tears slipped out, her face whitened, and her hands shook.

Van Patten quickly looked away, peeling off

his rubber gloves, aware that he was being curt. He remembered when he'd been warmer, more caring. Not that he was indifferent to the girl's suffering. But as he'd progressed upward through the medical hierarchy, he had gradually acquired a somewhat cynical view of the world — what one of his mentors had called a 'more realistic' view.

'You can't change things,' the professor had said, 'so don't waste your time and energy trying to be noble. Besides, sensitivity isn't worth shit to a search committee looking for a new chief of Ob-Gyn.'

Van Patten smiled to himself. He'd learned his lesson well. Yes, indeed. He was now well on his way to becoming chief. Only one more step up the ladder.

'Nurse, tell Admitting this patient will need a bed on the ward.'

'Yes, Doctor.'

'Oh, and have Dr. Morgan take her history and do a physical. I'm late for a meeting.'

After Van Patten left the room, the girl let go, her tears gushing forth as though a dam had burst, sobbing in despair.

Marie heard the sobs and came rushing in. She looked at the girl and then at the nurse. 'What happened, Stacy?'

Stacy drew her outside the examining room

and spoke softly. 'Van Patten told her she may need a pelvic cleanout. The kid's freaking.'

Marie's face clouded with anger. 'Men,' she seethed, her hand clenched into a tight fist. 'If he had his way, every woman would have a cleanout.'

'Hey, you act as if it's Dr. Van Patten's fault.'

Marie snorted derisively. 'Sure. What does he care? Another uterus yanked out. It's not his problem.'

Marie remembered the scalpel she'd seen lying on the counter in the examining room, the light playing off its shiny blade. She must be calm. She would show him yet. There was still time.

She smiled weakly at Stacy. 'You're right, honey. Of course it's not his fault. It's just that I'm mad, mad that this kind of thing has to happen. I needed someone to yell at. That's all.'

15

Victor was sitting in Dr. Westbourne's office when she returned from her morning rounds. He stood up as she entered the room. Holding his hands up in mock defense, he said, 'Before you say anything, Doctor, let me explain about the other day.'

'I'm not interested in your explanations. Please leave.' The psychiatrist sat down at her desk and began sorting through her mail, ignoring Victor.

'But it wasn't really the way it seemed.' He grasped for just the right words. 'What I mean is . . . it wasn't anything I said that upset Mrs. Evans.'

Olivia looked up, annoyed. 'The damage was done, Mr. Larsen. That's enough.'

'Is Mrs. Evans better now?'

'No, she's still very depressed, although I don't suppose we can blame you for that entirely.'

'I'm truly sorry.'

'All right. You've apologized. Now how

181

about letting me do my work?'

'Dr. Westbourne, please, I've really got to talk to you.'

Dr. Westbourne eyed the young reporter. 'All right, you obviously have something on your mind. Go ahead. What do you want?'

'Doctor, what kind of person would steal babies?'

'I beg your pardon?'

'I'm trying to develop a psychological profile on the person who kidnapped Mrs. Evans's baby.'

'But that was three years ago.'

'I know. What I'm going to tell you may sound crazy — my editor certainly thinks it is — but I hope you'll listen before you pass judgment.'

'I'll listen.' The psychiatrist's smile was wary, but she seemed friendlier now.

Victor took a deep breath and for the next ten minutes filled her in on the kidnapping in Atlanta two weeks before. He told her about the note the Atlanta father had given him and how it was almost identical to the one Janet Evans had received three years ago.

'I know it sounds absurd, but I have a strong feeling that the same person is responsible for both kidnappings. It there's even a chance those babies are alive, I want to find them.'

Dr. Westbourne responded thoughtfully. 'Making sense out of the absurd is my business,' she said, pouring herself a cup of coffee and offering one to Victor. He declined with a shake of his head, not wanting to interrupt her now that she had started to talk. 'So you think Janet reacted hysterically the other day because she recognized the note?'

Victor nodded. 'The problem is that I don't have any hard evidence yet for the police. Without both notes, they'll blame Mrs. Evans's hysteria on her mental state.'

'You're right,' the psychiatrist agreed.

'That's why I decided to talk to you, Dr. Westbourne. I hoped you would help me build a profile of the kind of person who might commit this type of crime. Then I'd have something to go on, somewhere to start. Right now I'm back at square one.'

Taken with Victor's earnestness, Olivia sat back in her chair. 'All right, let's see what you have so far. You think the same person stole newborn babies from at least two different cities, several years apart. Correct?' she questioned Victor.

'Correct.'

'Do we know if we are looking for a man or a woman?'

'Mrs. Evans thought she saw a woman the night Justine was kidnapped.'

183

'You seem to know quite a lot about her.'

'My father was one of the police detectives on the case back in Houston. He was obsessed with finding that baby.'

'And now the son is taking over where the father failed?'

Victor responded to this observation with a burst of anger that almost turned his lips white. 'My father died two months ago. Don't try to analyze my motives.' He squirmed under the psychiatrist's penetrating gaze, feeling guilty of some imagined crime. 'I'm a reporter. This case in Atlanta just happened to come up now and — '

'I'm sorry about your father, Mr. Larsen. I can see that his death must have been very painful for you. Please accept my apologies.'

Victor nodded and relaxed a bit.

'I just wanted to understand how you got your information,' Olivia said. 'Very few people are aware that Mrs. Evans thought she saw the kidnapper. Her husband was afraid she might be harmed if people knew she was a witness.'

'I understand. Don't worry about that. Nothing about her will get in the papers.'

'So,' she sighed, 'where were we?' Olivia ran one hand through her short auburn hair while she considered a possible psychiatric profile of the kidnapper. 'A woman. That certainly makes it easier to explain.'

'It does?'

'Yes. You see, sex-identity conflict is a fundamental doubt. This is true for both sexes. For women, having a baby is sometimes the ultimate proof that they are 'complete,' so to speak. That's still true, by the way, even in this age of feminism.'

Victor nodded, encouraging her to continue.

'Now, if we assume for the moment that a woman took those babies, I'd guess she'd be someone who couldn't have her own children. Perhaps she's infertile, or perhaps she's had a hysterectomy. Or she might be terribly afraid to go through childbirth herself. These stolen children would then represent the simplest proof of her femaleness.'

'I guess that could explain why the kidnapped children were both newborn infants.'

'Exactly.'

'What about the family background of the kidnapper?' he asked.

'I would imagine we're dealing with a woman who was inadequately mothered, although this is all speculation, of course. Perhaps she now wants to change her own personal history symbolically. This is her ultimate mastery. All human beings seek to undo parts of their personal history that are psychologically painful.'

'I see. But why did the kidnapper choose to take these particular children?'

'That's a hard question to answer if we assume they were not random choices. A deranged person might have imagined that the mothers were guilty of some kind of sin. You said they both received similar notes?'

'Yes. Janet's note said, 'Eye for eye,' and Laura Hill's said, 'Tooth for tooth.' '

Olivia considered this for several minutes. 'Hmmm. It sounds almost as though they're being punished. Is Laura Hill married?'

'Yes.'

'Possibly our kidnapper thinks Janet and Laura are bad mothers. Maybe they've had extramarital affairs. The kidnapper might believe that by taking their babies, she was passing judgment on them, making them pay for their sins . . . whatever. I would say that one of your first jobs is to find the connection between Janet Evans and Laura Hill. Whatever they have in common is more than likely the reason the kidnapper chose them as victims. So far your only link is those notes, and as much as I would like to help Janet Evans, I have to agree with your editor. Right now it's too much of a long shot.'

Victor stood up to leave. 'I realize that, but if I can find a pattern — a link between the two women, as you suggest — would you agree that this mystery woman is capable of stealing another baby?'

'Naturally. Anything is possible when you're dealing with insanity, Mr. Larsen.'

July 17, 1981
Friday

For the second time in five minutes, Bill Evans checked his watch. He'd have to hurry to catch his plane.

The game room was empty. Most of the patients were in therapy sessions. Mrs. Milsap had told him to wait here for his wife. He wondered what was keeping Janet.

Pacing back and forth he practiced his speech to her. Ten days. Was that all it had been since he was last here? But they both knew. They had been lost to each other for much longer than that — for almost three years now. He wondered if Janet was in any condition to understand how lonely he had been. Three years was too long to ask any man to wait. And Rebecca had been there when he needed someone. When *he* needed someone. Damn it! Why did he feel so guilty?

He started to sit down on the sofa.

'Careful, I haven't cleaned over there.' Carlotta Winchester hurried over with a dust cloth. 'I'm working all by myself again. You know what they say about a woman's work.'

Something about Carlotta's appearance — the smock over the nightgown, perhaps — put Bill off. He merely nodded and waited until she finished dusting before settling down to wait.

A few minutes later, an attractive young woman entered the room. 'Mr. Evans, I'm Anne Midlands, the nurse on ward one. I've brought your wife.'

Janet stood just behind Anne, obscured from Bill's view for a moment. Now she moved toward him. He sucked in his breath involuntarily, horrified at the change in his wife. Her long black hair was a wild tangle; her pink cotton robe hung haphazardly on her now gaunt frame. She was a stranger, almost unrecognizable. This was not Janet. Janet was lost to him. She was lost forever.

'Mr. Evans, if you'd like to be alone, I'll wait outside.'

Bill looked at Anne. What could this lovely young woman know of suffering?

'No, that's not necessary. I can't stay long, anyway.' He now felt uncomfortable being alone with his wife and welcomed the

188

presence of a third party.

Janet said nothing while Anne gently led her to the sofa. A kind of bond had developed between the two women. Janet seemed to respond to Anne's soothing, uncritical, almost maternal nature.

Bill pulled up a chair facing them. 'How have you been, Jan?' Suddenly he didn't know where to begin. Nervous, he lit a cigarette.

'If you don't mind, Mr. Evans, I'm allergic to cigarette smoke.' Anne smiled apologetically as Bill guiltily crushed the cigarette out.

Janet Evans looked at her husband. Her eyes — the eyes that had once been so expressive, dancing merrily in her impish face — were dull and vacant. 'Did Gus call?' she asked.

Bill held out his hands in a gesture of helplessness. The doctors had all said that she would recover someday, but he knew that a cure was impossible as long as she clung tenaciously to the hope that the baby was alive somewhere.

As if reading his mind, she said, 'Three years next Friday.'

Bill shook his head sadly at the memory of that long-ago night. 'I know, but you have to forget now. It's been too long. The baby's dead. Gus is dead. No one is working on the case anymore.'

Janet put her hands to her ears. 'No, it's not true. I won't listen.' She didn't scream as Bill expected, but began rocking back and forth like a child.

Anne put an arm around her shoulder, comforting her. 'You shouldn't upset your wife like that,' Anne warned, more harshly than she'd intended.

'You think *I* don't hurt?' he said. 'Having a child kidnapped can kill a parent. This isn't like death. You can confront death. This is worse. We'll never know if Justine is alive or dead. But after three years . . . ' He paused and then repeated the words. 'After three long years, I've given up hope of ever seeing my daughter again. I've got to believe she's dead. Otherwise I can't go on. I can't grieve anymore or I'll die, too.'

Anne felt a sudden sorrow for this man, so blond, so handsome, so self-assured. 'Mr. Evans, I've become very fond of your wife. I want to help her if I can.'

Janet remained impassive, hands still over her ears.

'I'm not really sure she wants to get better,' Bill said sadly. 'Anyway, I've given up. I came here to tell my wife that I want' — his voice cracked — 'I *need* a divorce.'

Anne looked stunned.

Bill quickly added, 'It's been over between

190

us for a long time. Believe me. Janet and I both know it.' He got up, self-consciously checking the time. 'I must leave or I'll miss my flight.'

He looked at Anne and started to say something more, but decided against it. Instead, placing his hand gently on Janet's cheek, he turned and walked out the door without another word.

July 17, 1981
Friday

Leaving work that evening, Anne was again startled to hear someone calling her name.

'Anne? Hi, Anne, how are you?'

'Fine . . . Mr. Larsen, and you?'

'You promised to call me Victor,' he said, smiling. 'I'm fine. I hope you weren't too angry with me the other night?'

She hesitated. 'No . . . '

'Can I make amends by taking you to dinner tonight?'

'It's really not necessary . . . Victor, I'm not angry — honestly.'

'There's a French restaurant in the marina. I've been meaning to try it, but I need just the right companion.'

Anne thought for a minute. 'I don't think

191

I'm dressed for it.'

'You look lovely.'

'No — really. I wouldn't feel right.'

'You're a very pretty lady, and I would very much like to spend the evening with you.'

Anne blushed.

'Please, may I take you to dinner?'

Again Anne considered. Finally she relented. 'All right, if it's not too late an evening.'

'I know,' Victor teased, 'you have to get your beauty rest.' He led her around the corner to his MG.

Anne gave him an indulgent look as he removed the press card from the dashboard.

Victor shrugged. 'I might as well use what little clout I have in this town. Of course,' he teased, 'once I'm famous, I'll have a gold Mercedes with vanity license plates so everyone will know me.'

'You plan to become famous?'

'Sure,' he replied, helping her into the car. As they drove away, Victor told Anne of his dream to become a great investigative reporter. 'That's partly why this kidnapping case is so important to me.'

Anne frowned.

'Please understand,' Victor quickly added, 'I'm not just out for personal glory. Now that I've met both Mrs. Evans and Mrs. Hill, I feel a certain responsibility to follow through on my hunch, even if McFadden thinks it's just a long shot.'

'Who's McFadden?'

'Harmon McFadden is my editor. A great guy, really, but kind of hard-nosed. He thinks I'm way off base about this case.'

'But you don't?'

'No, I don't.' He smiled at her. 'What about you?'

'Me?'

'Do you think I'm crazy? Am I too obsessed with this thing?'

Anne wasn't sure how to answer. 'I really don't have an opinion. Does it matter?'

Victor thought for a moment. 'Yes. It does.' He let his gaze linger on her a moment before turning his attention back to the road.

Anne studied him closely. The other night she'd been too nervous and self-conscious to appreciate how striking he was. Now, sitting across from him in the car, she couldn't help noticing his thick mop of sandy hair, strong mouth, and deep violet eyes. He looked strong and self-confident, yet gentle and sensitive as well. The combination had undermined her usual wariness. Surprised, she found herself feeling very much at ease and perfectly safe with this man.

Victor stopped in front of Danielle's in

Marina Del Rey and let the valet park his car. Inside the decor was elegantly understated — white linen tablecloths, soft, intimate lighting, Chopin nocturnes lilting from discreetly placed overhead stereo speakers.

Anne was impressed. 'This is lovely.'

'I'm glad you like it.'

The view from their table was breathtaking. The evening sky, awash with the yellows and pinks of the setting sun, served as a perfect backdrop for the homecoming sailboats drifting slowly toward the harbor.

Victor ordered coquilles Saint-Jacques, veau forestière, and a bottle of Cabernet Sauvignon blanc. In the dim candlelight they talked, enjoying an easy camaraderie for the first time.

Over coffee and dessert, Victor told her stories about his trials as a struggling writer. 'I started at the bottom and it was downhill from there,' he quipped.

Anne laughed in spite of herself. She was really beginning to like this man and his self-effacing honesty. And talking to him seemed so easy. There was none of the awkwardness that usually spoiled a first date.

'It sounds as though you haven't let rejection get the best of you.'

He smiled, violet eyes dancing. 'Not Victor Larsen. I've known what I wanted from life since I was a kid, and I'll find a way to get it.'

'Yes, the gold Mercedes.'

He shook his head. 'Not just the flashy car and a big house in Beverly Hills. I want it all.'

Anne was aware of his eyes resting thoughtfully on her.

'Someday I want to come home to a loving wife and a couple of beautiful children — just like their mother, of course,' he added, still watching her reaction, afraid he might have said too much, not wanting to frighten her away.

Anne's heart was thudding wildly now. She could feel the beginnings of a blush creeping slowly up her neck, toward her cheeks. It was absurd. Victor wasn't talking about her. He was speaking in generalities. 'You make it all sound so simple. Like a fairy tale.'

'It can be. I believe it really can.'

'You're a romantic, Victor Larsen.'

'You make romanticism sound like a curse. Without dreams, where would we be? Stuck with reality. Well, no thank you.'

Placing her fork across her empty dessert plate, Anne looked up at Victor, her voice bitter. 'And what happens when those dreams don't come true?'

'I don't follow.'

She sighed. 'Oh, I'm just thinking of Janet Evans. Her husband came to see her today.'

Anne told Victor about the visit. 'He wants a divorce. They were married for ten years. Ten years, two beautiful children and now . . . nothing. No more dreams.'

Victor noticed the beginning of a tear settle in the corner of one eye as Anne struggled for control. He wanted to reach out and take her hand, but held back. 'Anne, I really believe Janet's daughter isn't dead.'

She looked at him with sudden sadness. 'Don't you think you're carrying this a little *too* far?'

He shook his head. 'I met the parents of the baby that was stolen in Atlanta two weeks ago. If you'd seen them, you'd understand why I can't give up hope. You know, before I left Mr. Hill told me his wife was close to a breakdown. I can't help thinking she could end up like Janet Evans.'

'Did she see who did it?'

'No, she fell asleep in the park. Someone must have just crept up and taken the baby.'

'Unbelievable.'

'I know. The only clue we have is the note.'

'Note?'

Victor told her about the message Mrs. Hill had received when she was in the hospital.

'How does that tie in to the Evans case?' Anne asked, more and more caught up in Victor's investigation.

'Because the note was almost identical to the one Janet got.'

'You mean the same words?'

'Well, almost. Mrs. Evans's note said, 'Eye for eye,' Mrs. Hill's said, 'Tooth for tooth.' '

Anne's face went ashen, her expression one of disbelief. *No . . . it can't be . . .*

'Anne, what's wrong?' Victor put his hand on hers and squeezed.

Anne shook her head as if to clear her thoughts, then lifted her gaze toward him again.

'Are you all right?'

'It's . . . those notes. The words were taken from Deuteronomy, chapter twenty-one, verse twenty-four: 'Thus you shall not show pity: life for life, eye for eye, tooth for tooth, hand for hand, foot for foot.' '

'You do know your Bible.' Victor was clearly impressed. 'Does the quotation have some special significance that might help me?'

Anne ignored his question. 'Why haven't you gone to the police with this?'

'Because they'd never listen to me. My father was the detective on the Evans case, and he could never make anyone believe the note was important. Nothing's changed.' Victor told her how Bill Evans had destroyed

197

Janet's note, leaving no way to compare it with Mrs. Hill's.

'And when I showed Janet Mrs. Hill's note, she became upset. I'm sure she recognized it.'

'I think you're right,' Anne said thoughtfully.

'But I don't know what to do next,' Victor confided. 'I went to talk to Mrs. Evans the other day and didn't find any real answers. That's why I tried to get your help. I hope you understand.'

'I do now,' she said. 'Maybe I can get Janet to talk to me, but it will take time. I can't guarantee anything. She's very withdrawn.'

'I have no choice,' Victor sighed.

'Unless . . . ' Anne thought for a minute.

'Unless what?'

'Well, you said Mrs. Hill got her note when she was in the hospital. Right?'

Victor nodded.

'Is it possible that someone might have seen who delivered it?'

Victor's face brightened with enthusiasm.

'It's a long shot,' Anne said, 'but maybe you can track down someone who was in or around Mrs. Hill's room that day.'

'Anne, you're terrific. Why didn't I think of that?' He paused for a moment, considering. 'McFadden will never give me time off during the week, especially to work on this. I'll have

198

to catch the late flight to Atlanta tonight and check it out first thing in the morning.'

'You'd better take me home, then.'

'You don't mind?'

'Of course not,' Anne assured him truthfully.

'I promised myself that I'd make amends for last time, and here I go running out on you.'

'Victor, you don't owe me anything. It was a lovely evening. We're more than even.'

'I'd like to take you to dinner again.'

She didn't know what to say.

'Next week?'

Anne felt the blush return to her face, and she hung her head to hide her blazing cheeks.

'Come on. You can't refuse a good ol' Texas boy. Besides,' he added conspiratorially, 'you're involved in the case now. You'll want to hear about whatever I learn in Atlanta, won't you?'

She looked up, the blush fading. 'All right, I'll have dinner with you.'

'Great. Let's make it Wednesday evening. By then I should have some answers.'

She nodded.

Later, as he walked her to the door of her apartment, Victor leaned over and kissed her lips — a chaste, gentle caress. She did not resist, but neither did she respond — a fact that strangely pleased Victor. She was obviously a well-bred southern girl who waited to be approached. He knew his mother was going to be delighted with Anne.

Funny, he had to come all the way to L.A. to find the girl next door.

16

Atlanta
July 18, 1981
Saturday

The head nurse in obstetrics at Grady
Memorial was in no mood to deal with the
young man in a blazer and slacks who kept
hounding her as she tried to proceed with
morning rounds.

'We've had eight deliveries in the past two
hours, Mr. Larsen. This place is a madhouse.
You can see that yourself. I'm afraid I just
don't have time to talk to any more
reporters.'

'Look, Mrs.' — Victor read her name tag
— 'Mrs. Chapanis, I came all the way from
Los Angeles. This will only take a few
minutes, really. I must talk to the nurse
assigned to Mrs. Hill during her hospitalization.'

The head nurse eyed Victor suspiciously.
'The police already questioned EmmieLou.
She had nothing to do with the kidnapping.'

'I know that, ma'am. I just want to check
something out.'

'Well, it's up to Miss Madison,' Mrs. Chapanis finally relented. 'She's at the nurses' station down the hall.'

Victor followed her instructions to ward B. It bustled with frenetic activity: orderlies wheeled big-bellied women on stretchers through the swinging double doors of the delivery room while worried husbands in green scrub suits ran along-side; harried nurses carried newborn infants to mothers for their morning feedings; candy stripers handed out magazines to anxious relatives. Everyone was busy.

The center of all the confusion was the nurses' station. Several women in white were taking morning report.

'Excuse me,' Victor interrupted. 'I'm looking for EmmieLou Madison.'

An attractive brunette stood up. 'I'm Miss Madison.'

Victor explained that he was a reporter investigating the Hill case. 'I'd just like to ask a few questions.'

'Why don't we talk in the nurses' lounge? It's quieter there. I'm about ready to go off duty anyway,' she said, checking her watch.

Victor followed the petite nurse to a small room off the main corridor. Two nursing students sat on a counter beside a coffee pot, talking in low tones. They slid to their feet as

EmmieLou entered.

'Hi, Miss Madison. We were just discussing the in-service lecture you gave last week.'

EmmieLou smiled. 'Relax, girls. You're entitled to take a break once in a while.'

They giggled appreciatively and quietly continued their conversation in the far corner of the lounge.

EmmieLou turned to Victor. 'I have to keep remembering I was once that young myself.'

'You don't look old enough to be their teacher.'

'Thank you, Mr. Larsen. Would you like some coffee?' she asked, filling a Styrofoam cup with the thick black liquid.

'Thanks.'

EmmieLou poured herself a cup and sipped the bitter brew, then rested her head against the wall and closed her eyes.

Victor looked at her worn white shoes. 'Tough night?'

'Oh, it's not that bad,' she sighed. 'There's a lot of stress in this job, but it's got its rewards, too. Especially when the babies are healthy and *wanted*,' she added with emphasis.

'Does that happen often?'

'Does what happen often?'

'Babies that aren't wanted.'

EmmieLou opened her eyes again. 'It

doesn't happen so much here at Grady, but in San Antonio, where I trained, it was awful. Every other baby was an accident. Most mothers didn't even know who knocked them up.' She noticed Victor's raised eyebrows. 'Sorry. You get kind of hard in this business.'

'I understand.'

She reached into her pocket for a cigarette and offered one to Victor, who declined. She lit hers and took a long drag. The two nursing students deserted the lounge, leaving them alone.

'Now what was it you wanted to ask? You know the police already questioned me about the case. I couldn't help them.'

'You heard that Mrs. Hill received a strange note in the hospital?'

EmmieLou looked surprised. 'I read something in the papers, but I didn't realize she got it while she was at Grady. She never mentioned it to us.'

Victor took a crumpled paper from his pocket and handed it to the nurse. 'This is a copy of that letter.'

EmmieLou scanned the paper and shook her head. 'I don't get it. You think the kidnapper sent this?'

'Yes.'

'But why deliver it before the baby was stolen? Don't people usually leave ransom notes *after* the crime?'

'I don't think we're dealing with a routine kidnapping.'

'Could you be more specific? It's been a long night.'

'This is obviously not a ransom note. There was never any demand for money.'

'So why send it?'

'Perhaps the kidnapper felt Mrs. Hill should be punished and decided to warn her. The phrase 'Tooth for tooth' is part of a biblical quotation. It's from Deuteronomy.'

'Are you saying the kidnapper wanted to warn Mrs. Hill before the baby was taken?'

'Possibly. I can't explain this yet,' Victor admitted.

'How can I help you?'

'Did you see anyone suspicious around the ward the week Mrs. Hill was here?'

EmmieLou gave a short laugh. 'You saw this place today. It's a madhouse. I probably wouldn't flinch if Jack the Ripper walked by.'

She examined the note again, frowning. 'It's funny, though . . . this note . . . ' Then she remembered. 'When I was a nursing student, a woman gave birth to a stillborn child. It was awful. She was half crazy afterward. I remember because most of the patients wouldn't have cared one way or the other. Anyway, the next day, she started

205

screaming and carrying on. There was a note on the bed! 'Life for life' had been scribbled in red lipstick.'

Victor couldn't believe his ears. 'Miss Madison, Mrs. Hill's note was written in red lipstick. This is just a photocopy.'

'Incredible.'

Victor nodded. 'And better than that, 'Life for life' is part of the same biblical quotation.' He repeated the verse Anne had taught him: ' 'Thus you shall not show pity: life for life, eye for eye, tooth for tooth, hand for hand, foot for foot.' '

Another piece in the puzzle had fallen into place. Victor was ecstatic. 'Miss Madison, someone has been taking babies and leaving notes for their mothers. The notes are all part of the same biblical verse and all are written in red lipstick. That's hardly a coincidence. It's got to be the same person . . . '

'Wait a second,' EmmieLou interrupted. 'You said babies were taken. Then this case doesn't fit; the woman in San Antonio had a stillborn.'

Victor shrugged. 'Well, as I said, I haven't worked it all out yet. But that case has to be related to the others somehow.' He sipped his coffee, thinking of possible explanations. 'Maybe the patient in San Antonio wrote the note herself. Maybe she was so upset after

206

losing her child that she started stealing other women's babies.'

EmmieLou shook her head. 'Sorry. Good try, but that's not it.'

'How do you know it's not?'

'The San Antonio woman was Amanda Hodson, Councilman Hodson's wife. Six years ago he was just a poor law clerk, but now he's a successful politician, and they've got two healthy kids. I still read about them in the papers.'

'Were you the nurse who took care of her?' Victor asked, unwilling to give up.

She nodded. 'I was working the day shift on her ward.'

'Who had the night shift?'

'Gosh, I don't remember. It was so long ago.'

Victor pressed. 'Think, please, Miss Madison. It could be important.'

EmmieLou rubbed her temples. 'I'm sorry. I can't remember right now. It's really been a long night.'

Victor looked disappointed.

'Okay, tell you what. First I'm going to go home and get a few hours' sleep. Then I'll look through my nursing school yearbook. Maybe one of the pictures will ring a bell.'

'That would be terrific. I really appreciate your help.'

'I'm not promising anything.'

'I know. I'm grateful that you're willing to try. Listen, how about meeting me for dinner tonight at my hotel? I'm staying at Peachtree Center.'

EmmieLou considered his offer a minute, then said, 'Okay, sure, but is five o'clock all right? I have to start working tonight at eleven.'

'Fine. Can I give you a lift home?'

'No, thanks. I have to finish my charting. Besides, I live right around the corner in the Brighton Towers.'

'Very convenient.' Victor smiled.

'Very cheap.' EmmieLou laughed.

'All right, then. See you at five.'

As Victor and EmmieLou left the lounge together, they didn't see the woman lurking near the elevator, watching them.

July 18, 1981
Saturday

Although he'd slept little the night before, Victor was bristling with nervous energy when he got back to his hotel. EmmieLou Madison seemed like his last shot. Could she identify a nursing school classmate from six years ago who might be able to provide him

208

with some clue about the kidnapping? He laughed ruefully. If McFadden called him a schmuck now, Victor couldn't disagree. Who was he kidding? He really had nothing — nothing except a bunch of notes and a crazy feeling he was on the right track.

Parking his rented car, Victor entered the lobby of the Peachtree Plaza. Seventy stories high, it was the tallest hotel in the world. This morning he'd arrived after three o'clock, too late to appreciate the showplace that architect John Portman had designed.

Now he wandered around the seven-story atrium with its passing parades of people — even at 8:00 A.M. Enclosed walkways from the hotel led to the Merchandise Mart and Davison's Department Store, but none of the shops were open yet. There was nothing else left to explore, so he walked back to the half-acre lake in the middle of the lobby and sat down to enjoy a lakeside breakfast of coffee and a Danish.

Sipping the coffee, he overheard two men discussing the baseball strike. 'I got this from a very reliable source; it's gonna go on till August,' one of them confided.

Victor shook his head. If the man was right, McFadden would be in a foul mood for the next four weeks at least.

Suddenly feeling his overwhelming fatigue,

Victor decided not to fight sleep any longer. Wearily, he rode the elevator to the tenth floor of the cylindrical tower. Opening the door to his room, he now fully appreciated the floor-to-ceiling glass wall with its startling city panorama. The view reminded him to make a reservation for dinner. The Sun Dial, a three-level revolving restaurant at the top of the building, would be nice, he thought. It offered spectacular vistas at night.

Half an hour later, showered and shaved, he set his alarm for 4:00 P.M., settled between the crisp sheets, and fell into a deep, dreamless sleep.

July 18, 1981
Saturday

Sleep eluded EmmieLou Madison.

An hour after going to bed, she was still awake, poring over her nursing school yearbook. She hadn't looked at it in years. Seeing the faces of so many forgotten friends and teachers brought back memories of those times. A kaleidoscope of memories tumbled through her mind as she turned the pages of the book, stopping here and there to study the candid shots of the students going about their daily routine.

The chemistry lab . . . Oh, God, organic was a ball breaker . . . Learning how to give injections. EmmieLou laughed, recalling how they'd practiced first on oranges, then on one another . . . Pharmacology. Professor Singleton was a dreamboat. Too bad he was married . . . The wards. Bedpans and dirty dressings . . . she never thought she'd become a good nurse. The work was so hard. Final exams. She had been second in her class . . . Graduation . . .

Sighing, EmmieLou turned to the class pictures. She'd changed so much in six years. She'd worn her hair in short, tight curls then. Page by page, she carefully scanned the faces of her classmates, shaking her head. Where were they now? Which ones were married? Divorced? Did any of them have children? Were any of them dead? She shuddered, realizing how quickly the years seemed to pass.

She focused on one portrait she'd passed earlier. There was something about that girl's eyes . . .

Suddenly remembering, she grabbed the phone and dialed Victor's hotel. He'd be thrilled when she told him the good news. As she waited on the line, she heard a faint patter in the other room. A sound almost like soft footsteps.

'Who's there?'

She heard the noise again, in the living room.

'Who is it?' Her heart raced furiously. 'Wendy, is that you?' Her roommate wasn't due home from work until after six.

The bedroom door was open, and the living room was dimly illuminated by thin strips of sunlight that crept around and under the window shades. EmmieLou held her breath, listening. There was only silence.

This is crazy, she thought. She was just tired. It was her imagination working overtime.

EmmieLou's fear was understandable. There had been a few robberies in the building recently, and she was unusually nervous, often jumping at strange noises, looking for creatures lurking in the shadows.

As she listened to the ringing of the phone, EmmieLou's muscles gradually relaxed, and her heart slowed to its normal pace. She chastised herself for being such a ninny.

A new icy shiver moved up her spine. The sound, she heard it again. Oh, my God . . .

'Aquarius, you frightened me!' she screamed as her roommate's tabby cat scuttled over her feet. 'Damn cat. I thought you were asleep in your basket in the other room.'

'Peachtree Plaza,' the hotel operator interrupted in a nasal voice.

'Oh, uh, Victor Larsen, please.' EmmieLou turned back to the telephone, relieved that it had only been the cat that had scared her.

'I'm sorry, Mr. Larsen doesn't answer. Would you care to leave a message?'

'No, thank you. I'll call back later.'

EmmieLou was about to hang up when she heard something behind her. For a terrible instant she thought she felt someone's warm breath against the nape of her neck. Was she losing her mind?

In that same instant as EmmieLou turned, her face froze in horror, a savage two-handed blow landed noisily on her skull, cracking it. The attacker smiled, a hideous grin. She stuffed a corner of the sheet into the dying girl's mouth, muffling the scream that seemed about to escape. She thrust the pointed tip of her scalpel into EmmieLou's throat and, still smiling, slid the surgical blade from ear to ear. Impassively, she watched EmmieLou die, observing the nuances of expression that passed across her stricken face — first surprise, then terror, then puzzlement. Her own countenance expressed nothing but detached interest.

When EmmieLou was finally still, her satisfied assailant glanced again at the blood-soaked bed.

Aquarius returned, scampered over EmmieLou's lifeless body, then ran off, frightened.

Turning to leave, the woman snatched the open yearbook and took it with her. No need to leave any clues behind.

July 18, 1981
Saturday Evening

It was almost 6:00 P.M., and Victor still hadn't heard from EmmieLou. He dialed her number for the third time since five. Again the line was busy. Finally, he decided to drive over to her apartment. She'd said it wasn't far from Grady Memorial.

When he pulled up in front of Brighton Towers, it was nearly 6:30. Police cars blocked the parking spaces in front of the building, but he found a spot around the corner.

'Everyone back,' a policeman shouted to the crowd gathering outside. 'I want everyone behind the barricades or on the sidewalk.' He looked at Victor. 'That means you, too, buddy.'

'I'm a reporter.'

'Which paper?'

'*L.A. Tribune.*'

'Kind of a long way from home, aren't you?'

'I'm in town on a story.'

'Uh-huh. Got some I.D.?'

'Yes.' Victor pulled at his wallet and handed his I.D. card to the officer.

The policeman studied it and then nodded. 'Okay, come around.'

'Thanks.' Victor stepped between two barriers blocking the street and headed inside the building. He wondered what had happened as he walked to the mailboxes and found the name he was looking for: E. Madison, apartment 5-B.

Two plainclothes detectives were talking together by the elevator when Victor walked over. 'I'm a reporter,' he told them. 'What's going on?'

'Possible homicide.'

'Who was killed?'

'Don't know yet. We're on our way up. Got a call from a woman who said her roommate was dead.'

Riding the elevator, Victor felt the first knot of apprehension in his stomach. They had pushed the button for the fifth floor. That was EmmieLou's floor! No, he thought, she couldn't be the murder victim. As he stepped out into the dimly lit corridor, a uniformed policeman with gun drawn met him at the door.

'It's okay, Pete. He's a reporter,' the taller detective explained. 'Where's the woman who called in the murder?'

'Her name's Wendy Devlin. We sent her to the hospital. She was very upset. They probably had to sedate her. Wilson went in the ambulance, but he won't do any questioning until you guys get there.'

'Did you speak to her?'

'Yeah. Poor kid. She came home from work around six and found her roommate in the bedroom, dead. It's messy, Sarge.' The patrolman was obviously upset.

'Any ideas on what happened?'

'My guess is attempted robbery. There've been more than half a dozen burglaries in this building since June. The robbers usually strike while the tenants are at work. Unfortunately, this time someone was home.'

'Any evidence of a break-in?'

The policeman shook his head. 'According to Miss Devlin the door was locked, but she was surprised to find the cat inside wandering around freely. Apparently she keeps it shut in her bedroom during the day.'

'I don't get it,' the short detective interrupted.

'Miss Devlin is a secretary. She works nine

to five. Her roommate was a nurse on the night shift at Grady.'

Listening, Victor felt a sickening twinge in his stomach. 'Oh, my God,' he gasped. 'Officer, what was the murdered girl's name?'

'EmmieLou Madison.'

'Are you sure?'

'Miss Devlin made positive identification. Why, did you know her?'

Victor nodded. 'I've been working on a story about the Hill baby kidnapping. This morning I interviewed EmmieLou Madison at Grady.'

'Too bad Miss Madison came home today,' the policeman observed. Then, turning to the detectives, he asked, 'Wanna see the body?'

'Now's as good a time as any. Let's get this over with.'

Victor bit his lip. 'Mind if I come, too?'

'Suit yourself. I guess you reporters are used to this kinda stuff.'

Wishing that were true, Victor almost tiptoed into the living room. The others walked as slowly. No one was eager to see the body beyond the closed bedroom door. Cautiously, the officer pushed it open.

A heavy rubber bag lay unzipped beside the body. A photographer was snapping pictures, obstructing Victor's view. Two men talked nearby.

'Probably been dead no more than five or six hours.'

Victor felt the queasiness in his stomach again. He started forward cautiously, afraid yet compelled to look.

He inhaled sharply when he saw her. Staring at her in disbelief, he felt his heart pumping wildly. Jesus, it couldn't be! EmmieLou lay on her back, her now bloated body bathed in a pool of blood, her throat slit from ear to ear. The gaping wound gave the appearance of a hideous grin.

My God! Victor wanted to retch, but still he moved closer. Her wide eyes had a peculiar, almost puzzled look. Her mouth was open, too, as if a scream of agony were trying to escape. How she must have suffered in those final moments of life.

He wanted to move back, to run, to cry, but he froze in his tracks. His head swam, and his sight blurred; his chest ached as he tried to breathe. His body felt the evening sunshine warming the room, but his mind was filled only with the grotesque sight and the consciousness of death.

'A horrible way to die,' said the policeman, grimacing. 'I'll never get used to this kind of thing.'

'No, you never do,' the tall detective agreed.

'Any sign of the murder weapon?' the shorter detective asked.

'The coroner says the throat wound is too clean for an ordinary knife. He thinks some kind of razor-sharp instrument was used.'

'Got any ideas?'

'Could be anything really, but I'd put my money on a surgical knife.'

'You mean a scalpel?'

'Yeah, that's right.'

In a daze, Victor listened to their exchange. He tried to calm himself down. If he was ever going to make sense of all this, he couldn't panic. He had to stay calm and reason it out. What did all this mean? The policemen continued talking as he studied the blood-soaked room.

Victor spotted the phone, which was off the hook. Had EmmieLou been trying to call for help when she was killed? And why was she killed? The police suspected it was a botched robbery attempt, but somehow he didn't believe that.

Two white-coated attendants carrying a stretcher entered the room. 'You guys finished?' one of them asked the policeman.

'Yeah, she's yours.'

'Thanks a bunch.'

As they lifted EmmieLou's body onto the stretcher, Victor stole one more look. He was certain now about the expression on her face, it was surprise — as though she had known her killer. Shaking his head, he turned and left the apartment. Outside the crowd was restless. The promise of a horrible spectacle attracted them, and they pushed and shoved to get a better view. Their curiosity shocked and startled Victor, but he pushed his way through the mob and headed for the rented car.

17

Los Angeles
July 20, 1981
Monday

Anne had awakened with a splitting head-ache. Even now, as she sat in Dr. Westbourne's office about to start her therapy session, the pain persisted. Maybe the psychiatrist could help. Part of her wanted that help, but another part of her was afraid.

'Anne, during our session on Friday, you had trouble discussing your family. You were blocking. I think your feelings are buried in your subconscious mind. They may be too painful for you to deal with on a conscious level.'

Anne tensed slightly.

'Don't worry. That's perfectly natural. Everyone keeps some secrets buried. Some-times, though, these secrets may be the cause of our problems. Releasing them can be therapeutic. Today I'm going to try to help you relax so we can talk further.'

'Are you going to hypnotize me?'

'I'd like to try.'

221

Anne was uneasy. 'I don't know, Dr. Westbourne.' *Is it all right? Help . . .*

'Trust me, dear. Just relax and listen to the sound of my voice.' The doctor's tone was soothing. 'You will hear only the sound of my voice.'

Anne looked at her.

'I'll start counting, and when you hear the number ten, you will go to sleep.' The psychiatrist began a slow cadence. 'One . . . two . . . three . . . '

Anne felt a heaviness in her eyelids. She closed them, still aware of Dr. Westbourne's voice.

'Seven . . . eight . . . '

By the time she reached ten, Anne was completely relaxed.

'How are you, Anne?'

'Fine, Doctor.'

'Good, now I want you to sleep and to remember. Okay?'

'Yes.'

'I'm going to have you open your eyes. When you do, you'll be back home in Texas. Just your mother is there today. You're a little girl, only five years old. Do you understand?'

'Yes.'

The psychiatrist noticed that Anne's voice already seemed younger. 'Okay, open your eyes.'

Anne's eyelids fluttered, then opened.

'Where are you?'

'In Texas,' she replied.

'Where exactly?'

Anne frowned, thinking. 'No name . . . the desert . . . somewhere near Mexico, but I'm not sure. Mama says only crazy people would live in a place so hot and dry. That's why it's got no name.' She giggled at this memory.

'Tell me about this place.'

In her mind's eye, Anne could see the hard and dangerous land where she was born — dry, baked earth with clumps of sage and tumbleweed here and there. She unfastened the top button of her blouse.

'It's too hot. I hate it here, Mama.'

In that open and empty place it was always hot. The blazing sun beat down on the barren hills relentlessly. Inside the tiny cabin the heat was almost suffocating. Certainly one of the world's most desolate spots, the area was overburdened with filth and mosquitoes. The wind swept down from the hills, blowing dust across hundreds of square miles of dry land with nothing to slow or break its path.

Despite the oppressive heat, a cold sweat covered Anne's body. Her eyes were frightened.

'Anne, where is your mother?'

'In the rocking chair.'

223

'What is she doing?'

'Singing hymns.'

'Where are you?'

'Hiding.'

'Where?'

'Underneath the house. After supper, when Mama rocks herself in her chair, I come to this hiding place. It's so peaceful here.' This was Anne's sanctuary — where she would lie for hours, thinking and listening to the wind, dreaming of happy things. Sometimes, as the evening shadows grew deep, she would imagine all sorts of demons in the deserted hills, but even they were less fearsome than the broom closet behind the kitchen.

'No, Mama, please don't make me go in the closet again,' she whimpered.

'Why do you have to go in the closet, Anne?' the doctor asked.

'Mama says I need a lesson.'

'What did you do?'

'I sinned.' She could hear her mother's voice, quoting Ezekiel: ' 'Therefore, thus says the Lord God, because you have forgotten me and cast me behind your back, bear now the punishment of your lewdness and your harlotries.' ' *What did I do? I wasn't touching myself* . . . 'No, Mama, don't hit me.' Anne's hunched shoulders trembled, and tears trickled down her cheeks. She could feel the blows.

Dr. Westbourne felt the session was becoming too traumatic and decided to wake her. 'Anne, I want you to close your eyes and listen while I count backwards from ten. When I get to one, you'll wake up feeling refreshed. You won't remember anything that has happened since you went to sleep. Do you understand?'

'Yes.' She answered without emotion, her eyes already closing as she listened to the psychiatrist. On the count of one she opened her eyes. 'What did I say, Doctor?' she asked fearfully.

Dr. Westbourne smiled reassuringly. 'Just things about Anne as a little girl. It sounds as though you spent a lot of time by yourself.'

Anne's heart raced.

'You must have been lonely.'

Anne gazed down at her hands for a moment before answering. 'A little.'

'Did you have many friends?'

Anne shook her head. 'I wanted to, but all the other houses were too far away. Besides, Mama said they were the wrong kind of children. She told me I'd pick up bad habits and catch terrible diseases from them.'

'Why were they the wrong kind of children?'

Anne sat very still, anxiously rubbing her hands together. 'They weren't Baptists like us.'

'Was your mother religious?'

'She tried to go to church every Sunday, but sometimes she had to work.'

'Where did she work?'

'She was a waitress in a roadside café about five miles away.'

'Did she talk much about her childhood?'

'Sometimes.'

'What did she say?'

'That she was an orphan. Her mother abandoned her when she was a baby.'

'Who brought her up?'

'She was raised in a Baptist orphanage near El Paso. That's where she learned religion.'

'Did she tell you anything about her parents?'

Anne was silent. Dr. Westbourne repeated the question.

'Mama said her mother was a . . . a bad woman.' Anne's voice faltered.

'You mean her mother was unmarried when she became pregnant?'

Anne nodded. 'Mama was always telling me how lucky I was because I had a mother and a father. She said my life was easy compared to hers. I never suffered like she did.'

226

'How did your mother suffer?' the psychiatrist asked.

'She told me many times how much she suffered giving birth to me. She said she was nauseated the whole time she was pregnant. During labor she almost died; it lasted more than two days, and there was no doctor. Mama never really regained her health and strength after I was born.'

'Did you feel guilty?'

'What do you mean?'

'Did you feel responsible for her suffering?'

Anne was silent for some time. 'I guess I did, more or less. She always blamed me for everything.'

Immersed in her past, Anne was becoming more visibly agitated. Her hands shook; tears filled her eyes. 'And Mama said I killed him.'

Olivia sat up. 'Who, Anne? Who did she say you killed?'

'My father,' she sobbed. 'If it hadn't been for me, he'd never have shot himself.'

This revelation surprised the doctor. Their session was nearly over, but she wanted to continue. 'When did your father die?'

'The day I was born.'

Watching her face, the psychiatrist felt a sense of sadness. Piece by piece the pattern of an isolated, frightened, guilt-ridden childhood was emerging. She desperately wanted to help this troubled girl. At the same time, she knew it would be improper to express the feelings, the need to love and comfort, that Anne aroused in her. The discipline of long years of training and experience told her to maintain a degree of professional distance. Still, she tried subtly to communicate her compassion to Anne.

'I'm sorry, Doctor.'

'For what?'

'For crying.'

'My dear, you should never be sorry for showing your feelings.'

Anne removed her glasses and wiped her eyes with a fresh handkerchief. Though she looked somewhat relieved, she said nothing.

'I think your headaches are caused by the kind of painful memories you relived today. You'll have to trust me, but once we uncover them, I know you'll begin to feel better.' Dr. Westbourne rose from her desk. 'Next time we'll talk more. Don't worry. We'll work this out together.'

Anne forced a weak smile. What had she told the doctor to earn such a look of pity? 'Thank you. I'm very grateful to you.'

July 20, 1981
Monday

McFadden was already hunched over his desk when Victor entered the newsroom Monday morning. 'Have a nice weekend?' he asked.

'It was okay,' Victor replied warily, detecting the sarcasm in the editor's voice.

McFadden puffed furiously on his cigar, his face slowly reddening until he looked like Vesuvius ready to erupt. 'Where the hell have you been?' he demanded.

'I signed out,' Victor stammered.

'Signed out? God, tell me I'm hearing things. This is not some nine-to-five job. A reporter does not *sign out*. He's on call twenty-four hours a day, seven days a week.' He glared at Victor. 'You *do* want this job, don't you?'

'Did I miss something?' Victor asked sheepishly.

'Oh, no, nothing important. Just a near-riot in East L.A.'

'What happened?'

'Yesterday a cinder-block wall collapsed in one of those run-down tenements on Alvarado. Crushed a five-year-old boy.'

Victor was shocked. 'Did he die?'

'His condition is critical. He's in the intensive care unit at L.A.U.'

'I'd better get over there.' Victor started to turn.

'Don't let me interrupt your busy schedule,' the editor said wryly. 'I can assign someone else. I just thought this tenement story was your baby.'

'Look, I'm sorry, Chief. I didn't realize. I —'

McFadden waved him away. 'Save it, kid. I'm not interested in excuses. I want something by three o'clock for the evening edition, so you'd better get a move on.'

Victor hurried out, glad he hadn't told the editor about his trip to Atlanta and EmmieLou's murder. After all, he thought, walking to his car, what was there to tell? A young woman surprises a burglar in her apartment. The police called it a routine homicide. Such crimes were occurrences in every city across the country. Victor could hear McFadden now: 'Larsen, a routine homicide in Atlanta is hardly news in L.A.'

But EmmieLou's murder was anything but routine. Victor was certain of that. For the past thirty-six hours, he'd gone over and over the details in his mind.

First, there was the problem of suspected burglary. The police said the thieves were probably professionals who usually robbed apartments whose tenants were out during the day. EmmieLou always worked the night shift, and anyone who bothered to case the place beforehand would have known that.

Okay, then, maybe it had been a copycat burglary done by amateurs who had heard of the recent rash of break-ins. That was certainly possible.

Still, nothing seemed to be missing from the apartment. EmmieLou's wallet and jewelry were in plain sight on her bureau, apparently untouched. The police suspected that EmmieLou had surprised the killer during the robbery. The intruder had killed her and then fled in panic, taking nothing.

But Victor didn't buy that explanation. First, if the slaying had been the result of panic, the killer would have used any handy weapon, not a razor-sharp scalpel. And EmmieLou would not have had such a thing in her bedroom. Also, it just seemed too coincidental that EmmieLou should be the victim of a bungled robbery attempt on the very day he came to talk to her about Mrs. Hill.

And what about the yearbook? Had she found it? Did that have any bearing on her murder? Could anyone have known exactly why she was looking through pictures of her nursing school classmates? Could someone have killed EmmieLou to stop her from giving Victor information that might help his investigation?

As he sped toward L.A. University, he reviewed the facts one more time, recounting the improbabilities. He wasn't sure what had happened during the last few minutes of EmmieLou's life, but he was sure there was more here than a random robbery attempt.

July 20, 1981
Monday

It was hot outside, and hotter still inside the tiny apartment. The stagnant air was so thick and close that Juanita felt she would suffocate. Every breath was difficult.

She pulled the window open just a crack, hoping for a breeze to ruffle her hair and dry her sweaty face. Instead, the foul stench of overripe garbage assailed her. Still, she thought, this is better than no air at all. A fly settled on her nose, and she brushed it off indifferently.

The loneliness was as oppressive as the heat and the filth. Since the attack in the laundry room, Juanita had been afraid to go out of her apartment. For days she had hidden behind locked doors. Marie Fontaine was her only connection with the outside world.

Juanita wondered why her friend hadn't visited her over the weekend. She'd dialed Marie's number several times, but there was no answer. She prayed Marie was all right, both for Marie's sake and for her own.

Wearily, she sat down on the couch, her swollen feet spilling over the straps of the cheap rubber sandals she'd bought at the Pic and Save. As always happened when she was sitting quietly, she could feel the child's impatient kicking. Her back ached constantly; the baby was growing so heavy.

Soon, she thought, my little one will be born — an American citizen. She smiled at the notion; it helped ease the pain of her loneliness.

Sitting there, Juanita leafed through the booklet Dr. Van Patten had given her. Titled 'Now You Are Pregnant,' it showed pictures of a child like the one that was growing within her. She marveled at the developmental process from egg to human being.

As she looked at the pamphlet, a frightening thought struck Juanita. What if Marie stopped coming to see her? Who would help her with the baby? What would she do? Hugging her belly as if to comfort the child inside, she decided that she'd go back to the clinic if Marie didn't come soon. She would find some way to make sure her baby came into the world safely.

July 20, 1981
Monday

'Oh, it's you again.'

'Sorry to bother you, Dr. Westbourne, but do you think our mystery woman could be a murderer as well as a kidnapper?' Victor stood in the doorway, breathless.

'Why don't you come in? You look as if you could use some coffee.' The psychiatrist started to pour a cup.

'No thanks, Doctor. I don't have time. I'm on another story for the paper. I just stopped by for one quick question.'

'Well, at least have a seat.'

Victor sat down. 'Thanks. I had to talk to someone. I've been so upset since the murder — '

'Wait . . . Why don't you start at the beginning?'

Victor described his trip to Atlanta and his conversation with EmmieLou, explaining that she'd hoped to find a year-book picture that would help identify the kidnapper. 'We were to meet for dinner. When she didn't show up,

234

I went to her apartment. She'd been murdered.' His voice shook, reminding Victor how much the events of the past two days had affected him.

'Here's what I need to know, Doctor: Could the kidnapper also be capable of murder?'

'You're asking a hypothetical question, Mr. Larsen. I can only make a guess based on experience, but as I said the other day, anything is possible when you're dealing with insanity, except that . . . ' She hesitated.

'Except what?'

'Well, we developed a profile of a woman with a delusion about children. She needs babies so much that she steals them. That profile doesn't suggest a murderer.'

'Why not?'

'Because generally when a delusion is as sharply focused as hers seems to be, there tends to be little deviation.'

'Suppose she thought EmmieLou could identify her?'

'I guess the fear of being caught *could* drive her to commit murder. She might feel cornered now, trapped. Still . . . '

'Please, Dr. Westbourne, any information would be helpful.'

'I've always felt that murder is a demented effort to destroy one's self and the parents

235

who created that self.'

'What are you saying?'

The psychiatrist looked at him. 'I'm saying that you can't predict what she might be capable of if she's now under stress. Whatever pattern she's developed thus far may change.'

'I see.'

'Have you gone to the police yet?'

'So far I have nothing concrete to present to them. Just a hunch, one note, a hysterical reaction from Mrs. Evans, and now a seemingly unrelated murder. My editor may be right, after all; I could be way off base. Maybe I *am* just an overanxious reporter trying to create a story out of thin air.'

Dr. Westbourne looked at him. 'You don't believe that, do you?'

'No,' Victor said softly. 'I don't.'

July 20, 1981
Monday

'Tony? Tony, can you hear me? Can you wiggle your toes? Come on,' the doctor intoned.

The dark head lying on the pillow did not move. A respirator clicked rhythmically beside the bed. From overhead, blood flowed

236

downward through a plastic tube inserted in the child's arm.

'Tony . . .'

The neurosurgeon pulled back one of the boy's eyelids and shone his light through the dilated pupil, onto the retina. The pupillary response was sluggish, indicating some abnormality in the sensitive optical circuitry deep within the brain of the comatose child.

Hunched over the bed, the mother anxiously watched the doctor's reaction. 'Will he be all right?'

'I don't know yet, Mrs. Gonzalez. I haven't finished my examination.'

The mother stepped back as he moved to the foot of the bed, fishing a rubber-tipped reflex hammer from his black bag. She watched the boy's face as the neurosurgeon pressed the metallic end of the hammer against the bottom of the boy's heel and drew it upward toward the toes. Although the scraping was forceful enough to leave a long white mark, Tony didn't flinch. The neurosurgeon repeated the procedure on the other foot, again without getting a reaction.

A nurse came in and quietly checked the strong, steady blips moving across the cardiac monitor. 'Blood pressure is one hundred over sixty,' she reported. She deftly manipulated the valves and switches of the respirator, adjusting the mixture of oxygen and moist air being pumped into the boy's lungs.

'Tony, can you hear me?' the neurosurgeon continued loudly, running his long fingers through the child's dark hair, feeling for damage to the skull.

'Please, Doctor, how is he?' the mother pleaded.

'I'm sorry, Mrs. Gonzalez; it's just too early to tell.'

'Is he sleeping?' she asked, desperate for reassurance.

'He's in a coma. It's a kind of sleep.'

'When will he wake up?' She didn't want to believe what she was hearing.

'We just don't know, but at this stage I'm very optimistic. He could recover completely. We'll just have to wait and see.'

A technician came into the room with an electroencephalograph and began setting it up.

'What is he doing?'

'He'll give Tony an EEG to check the activity in the boy's brain. It won't hurt him, I promise.'

'You think he's going to die, don't you?' Suddenly all of the mother's pent-up fears overflowed. She began to sob quietly.

Victor, who had been watching from outside, entered the cubicle and put a comforting arm around the frightened woman. 'Let me buy you a cup of coffee. There's nothing you can do now. Tony's in good hands.'

'Are you a member of the family?' the nurse asked Victor.

'No. I met Mrs. Gonzalez last week while I was doing a story. I'm a reporter from the *L.A. Tribune*. How soon will you know more about the boy's condition?'

Victor held the sobbing mother against his chest so that she didn't see the nurse shrug and shake her head ominously.

God damn it, he thought angrily. He would make that landlord pay, if it was the last thing he ever did.

18

July 21, 1981
Tuesday

'Well?' The receptionist eyed Juanita impatiently. 'Are you checking in or what?'

'Uh . . .'

'You're Dr. Van Patten's patient, the one without insurance, right? I wondered when you'd come back. Did you get things straightened out?'

'Uh, no, not exactly. I'm looking for Marie Fontaine. She's a nurse here.'

'Oh, yeah, Miss Fontaine. She's busy now. You'll have to wait.'

'That's all right.'

Juanita took a seat in the waiting area.

A woman fanned herself with a torn copy of *Parents* magazine. '*Caliente.*'

'*Sí*' Juanita agreed.

The air conditioning was broken. Damp wisps of gray hair fell over the woman's right eye and hung limply against her cheek.

Juanita waited for almost an hour before she finally caught sight of Marie leaving one of the examining rooms.

'And don't forget,' she was telling her young patient. 'If you need anything, just give me a call at home — any time.'

The girl nodded. 'See you next week, and thanks for everything.'

Slowly, Juanita got out of the chair and approached Marie. 'Hi,' she greeted her friend. 'I'm glad I found you.'

'What are *you* doing here?' Her voice was stern and cold.

'I, uh . . . I was worried when you didn't come the last few nights. I thought maybe something had happened to you.'

'You have my home number. Why didn't you call?'

'I did, but no one answered. I was worried.'

'You must have dialed the wrong number,' Marie countered, her irritation quickly dissipating. 'Don't worry. It's okay now.'

Juanita studied Marie's face, unnerved as always by her friend's changeable moods.

'You go home and get some rest now,' she said. 'I'll stop by and see you later. You shouldn't be traipsing all over town. Our baby will be here any day now. You want to be well rested when he arrives, don't you?'

'Do you really think it will be a boy?' Juanita asked eagerly.

'Absolutely.'

Pleased, Juanita thanked her friend and turned to go. Then she stopped and faced Marie. 'I *am* sorry to have bothered you, Marie,' she said. 'Forgive me?'

'*De nada*. Now go on home.'

Watching Juanita disappear down the corridor, Marie smiled to herself. Everything was going well.

At the same time, Stacy stepped farther back into the shadows where she had been observing the scene. Why would a patient come to the clinic to see Marie? And why did Marie speak of 'our baby'? For an instant she had an extremely uneasy feeling in her gut. Funny woman, this one, no matter how highly Baxter regarded her. Stacy would have to keep an eye on Marie Fontaine from now on.

July 21, 1981
Tuesday

Sy Goldblatt met Victor for a late lunch at a café near the hospital.

'How's the Gonzalez kid doing?' Goldblatt asked as they sat down.

'I don't think he's going to make it, Sy.'

'Oh, no. That's terrible. But I may have something that'll cheer you a little.'

'I don't think that's possible,' Victor said glumly.

'Guess who owns that property on Alvarado,' he baited.

'I can't. Tell me.'

'None other than Orson Pepperton.'

Victor was speechless. 'You mean State Senator Pepperton, the crusader for liberal causes and people's rights?'

The lawyer nodded.

'I don't believe it! That self-righteous bastard!'

Goldblatt gave Victor a satisfied smile. 'It's true. I went down to the Hall of Records and looked up the original deeds of trust. Of course, Senator Pepperton is no amateur. He used a bogus corporation called Theta Enterprises to buy the properties. I have a friend at the State Corporations Commission who checked it out for me. Pepperton is Theta's chairman of the board.'

Victor rubbed his hands together. 'Sy, you just made my day. This is going to be one helluva story.'

Goldblatt chuckled. 'When our busload of tenants marches up Rodeo Drive, Senator Pepperton is going to have a lot of explaining to do. I hope you'll have a photographer there. Oh,' he gloated, 'I can't wait to see a picture of him with his foot in his mouth.'

'Don't worry. When McFadden hears about this, he'll pull out all the stops. This will be front-page news.'

'How about holding the demonstration on Friday. I know that's only three days away, but I think we should strike while the iron is hot.'

'Sounds great.'

July 22, 1981
Wednesday

Dr. Westbourne had spent several hours reviewing her notes on Anne before their Wednesday session. So far she knew Anne's real father had killed himself on the day of her birth, and her mother, Lucinda, somehow blamed the child for this death. Lucinda had gradually spun a web of guilt and loneliness that enveloped Anne during her formative years, ultimately producing a shy, withdrawn, self-conscious adult.

Observing Anne now sitting across from her, Dr. Westbourne was amazed that she had turned out as well as she had. Everyone on the staff agreed that Anne Midlands had a natural ability to work with patients who were disturbed. It was truly astounding how she had been able to help Janet Evans.

244

'You remember how we worked with hypnosis on Monday?' the psychiatrist asked.

'Yes.'

'I want to try that again. Now, just relax and listen to the sound of my voice. You'll become very sleepy, but you'll be able to hear me and answer all my questions. Okay?'

'Yes.'

From Monday's session it was clear that Anne had suppressed some memories that were too painful for her to confront consciously. Olivia planned to use hypnosis until she could discover what had upset Anne. Then perhaps they could resolve it together in therapy.

She started counting, 'One . . . two . . . three . . .'

Anne felt her eyelids grow heavy. When she slipped into a relaxed, hypnotic state, Dr. Westbourne began questioning her.

'Anne, we haven't talked much about your stepfather yet. What did you say his name was?'

Already beginning to feel uneasy, Anne replied hesitantly, 'Luke Midlands.'

'How old were you when your mother remarried?'

'Five.'

'You're doing very well, Anne. How do you feel?'

'Fine.'

'Good. I want you to go back to Texas. You are five years old. Your mother has just met Luke Midlands. Do you remember that day?'

'I'm not sure,' she answered slowly. 'I think he came into the restaurant where she worked.'

'Where were you?'

Anne wrinkled her brow, trying to remember. 'Mama made me stay in the kitchen of the restaurant. I had been bad . . . Now I remember . . . He told Mama he was on his way to Longview.' The scene was being replayed in Anne's head. She had been sitting on the floor, listening to them . . .

'Where's Longview?' Lucinda had asked.

'A ways down that road,' he replied, nodding toward the dusty highway. 'The name's Luke Midlands.' He smiled, looking Lucinda over. Although she wore her hair pulled away from her face in an unbecoming way, there was still a hint of her former prettiness in her weatherbeaten face. 'What's your name, girl?'

'Lucinda.' Anne's mother had hesitated, distrustful of strangers. 'Why are you going to Longview?'

'Are you kidding? You mean you haven't heard about the greatest oil find ever?'

Lucinda shook her head, ashamed of her ignorance.

Luke explained. 'More than twenty years ago, Dad Joiner made his famous find — the Daisy Bradford number three. Since that time they've struck oil in every direction from the original site. I've been waiting all my life to have my go at one of those wells. I tell you, honey, you're looking at a rich man.'

'You mean you own the well?'

'No, girl, I'm a wildcatter. I only want a piece of the action. Even after all these years, I figure there's plenty of oil still in the ground.' Suddenly Luke put his arm around Lucinda and said impulsively, 'I been lookin' for a good woman. Why don't you marry me. Let me take you away from all this.' He waved one hand at the dust-covered restaurant.

'I think you must have sunstroke, Mr. Midlands.' Lucinda seemed to be appalled by the man's aggressiveness. She backed away. 'I'm a God-fearing woman with a daughter to raise.'

'Sorry, ma'am. Didn't see a weddin' band. Forgive me.' Luke turned to leave.

'I'm a widow. My husband died more than five years ago.'

'Why, then, you *do* need someone. A pretty woman like you shouldn't be stuck in this godforsaken place. But I'm in a hurry, girl, so make up your mind.'

That was true. Within two days of their meeting, Lucinda and Luke were married by a justice of the peace. They set out with Anne for Longview in Luke's 1948 Chevy.

Five-year-old Anne had buried the memory deep within her as she had all her childhood unhappiness.

'What was your stepfather like, Anne?' the psychiatrist asked.

'He was a big man,' she said softly, trying to remember Luke now: big and beefy like a prizefighter. Luke Midlands — the stereotypical wildcatter — a man geared to taking risks, who enjoyed life on a tightrope.

'Did he get along well with your mother?'

'I guess so.'

'Did they argue much?'

'No, not at first,' she replied, fidgeting nervously.

Even under hypnosis she seemed to resist this line of questioning. Olivia didn't want to press her, but she needed more information.

'Anne, you are getting older now. You are ten years old. Do you understand?'

'Yes.'

'Where are you living?'

'We keep moving from town to town. I can't remember all the places.'

'Why do you keep moving?' the doctor asked.

'Luke's well went dry. He needed work. There was nothing for him to do in Longview.'

'And what happened?' the psychiatrist gently coaxed.

'He began to drink.' Anne twisted her hands together in her lap as she spoke. More and more Luke had turned to alcohol to salve his injured ego. Lucinda had met him during one of his dry spells. She didn't know he'd spent much of his adult life in an alcoholic stupor.

'Is he ever violent?' the doctor asked.

'Sometimes . . . sometimes he beats Mama.' Drunk or sober Luke was a violent man. He became a bitter and disappointed man whose rough, reddened features were often clouded in anger.

'Does he ever hit you?'

Anne was silent. Dr. Westbourne repeated the question.

'He always wears cowboy boots,' she replied so softly that the psychiatrist wasn't sure she had understood.

'Cowboy boots?'

Anne nodded. 'Sometimes he kicks me.' She visibly cringed remembering the feel of those heavy heels.

Dr. Westbourne was stunned. She wanted to comfort this poor girl. At the same time she recognized that Anne needed to work through her own pain. 'Is he ever affectionate toward you?'

Anne's body tensed. 'Not really.'

'Okay, Anne, let's move on. You are thirteen now. Do you remember thirteen?'

'Yes.'

'Where are you living now?'

'Near Laredo somewhere. I don't know exactly, but Luke is working as a ranch hand. He hardly ever brings home money anymore.'

'Do your parents sleep together?'

Anne didn't know where the questions were leading, but she was afraid. 'Mama is too ill.'

'Where does she sleep?'

'She sits up all night in the rocking chair, singing hymns and seeking absolution for marrying an infidel.' There was a long pause. 'Luke says he's going to put her in the hospital if she doesn't stop.'

'He did put her in a hospital, didn't he?'

'Yes,' Anne whispered. 'He said he had to put her away.'

'Did you live alone with your stepfather after that?'

'Yes.'

'Did you stay in the town near Laredo?'

'No, Luke took me to San Antonio.' Her face was twisted with pain. She began to massage her temples.

'What's the matter, Anne?'

'My head. It's aching.'

Olivia leaned forward, observing the girl. 'Do you remember when your headaches began?'

'April,' Anne replied. 'April fourth.'

'Are you sure?' The psychiatrist was genuinely surprised by this answer. Most migraines began gradually; she had never heard of a case where the onset of the headaches could be pinpointed to a particular day. 'Is there some reason why you remember the date so precisely?'

Anne twisted and untwisted the handkerchief. 'I just remember.' *Please, make her stop. I don't want to think about it anymore* ... A dull pressure continued to gnaw at her temples.

'Anne, I know this is difficult for you, but I want you to try to remember that day again. It is April fourth. You are thirteen years old, and you're living in San Antonio with your stepfather. What happened that day?'

She shuddered.

'Do you remember?'

'Yes. It's fiesta week. Everybody is out celebrating.'

'Are you?'

'No, I stayed home tonight. I have to study for a test in school.'

'Where is your stepfather?'

'Out drinking.'

'Okay, he's coming home now. Is he drunk?'

'Yes.' Anne began to whimper. 'He wants to hurt me . . . *Stop it. Don't touch me. Mama, please!*'

Anne could picture him, laughing as he reached for her, pushing her back on the bed. She could feel his hands all over her body, and she wanted to die. Without a word he had pulled up her thin dress and pried her legs apart with his rough hands. He held her throat with one hand and with the other he unzipped his pants and let his erection spring free. Hunched over her, he looked like a great beast. Within seconds Anne felt a searing pain as he pushed his way into her, tearing her virginity. Finally, he grunted and rolled off her.

'He's hurting me, Mama, please!' Anne cried the same tears of shame and rage that had burned down her cheeks all those years ago.

'Did he ever hurt you again?' the doctor asked cautiously.

'Yes, after that he came to my room almost

every night. Sometimes he brought friends.'
Anne sat quietly for a moment. Then
suddenly, she jumped up and began to pace
about the room. 'They raped me!' she
screamed.

Without thinking, Olivia ran to her and
enfolded her in her arms.

'Oh, Mama, please help me. They hurt me.
Now I can never — ' Choking on tears, she
stopped trying to speak.

'It's all right now, Anne,' the psychiatrist
soothed. 'You're safe. Luke's gone. No one
can hurt you anymore.'

July 22, 1981
Wednesday

'Am I glad to see you,' Victor said, catching
up to Anne as she came out of the Institute
that evening. 'I looked for you on Monday
while I was here on a story.'

At first she didn't look up, but rather,
acknowledged him with the slightest nod of
her head.

'Are you all right?'

'Of course,' she snapped. 'Oh — I'm sorry,
Victor. I guess I'm a little preoccupied.'

'You didn't forget our date tonight, did
you?'

253

'Our date?'

'Dinner tonight?' He looked at her more closely. 'You sure you're okay? You look beat.'

Blushing, Anne stammered. 'It's been a really rough day. I'm afraid I did forget about tonight.'

'Look, we don't have to go out. To tell you the truth, I've had a pretty tough day myself. How about if we get some Chinese food? We could eat at your place if you don't mind.'

He saw the indecision on her face. 'Come on. It'll do us both good to relax for an evening.'

'All right, but — '

'I'll leave as soon as the dishes are done. Scout's honor.'

In the car, listening to Victor's account of EmmieLou's murder, Anne soon forgot about her therapy session of earlier that day. She became engrossed in his tale.

'It's awful. That poor girl, dying that way. Did the police catch the murderer?'

'The police think EmmieLou was murdered during a burglary attempt. I don't,' Victor declared.

'You don't?'

'No, I think her death is connected somehow with the kidnapped babies.'

Anne looked shocked. 'What?'

'I know it sounds crazy, but listen to the

254

whole story. Then tell me what you think.'

By the time they arrived at Lo Mein's in Hollywood, Anne was convinced. 'It certainly sounds as if someone wanted to keep EmmieLou Madison from identifying her classmate.'

'I'm glad you think so, too.' Victor felt a sense of relief knowing Anne agreed with him. He got out of the car and opened the door for her. 'I don't know about you, but all this detective work has really made me hungry.'

Anne managed a weak smile.

The decor of Lo Mein's was appropriately Chinese-American eclectic: bamboo and enamel screens, chopsticks, Corningware dishes, Chinese waiters, and Muzak.

'Try the moo shoo pork. It's their specialty,' Victor suggested.

'I'm not exactly an expert on Chinese food,' Anne said, 'so you decide.'

'Well, to be honest, this isn't really authentic Chinese. You'd have to go to Hong Kong, Taipei, or the mainland to get real home cooking.'

'Have you traveled to the Far East?' Anne was intrigued, never having left Texas until this year.

'After my sophomore year of college, I got restless and decided to drop out for a while and see the world. My father was furious. No son of his had ever dropped out of anything.'

'I would imagine the trip was great experience for a budding writer.'

'That's just the point,' Victor explained. 'My father hated the idea of my writing. He wanted me to be a cop like him and my three older brothers.'

'Sir?' An Asian waiter interrupted them.

'Okay, let's see what we want.' Victor scanned the menu. 'Could we have one order of cashew chicken, one moo shoo pork, one shrimp in lobster sauce . . . and some pork fried rice.' He turned to Anne. 'Anything else?'

'I hope you're hungry. That's far too much food for me.'

Victor laughed. 'You know us southern boys, ma'am. We like to eat hearty.'

Waiting for their order, Victor told Anne more about his travels. He'd been everywhere, it seemed. He'd even visited exotic-sounding places like Sumatra.

'You really saw cannibals there?' Her eyes widened with fascination.

'Well, not exactly. Cannibalism was outlawed back in the thirties. That's when the last missionary was eaten. The Batak people I met several years ago on Samosir Island are the grandchildren of cannibals. They're quite

256

respectable farmers now.'

'Still, imagine eating another human being.' Anne shuddered at the thought.

★ ★ ★

On the way to Anne's apartment, Victor told her about his tenant story. 'It started out as a routine feature. I even fought McFadden on it because I didn't much want to do it. But after the fire and now Tony Gonzalez's accident, it's turning into front-page news.'

Victor's enthusiasm was evident in the way his violet eyes danced as he talked. More and more Anne found herself drawn to him. Somehow he made her forget her shyness. 'You really love your work, don't you?' she observed.

'Maybe I feel as though I'm finally doing something important. I really think my story could change conditions for those people. And Friday's demonstration should make a ruckus all the way to Sacramento.' He looked at Anne. 'Want to come along?'

'Sorry, I can't. You forget that I'm a working girl.'

'Too bad. You'll miss quite a show.'

'I expect a full report,' she said in mock seriousness.

'Yes, ma'am.'

Moments later they pulled up in front of a building on Havenhurst. 'You're lucky you found this place,' Victor said. 'Apartments in L.A. are at a premium.'

'Actually it's funny. I found the ad for it stuffed in my purse, but I don't remember clipping it out of the paper.'

'Sounds as if you're losing your mind,' Victor teased.

'That's not funny,' she snapped, catching Victor by surprise.

'I was only kidding,' he said. 'Please don't be angry.'

They found the door to Anne's apartment slightly ajar.

Victor shrugged. 'You probably forgot to lock it.'

Anne didn't answer, but the instant she pushed open the door, she knew something was wrong. The cloying scent of an unfamiliar cheap perfume filled the air. The apartment looked as though a tornado had swept through it, and Anne's books and magazines were pulled from the bookcases on the far wall and strewn on the floor. Her coffee table and lamps were overturned. Only the portable TV had been left untouched. Several crushed cigarette butts filled the normally unused ashtrays.

Standing just behind her, Victor surveyed

the destruction. 'My God, what happened?'

'I . . . I don't know.' Anne was stunned. When she started to go inside, Victor held her back.

'No, let me check around first to make sure nobody's still inside.'

He quickly surveyed the tiny one-bedroom apartment, reassuring himself that the intruder had left. If possible, Anne's bedroom was even more of a mess than the living room. The drawers in the bureau had been pulled open, and their contents were scattered all over the room.

'Okay.' He returned to the living room. 'You'd better come in and see what's missing. We'll have to call the police.' He picked up the phone.

Anne didn't seem to hear him. She stood in the doorway, her eyes registering something between shock and terror.

'Are you all right?'

'I . . . I'm fine. Don't call the police. It's not necessary. Nothing's missing.'

Victor was annoyed. 'How do you know? You haven't even checked.'

'What do I have to steal?' she asked flatly. 'No — the police won't help. You told me they didn't do much about EmmieLou Madison, and she was murdered.'

Victor put down the receiver, concerned

about Anne's reaction. 'Look, you're upset. Let me help you put your things back. Then we can decide what to do.' He bent down and started replacing the books on the shelf.

Anne grabbed them out of his hand. 'I'll do that.'

Victor looked at her, again confused.

'I know where everything belongs,' she said with exasperation.

The phone rang. Anne jumped at the sound.

'I'll get it,' Victor said, picking up the receiver. 'Hello?'

There was no answer.

'Who is this?' Victor demanded as the caller hung up. 'Probably a wrong number.' He shrugged and put the receiver down.

Anne didn't mention that this was the third such call she'd received in the last week, but from the look on her face, Victor knew she was terribly frightened. Someone was trying to frighten Anne Midlands out of her mind. But why? He was about to say something when he saw her pick up an envelope from the floor, her face ashen. 'Anne, what is it?'

'The letter I wrote to my former supervisor asking for job references. It's still here.' There was wonder in her voice.

'So? I don't understand.'

Anne shook her head. 'I *mailed* that letter

last week . . . or at least I thought I did.' Tears filled her eyes and began to spill down her cheeks. 'What's happening to me? Maybe I *am* losing my mind.'

Victor took her hand and sat her down on the couch. 'Anne, forgetting to mail a letter is nothing to get upset about. I forget things all the time; we all do. It's perfectly normal.'

Anne wiped her eyes with a fresh handkerchief. 'I'm sorry. It's just that — '

'Stop apologizing. I understand. Listen, maybe you should stay at my place tonight. I'm worried about your being here alone.'

Anne shook her head. 'No, please. I'll be all right. They're not going to come back. They already know I don't have anything worth stealing.'

'You sure?' She really was a mystery. Watching her cool, almost indifferent demeanor, he didn't know what to say to her. A moment ago he'd been about to take her in his arms. Now she had wiped away the tears and was in control again. Or so it seemed. Was she secretly terrified? Was this indifference a defense mechanism? Did she want him to console her or did she really prefer to stay here alone?

'I'm sure,' she replied. 'I'll be okay, but would you mind if we canceled our dinner tonight? I've got a little headache, and I'd like to lie down.'

He was about to protest when he saw that she had her mind made up. 'All right, then. After I leave, I want you to lock and bolt the door securely. Okay?'

She nodded.

'And give me that letter. I'll mail it for you.' Reluctantly, he turned to go, still feeling there was more to say. As he stepped into the night, he heard her shut the door and lock it.

19

Victor spent a sleepless night worrying about Anne. Several times he was tempted to get up and drive over to her apartment, but he was afraid she would misunderstand.

He couldn't stop thinking about her. She was proud and honest and gentle. He valued those qualities very highly. She was also painfully shy. Most women warmed up to him right away. But not Anne. With her he had to do all the work.

Perhaps that was part of her appeal: the challenge of coaxing her out of her shell. Now, just as she had started to warm up, she'd pulled away again, afraid of getting close to him or to anyone.

Why was she so fearful? Maybe she'd had a bad experience in the past. That was certainly possible. She needed to act indifferent to conceal her vulnerability.

The luminous dial on the bedside clock blinked 2:00 A.M. He was exhausted, and yet he couldn't seem to close his eyes. Who had ransacked Anne's apartment? Why? He felt so emotionally drained: the baby kidnappings, meeting their mothers, the fire, EmmieLou's murder, Tony Gonzalez's accident — and now tonight. It was just too much. He wished he could turn off his mind.

Toward dawn, Victor fell into a fitful sleep. He dreamed someone was watching him wherever he went. Someone was following him to Atlanta . . . to EmmieLou's . . .

He woke up in a cold sweat. Suppose someone *had* followed him and had somehow found out that EmmieLou might be able to provide information about the kidnappings? What if that someone had also followed him to Anne's apartment last night? He checked the clock again: it was almost 7:30. So what if he woke her up, he thought as he dialed the number she had given him. Come on, Anne, answer.

At the sound of her voice, a wave of relief swept over him. 'I called because I was worried about you. I hope you didn't have any more visitors after I left.'

'No, you were the last,' she said softly. 'Victor, I'm sorry I was so abrupt last night. I was being silly.'

Victor smiled. 'Never mind. I just hope we can try that dinner again soon.'

'That would be nice.'

'Would you mind if I call you later? Just to make sure you're okay? I've got to go down to Alvarado Street to work on the placards for the demonstration. Otherwise, I'd insist we make that date tonight.'

'Go ahead,' Anne replied. 'I'll talk to you later.'

July 23, 1981
Thursday

Glynnis McCombie began to get dressed after her weekly clinic visit. 'How's the baby?' she asked Marie.

'Fine, honey. As a matter of fact, you're almost in the home stretch.'

'But I'm not due until the end of September. That's more than two months to go.'

Marie smiled enigmatically. 'Some babies come early, especially in young mothers.'

Glynnis looked worried. 'Is that a problem?'

'Not if you follow all my instructions. I've talked it all over with Dr. Van Patten, and he agrees that from now on I should visit you at home.'

'You mean I'm not going to have the baby in the hospital?'

265

'Of course you are, honey. But I'm going to make home visits until you're ready. Then we'll bring you here for the delivery.'

Glynnis nodded. She wasn't at all sure she understood, but she trusted Marie. After all, without Marie Fontaine, she'd be all alone.

'Now, give me your address and phone number. I'll stop by early next week to check on you.'

Glynnis wrote down an address on Vermont Avenue and a telephone number, and Marie pocketed the slip of paper.

'All right now, honey. You go on home and get plenty of rest. We want our baby to be healthy, don't we?' Marie squeezed the girl's arm affectionately.

As soon as Glynnis left, Marie entered the nurses' locker room and looked around to make certain that no one was there. She opened her locker and furtively removed the surgical scalpel she had stolen from Dr. Van Patten's examining room. She studied the razor-sharp edge of the stainless steel blade for a long moment. He shouldn't have done it, she thought. If only he hadn't done it, everything could be different. But there was no point in crying over spilled milk.

She replaced the scalpel on the top shelf of her locker and carefully covered it with her hood. Then she checked to make sure she had

Glynnis's address and telephone number. Satisfied that everything was in order, she left, unaware that Stacy Gardner was peering through a crack in the door, puzzling over Marie's odd behavior.

20

July 24, 1981
Friday

After lunch, Anne sat with the patients, who had gathered in the game room.

'Where's Tanya?' Sarah Lungren asked. Ever since the previous week's group therapy session, this forbidding, husband-murdering woman had taken the young drug addict under her wing. Perhaps the girl represented the daughter she had never had, but whatever the reason, Sarah poured all her frustrated love into Tanya. She helped her with her weaving, showed her how to bake bread, even taught her a few songs from the old days.

'Didn't Tanya tell you? She's being discharged today,' Carlotta Winchester reported, continuing her dusting.

'Discharged?' Sarah looked pained.

'She's going to be in the outpatient program. You'll still see her in group.'

'I guess she didn't have time to say good-bye.' Sarah tried to mask her disappointment, but Anne could see the pain the robust woman was trying to hide.

'Sarah, why don't you see if Tanya's still on the ward?' Anne suggested. 'Maybe she's in her room packing.'

Sarah pressed her lips together. 'No, it doesn't matter. If she wants me, she knows where to find me.'

'Shut up over there,' Aggie Barlow called over her shoulder, then resumed intently watching 'Days of our Lives.'

'Baseball commissioner Bowie Kuhn states no new talks are scheduled for a few days,' Deborah Fortune announced in a clear voice.

'Will you pipe down!' Aggie shouted.

Deborah got up and made an exit worthy of any professional actress. 'I'm going to my studio. Hold my calls.'

Anne continued to observe Sarah sitting dejectedly in a corner near Janet Evans. In a sense, she thought, both women had lost their children. Of course, it wasn't exactly the same; Janet had lost her real child. It was such a pity. And no one would ever know if the child was alive or dead.

Thinking about it made Anne's temples throb. She moved closer to Janet, surprised to find her, head bowed, deeply engrossed in a book.

'What are you reading?'

Janet gave her a long glance. 'The Bible.'

Anne's heart skipped a beat. Leaning over

Janet's shoulder, she noticed that the volume was open to Deuteronomy, chapter 21, verse 24. Anne removed her glasses and massaged her temples. *Stop . . . Please . . .*

'Why did she take my baby?' Janet's voice was edged with hysteria. 'Why did she want to punish me?'

'Who?'

'The woman who took my baby.'

Anne put a comforting arm around Janet, who was trembling. Perhaps she ought to call Dr. Westbourne. 'No one wants to hurt you.'

Janet shook her head. 'You're wrong. I'm a sinner . . . That's what the note said. Eye for eye . . . She — ' Janet had begun rocking back and forth, her eyes wide with terror. 'Those eyes! She took my baby!'

Anne looked where the hysterical woman pointed. Catching her breath with a scarcely audible gasp, Anne whispered, 'It just can't be.' *Please, no . . .*

In the window of the double doors on the far wall she could see the reflection of a woman. Someone must be standing at the door. Without her glasses, Anne could make out little more than an outline. Only the eyes were clear. She shuddered, looking into them, feeling their power. There was cold, cold anger in those eyes.

Quickly she slid her glasses back on, but

270

the vision was gone. She turned to look toward the door, but no one was there.

'I saw her,' Janet whimpered hysterically. 'She *was* here. You believe me, don't you?'

Anne didn't answer. There was nothing to say. Of course she believed her; she had seen those eyes, too.

July 24, 1981
Friday

The atmosphere in the crowded bus was one of quiet anticipation. Most of the forty people on board were women and children, including half a dozen babies, and all sat elbow to elbow. All were Mexicans — some American citizens, most not — of assorted shapes, sizes, and demeanors. Although they were all dressed in what they considered their best clothes, for the most part they looked shabby.

Victor studied their earnest faces as they listened to Goldblatt's instructions. Carmen Gonzalez was there. He knew she'd left her comatose son's bedside to join the demonstration. Angela, the child Victor had rescued from the fire, sat on her grandfather's lap. They both smiled shyly at him.

Victor wondered for a moment why he had come. Was he looking for a story, a way to

271

further his career, or did he really care what happened to these people? For the first time he realized that except for Angela, her grandfather, Tony, and Carmen, he didn't know any of them as individuals. How could a boy from a middle-class family in Texas feel the weight of poverty and suffering they carried on their stooping shoulders?

'Okay, *compadres*,' Goldblatt exhorted, 'today's the day we show Orson Pepperton he can't push us around any more. He's going to have to listen and respond to our needs.'

'Way to go, man!' a group of rowdy teenagers in the back of the bus yelled. They were dressed identically in skintight jeans, T-shirts, and sneakers.

'You think this is gonna work, Señor Goldblatt?' an older man asked hopefully, grinning a toothless grin.

'Of course it will work. We just have to stick together, that's all.'

With a whistle around his neck and a baseball cap atop his head, Goldblatt looked more like a camp counselor than a lawyer.

'Now, when we get to Beverly Hills,' he continued, checking information from a clipboard, 'the bus will drop us off about a block from the senator's house. Everybody will get a sign to carry.'

'What if people get tired?' Angela's

grandfather asked in Spanish.

'There'll be a command post set up near the corner where we can get coffee and juice. We also brought a medical emergency kit in case . . . uh . . . anything should happen.' He hesitated to mention the possibility of violence, although it was always something to consider in any demonstration. The kit he brought contained rolls of bandages and iodine.

One of the teenagers — a boy with slicked-back hair, dark, nervous eyes, and a gold earring in his right ear — stood up. 'I don't believe you, man. You really think that if a bunch of poor Mexicans from the barrio march around some senator's fancy mansion like good boys and girls, he's gonna give us all new houses? Tell me why should he do that? Because he knows it's right? No way, Mr. Lawyer. His kind of people only understand one thing.'

The boy thrust his fist in the air to emphasize his point. The other teenagers followed, raising their fists as well.

'You're right about one thing, Juan,' the lawyer interrupted. 'Senator Pepperton won't listen to what we say because it's right or fair. But his kind of people do have a healthy respect for reality. They know when their backs are against the wall. Show them a situation they can't wriggle out of and surprising things can happen.'

'Like what?' Juan challenged.

'Like giving in to our demands. When the senator's picture appears on page one of the *L.A. Tribune* along with photographs of our group picketing in front of his Beverly Hills mansion, he's not going to have a choice.'

There was a general murmur of agreement from the adults, but the teenagers were still not convinced. A chorus of jeers erupted from the back of the bus.

Victor walked over to Goldblatt and whispered, 'Who's the kid?'

'Juan Garcia. He lives with his mother and five sisters in a tiny, crowded, rat-infested two-bedroom apartment on Olivera Street.'

'He looks like a gang member.'

'He is,' Goldblatt replied matter-of-factly. 'They call themselves the Grips. Juan is their leader.'

Victor shook his head. 'I don't believe it, Sy. We planned a peaceable demonstration, remember? When you invite hoodlums, you're asking for trouble.'

'Don't worry. Juan's just flexing his muscles for his friends. It makes him feel important. When it comes time to demonstrate, he'll behave himself. He and I are old friends from the days when I worked in juvenile hall. Believe me, he wants a better home for his mother and sisters as much as anyone here.'

'I hope you're right,' Victor said without conviction. He didn't realize it, but Goldblatt was also concerned. Although they had a permit to march, the police would undoubtedly be present in large numbers. He just hoped they'd be able to make their point peaceably.

There were audible gasps as the bus turned north off Sunset onto Rodeo Drive. To the shabby group from East Los Angeles, it was like taking a field trip to an opulent fantasyland. Everything appeared flawless here, immaculate. The afternoon sun was a shimmering golden bauble in a cloudless sky. Palm trees lined the broad avenue. And the houses — none of them had ever seen anything to compare to the huge mansions with their meticulously manicured lawns behind securely gated drives.

When they reached Senator Pepperton's neighborhood, Goldblatt told the driver to pull over to the corner. After everyone had stepped off the bus, he distributed placards bearing carefully hand-painted slogans — slogans obviously designed for media exposure: Fat Cats Breed Rats; Our Children Are Dying in Your Houses; Slumlords Make Money

While We Lose Lives; and Your Children Sleep with Teddy Bears, Ours Sleep with Rats.

Armed with the signs, they began to march slowly up and down the street, following Goldblatt's directions. After fifteen minutes, they were to congregate in front of the senator's house.

'Remember,' he reemphasized, 'this must be a peaceable demonstration. That's the only way we'll make our point.'

'What about the dead rats and roaches we collected?' Juan called out. 'You didn't forget them, did you, man?'

'When we get to the house, I'll ring the bell,' Goldblatt answered. 'I know the senator is at home this week working on his campaign speech for renomination to the state legislature. I'll have him step outside, Juan, and you can deliver our pets to him. Just wait until he's outside; I want the *Trib* photographer to get a good picture.'

'You mean I'll be in the papers?' the boy asked warily.

'Of course. You're a leader of this demonstration, aren't you?'

The boy obviously appreciated his new importance, and once again Victor was impressed with Sy's strategy. By placating the gang leader, he ensured the peaceable involvement of the other members. He watched as the placard-carrying procession moved up and down the street. Everyone was orderly; even the babies behaved themselves.

A few passersby stopped to stare at the group approaching the senator's house, but no one commented. The demonstrators looked angry, tough, and very much as though they meant business. A matronly woman in a maid's uniform wheeling a plump infant in a pram even hurriedly crossed the street to avoid a possible confrontation.

The senator's house was a handsome Spanish colonial built in the twenties. Full-blooming bougainvillea and wisteria in brick planters lined the circular driveway, and geraniums filled clay pots on either side of the double entrance.

When he saw the group approach, the Mexican gardener put down his pruning shears.

'Is Senator Pepperton at home?' Goldblatt asked.

The gardener shrugged, and the lawyer repeated the question in Spanish. '*Si*,' the gardener replied hesitantly.

The housekeeper answered the door and listened to Goldblatt's request with surprise before shaking her head. 'I'm sorry, sir, but the senator asked not to be disturbed.'

'Perhaps you'd better tell him that there are forty people here with a marching permit. We're prepared to camp on his doorstep until we see him. Maybe he'll change his mind when you mention that Victor Larsen from the *L.A. Tribune* is also with us. He's writing the series on slum landlords in East L.A.' Goldblatt smiled ingratiatingly as he added, 'We'll only take a minute of the senator's valuable time.'

The woman shut the door, promising to return with an answer.

One of the Beverly Hills squad cars that had been cruising the area pulled up. A patrolman got out and threaded his way through the group of marchers. A small crowd gathered on the opposite side of the street, waiting to see what would happen. 'May I see your permit?' he said to Goldblatt.

The young lawyer presented his signed permit to the officer.

'This looks to be in order,' the policeman said, carefully inspecting the document. 'Keep it orderly, okay? We don't want to make any arrests.'

Goldblatt assured him, 'This is a peaceable march. We won't cause any problems.'

At that moment, Orson Pepperton opened the front door. At forty-five, he could easily

278

have been a Hollywood heart-throb — his square face implacable, as if hewn from stone, his eyes a shade of blue even Paul Newman would envy, his closely cropped jet-black hair lightly dusted at the temples with gray. It had been more than twenty years since he'd played quarterback at Stanford, but he still had the rugged handsomeness of a jock. After college, he had turned down a pro football career in favor of law school and had finally chosen a life of politics.

Now, filling the imposing doorway of his home, impeccably attired in an Italian-style Eric Ross pin-stripe suit, he appeared every inch the successful gentleman.

'Sorry to have kept you all waiting, but I was delayed,' the senator commented, his face settling into the easy smile of a politician. Goldblatt knew, of course, that Senator Pepperton was not sorry at all. The lawyer suspected that underneath the handsome exterior lived a cold and ruthless man. Right now he was probably furious at this impertinent young lawyer who had sent a message he was forced to acknowledge.

'Now, Mr. — ' He looked at Sy.

'Goldblatt.'

'Mr. Goldblatt, what can I do for you and your . . . uh, friends?' As he viewed the group, the senator seemed perfectly calm. Only the

279

hard lines around his mouth betrayed his anger.

Goldblatt spoke. 'We're here today, Senator, to demand better, safer, cleaner housing in East Los Angeles. These people have traveled a long way to bring you their message. I don't think I can say it more eloquently than little Angela Nunez over there who almost died last week in a fire caused by inadequate kitchen facilities in her building, or Carmen Gonzalez whose son now lies in a coma after being crushed by a cinder-block wall that collapsed on him.'

Pepperton smiled, aware that a TV camera crew had appeared. 'No one is more concerned than I am about the need for better housing and stricter enforcement of the present laws,' he intoned, turning to the right to take advantage of the more flattering camera angle.

'Unfortunately, it's a question of priorities. Right now we're working on legislation to improve substandard conditions, but that sort of thing takes time.'

As the senator spoke, Goldblatt noticed several newcomers moving into the crowd, their pencils racing over open notebooks. The senator, he knew, would seize this opportunity to give his reelection effort a plug. Goldblatt almost smiled when Pepperton went into his pitch.

'Now if I'm elected to another term in the California Senate, I swear — '

'Cut the crap, man,' one of the Grips taunted.

The remark was the first note of antagonism, and one of the policemen took a step toward the teenagers. Goldblatt turned sharply, raising a hand in caution, and Juan quieted his gang.

'What we're doing today,' the young lawyer explained, 'might be called an act of faith.' He paused for effect. 'Faith in the system.'

The crowd drew closer, their conversation muted, as Goldblatt continued.

'Senator, you're always talking about lifting up the common man. I've heard you say that all Californians should have the same opportunities. I'm sure you'd be appalled if you could see for yourself the conditions these poor people are forced to live in.'

He gestured to Juan to come forward. The boy brought the container of rodents his gang members had collected over the past few days. At Goldblatt's signal, he opened it, spilling everything at the senator's feet. A collective gasp escaped from the spectators.

'What's the meaning of this?' Pepperton's face became suffused with rage, and the artery at his temple throbbed. At that instant,

281

the *Trib* photographer snapped a picture.

'One of these rats bit my little Tina,' a middle-aged woman in a silk mantilla cried.

'These are the cockroaches that come out of my bathtub,' another woman said in broken English.

One by one, members of the group came forward, pointing to the vermin, each telling a story of the filthy living conditions in the run-down buildings.

When they finished, Goldblatt leaned over and whispered something to the senator. The blood drained from his face. Pepperton cleared his throat nervously. 'Friends, you've made some very interesting points this morning,' he announced. 'Let me look into the matter further. My people will get on it right away.'

Goldblatt gave him a meaningful look.

'And, uh, I'm sure I can arrange funding for those of you who are homeless because of the fire.' Pepperton paused as if measuring the crowd's reaction, then continued, 'I promise, your case will be given attention immediately, even if I have to contribute from my personal funds.'

A rousing cheer went up from the crowd. Even the young gang members joined in.

'God bless you, *señor*.'

'Way to go, man.'

The senator rose to the occasion, shaking hands and kissing babies, all the while making sure he was on camera.

Later, as everyone climbed aboard the bus, Victor cornered Goldblatt. 'What exactly did you whisper to him back there?'

Sy gave him an innocent look. 'Oh, I just told him that we know who really owns Theta Enterprises. I also said that if legislation isn't introduced pronto, the whole story of Theta will appear in the *Trib*.'

'I see.' Victor laughed.

Goldblatt slapped him on the back. 'Come on, we'll drop you off at your office on the way back. You've still got a helluva story to write.'

21

Only under hypnosis could Anne reveal her long-repressed memories of being raped by her stepfather and abused by his friends.

A veteran student of aberrant human behavior, Olivia Westbourne had assumed that she was beyond revulsion, yet the pitiful sobs of the young nurse had been heartrending. Since Wednesday the psychiatrist had been able to think of little else.

Anne sat quietly, her eyes expressionless, her shoulders hunched, looking apprehensive and miserable.

'Anne, do you remember your dreams?'

'Sometimes,' Anne replied softly.

'What do you dream about?'

'I don't remember.'

Don't or won't? the psychiatrist wondered. 'Do you ever dream the same dream more than once?'

Anne twisted her handkerchief. 'I think so.'

'Do you want me to help you?'

'I . . . I don't know.'

Dr. Westbourne eyed her frankly. 'Anne, I think it's time to clean house, get rid of some of the cobwebs in your mind. What do you say?'

Anne was silent. *Please . . . stop . . .*

'Just listen to the sound of my voice. Only that.' By now Olivia could hypnotize Anne easily. Within moments she was completely relaxed. 'How are you?' the doctor asked.

'Fine.'

'I want you to stay in this deep sleep.'

Anne nodded.

'Your dream is beginning now, Anne.'

Anne's eyelids fluttered.

'Where are you?' the doctor asked.

'I don't know.'

'Look around. What do you see?' Dr. Westbourne waited patiently.

'Lights. Hot lights.'

'Where?'

No answer. Anne wrinkled her nose. 'I can smell alcohol . . . Everyone's wearing masks. They're looking down on me.' Anne's breathing became more rapid. She began to gasp for air. 'What are you going to do to me?' she cried, looking around wildly.

Olivia leaned forward, seeing the girl's pain but knowing she must continue her questions. 'Anne, are you in an operating room?'

'I . . . ' Her voice was filled with a kind of

285

horror. 'Yes, and they have to operate. The doctor says — ' She began to whimper.

'What is it, Anne?'

Anne let out a pained cry.

'What did the doctors say?'

'Too much infection. There's nothing they can do. I need to be cleaned out. Aaah . . . '

The psychiatrist watched Anne writhing in agony as the scene unfolded in her memory.

'It hurts, Doctor. Please . . . '

'Was it a hysterectomy?' Dr. Westbourne spoke in a whisper.

'What?'

'A pelvic cleanout. Isn't that what the doctor had to do?'

'No, no!' she shouted hysterically. 'That's not it.'

'Yes, yes, that's what it was,' Olivia said, as much to herself as to Anne. 'Luke and his friends infected you. That's why the doctor had to perform a hysterectomy.'

Anne was rolling back and forth, arms wrapped protectively around her waist. 'Mama, please don't let them hurt me,' she moaned.

Anne was still trembling, with both fear and relief, from her afternoon session with Dr. Westbourne when she pushed open the door to her apartment. The interior looked dark and uninviting. Instead of turning on the light, she waited for her eyes to accommodate to the darkness.

She wished Victor were there. It was the first time she had wanted his comfort. She needed to feel his arms around her. Yesterday when they'd talked on the phone, he'd told her he loved her. She hadn't answered then, but she knew she was falling in love with him as well — even though part of her continued to hold back.

But what was the point of letting go? It would never work. She could never let herself fall in love, not after all the things that had happened.

She walked into the living room, flicking on the table lamp. 'It can't be,' she cried, surveying the room. Everything was over-turned again, books and clothes scattered haphazardly about the apartment. Someone had been there.

She rushed to the door, terrified. She had locked it. Panting, she stood there for a moment, afraid to move, feeling weak and tired. She closed her eyes, rubbing her forehead with her hand. Another migraine was beginning.

'What's happening to me?' she kept asking herself, but she couldn't think. Shaking violently, she picked up the phone, dialed Victor's office, and waited. Her lips were chapped and cracking, and she licked them nervously. The telephone rang once, twice . . . Oh, let him be there, she prayed.

'*L.A. Trib*, city desk.'

'Victor Larsen, please.'

'Sorry, he's out on a story. Can I help you?'

Anne was about to reply when she saw the note. It was lying in the middle of the floor. 'No . . . please,' she whispered, dropping the receiver. 'Hand for hand,' it said, the words slashed with angry strokes in bright red lipstick. Anne began to shake uncontrollably. Then, exhausted, she slid to the floor unconscious, the note clutched tightly in her hand.

July 24, 1981
Friday

McFadden paced around Victor's desk. 'You did *what?*'

288

'I told you, Chief. I had to kill the story about the senator owning those buildings. Goldblatt made me promise.'

'Since when does some lawyer from the ACLU make the decisions around here?' the editor fumed. 'I don't understand you, Larsen. I thought you wanted to get Pepperton, and you had all the ammunition you needed.'

'That was before Goldblatt gave me a lesson in politics,' Victor replied. 'Sure, we might destroy the senator's political career with that scoop, but then again we might not. The man comes from one of the oldest families in California; the Pepperton influence touches every aspect of the state power structure. I wouldn't be surprised if their tentacles reach right into the board of the *Trib.*'

McFadden stopped his pacing. Perhaps he had something there. It was a fact that the Pepperton family was more than just socially prominent. He had often heard rumors that they had a hand in running the paper, although nothing had ever been confirmed.

'All right, let's say you're correct — that the story would fall on deaf ears. What do you hope to accomplish by *not* printing it?'

'Exactly what Goldblatt set out to accomplish — better housing for those poor people in East L.A. I think the cattle prod we used on the senator today will get him moving pretty quickly on that legislation. Besides, we reminded him that we could still print the story any time.'

'Great, now you're into blackmail,' McFadden bristled, but he was clearly impressed with Victor's reasoning. He quickly scanned the finished story on the screen. ' 'Acknowledge' has only one *c*,' he corrected.

'*That's* your only criticism?' Victor was both surprised and pleased. McFadden was one of the toughest editors in the business. A story rarely passed his inspection without several major rewrites.

'Don't get a swelled head. I've got a deadline to meet, and the story's *not bad*. I'll let it pass.'

Victor secretly smiled. 'I understand,' he said, trying to sound chastened.

'Now I suppose you'll be looking to get into more mischief. Are you privy to any other hot news items or shall I just assign you a story from the sheet like we do with the rest of the staff?' McFadden asked sarcastically.

Victor stopped his typing, debating with himself. Should he tell the chief what had happened in Atlanta? No, what was the point? He still didn't have much to go on. He had no hard facts, and only his imagination; he already knew what McFadden thought about that. 'Where's the assignment sheet?'

The editor smiled. 'You just might make it in this business, Larsen.'

★ ★ ★

At ten o'clock that night, Victor boarded a flight to San Antonio. He had to check Amanda Hodson's medical records from six years ago to find the name of that nurse.

Before leaving, he dialed Anne's number. Still busy. Oh well, if she's talking on the phone, she must be all right. He'd call her in the morning.

22

At 1:00 A.M., the corridors of the Psychiatric Institute were empty; everyone had been tucked into bed hours ago. Only an occasional cough or snore disturbed the silence, drifting through closed doors, echoing off the cold tile.

From the double doors of the Ob-Gyn clinic, the woman peered into the ward. The floor lights were dimmed. She pulled a flashlight from the pocket of her hooded cape and switched it on, illuminating the silent psychiatric wards. This was a good time to go in; all of the patients would be deep in drugged sleep. She entered and made her way through the ward, casting her light on each sleeping patient.

She heard a footstep and stiffened with alarm, but the sound trailed off in the distance. A glance behind her confirmed that she was unobserved. She slipped along the row of beds until she came to the last one. Then she bent over the sleeping patient.

'Mrs. Evans,' she whispered.

Janet stirred in her sleep.

'It's too late, Mrs. Evans.'

Slowly, Janet realized what was happening. Her mind was still drugged, both with sleep and with the medication she had been given, but even in her dazed state she recognized the fact that loomed before her.

'You shouldn't have remembered me,' the woman said. 'I wouldn't have had to do this if you hadn't remembered me.'

Janet struggled to her feet, staggering in shocked recognition.

The woman's smile was mocking. 'It's too late, Mrs. Evans. There's nowhere for you to hide anymore.'

Janet knew she had to run for her life. She pushed past the woman, fled the length of the ward, and threw herself against the double doors leading to the Ob-Gyn clinic, pushing with all her might. The doors swung open. Trembling, her gait unsteady, she stumbled into the darkened clinic and groped her way through the unfamiliar room.

The voice behind her kept repeating, 'There's nowhere to hide. You can't get away from me.' The woman flashed a beam of light in Janet's face, momentarily illuminating the corridor. The door to the stairwell was only a few yards away, and Janet ran toward it. As

293

she ran, she held her hands to her ears, trying to block out the hideous voice. But it rang through the empty hall, growing louder and louder, echoing in her brain. 'No,' she cried out. 'She wants to kill me! Someone, please help!'

Abruptly, the light flicked off, and once again Janet was immersed in total darkness. Terrified, she crouched against the wall, searching the blackness, her breathing ragged. Perspiration poured from her body. Her head ached from fighting the tranquilizing effects of the antidepressants. Carefully she inched her way along the wall to the stairwell door, her progress slow and labored.

'You're trapped,' the voice called. 'I'll catch you sooner or later.'

Shaking violently, Janet tried desperately to get hold of herself, to think clearly. Every muscle in her body was tensed with the exertion. Choking for breath, she continued her deliberate flight, staying close to the wall, moving one slow step at a time until she reached the door.

Frantically, she tried to turn the knob. Her fingers fumbled clumsily until she managed to turn it enough to force the door open. Her pulse raced as she slid through the door and into the stairwell. But it was no use — the woman had followed her.

'There's no escape, Mrs. Evans.'

Janet grabbed the railing when the woman came up behind her. Cold hands seized her in a powerful grip and thrust her over the metal rail and down into the stairwell. She tumbled into the blackness, gathering momentum until she struck the concrete floor at the bottom with a sickening thud.

The woman in the hood watched from the top of the stairs. 'Pleasant dreams,' she whispered before turning to leave.

San Antonio
July 25, 1981
Saturday

It was 3:00 A.M. when the taxi arrived at the emergency room entrance at San Antonio General.

'This is it, bub.' The driver nudged Victor who was asleep in the back seat.

Bleary-eyed, Victor pulled a five dollar bill from his wallet. 'Keep the change.'

'Hey, the fare was six-fifty. You only gave me a five,' the cabbie sneered.

'Oh, sorry,' Victor apologized, handing the disgruntled driver a twenty.

The man nodded toward the hospital. 'If

you're not well, you're certainly in the right place.'

'Yeah,' Victor replied, ignoring the joke. 'Thanks.'

'Don't mention it. Hope you feel better, fella.'

The taxi driver pulled away before Victor realized he hadn't gotten change. 'Bub' was right, he thought glumly.

Straightening his clothes, Victor tried to shake himself awake. What he needed was a cup of strong black coffee. He'd been traveling since ten — two hours to Dallas, then a two-hour layover before the fifty-minute flight to San Antonio, then nearly a half-hour to find a cabbie who would risk the drive to the rough side of town at this late hour. McFadden had been right: being a reporter was a twenty-four hour job.

He walked into the emergency room and nervously glanced around, relieved that his entrance had gone unobserved. The guard near the door never even looked up from his crossword puzzle. A young couple slept in the waiting area, their heads together, undisturbed by the noisy static from the overhead TV set.

The emergency room itself was a flurry of activity. Two doctors and three nurses were busy caring for an elderly woman who appeared to be dying despite their substantial efforts. Their backs were to Victor, who watched unseen.

That's when he saw his chance. One of the doctors had draped his white coat over the back of a chair. Affecting nonchalance, Victor sauntered over, picked up the coat, and strolled through the double doors into the main corridor of the hospital.

It was deserted, but even so, Victor's heart raced. On the plane his scheme had appeared flawless. Now, suddenly, it seemed risky. But it was too late to back out.

He put on the coat; it was a passable fit. Locating a bank of elevators at the end of the dimly lit hall, he rode to the basement. With little difficulty, he found the chart room — a huge area filled from floor to ceiling with metal shelves jammed with hundreds of thousands of manila folders.

'Can I help you?' A pretty girl of eighteen or nineteen sat behind a desk reading a novel.

'I need a chart.' He tried to sound authoritative.

'Are you one of the new interns?' the girl asked, giving him a frank once-over. 'It's hard to get to know everyone; there are so many of you guys.' She smiled, evidently pleased with what she saw.

Victor nodded. 'I'm Dr. Larsen.'

The girl seemed unaware of his discomfort. 'Judy Taylor. I'm a freshman at Piedmont Junior College. This job helps pay my tuition.'

'Look, I'm really sorry,' he apologized, 'but I've been on duty since yesterday. I'm afraid I'm in a little hurry.'

'Sure. Whose chart do you need?'

'Amanda Hodson. She'll be in tomorrow, and I need to review her case.'

'I get it. You want to impress your attending with the answers before he asks the questions. Pretty tricky.'

'Something like that.'

The girl leafed through several charts and finally removed a thin one. 'Your patient must have had only one previous admission,' she said, handing Victor the file.

He nodded. According to EmmieLou, Mrs. Hodson's last two babies were delivered uptown. Only the stillborn infant was delivered at San Antonio General.

'You can work back in the supervisor's office,' Judy offered. 'I'm alone here at night; you won't be disturbed. There's even coffee if you want it. I made it myself.'

Victor thanked her, welcoming an opportunity for privacy. He found a glass-walled cubicle with a desk, a bookcase, and a fresh pot of coffee. Pouring a cup, Victor began looking over the chart.

Feeling as if he'd stepped out of his element, he quickly reviewed the chart's organization. The order sheets were first, followed by graphs of the patient's vital signs. Next came the history and physical examination on the day of admission. The rest of the chart included progress notes, labor and delivery notes, nurses' notes, innumerable laboratory values, X-ray reports, and the results of other tests and procedures.

To make sure he didn't miss anything vital, Victor decided to start at the beginning. From the history and physical reports, he learned that Mrs. Amanda Hodson, twenty-four years old, had entered San Antonio General on July 13, 1975, at 1:00 P.M. Based on his examination, the intern on duty estimated the infant's birth weight at 8½ pounds. Fetal heart tones were clearly detected and noted. Victor scanned the page: 'Fetal heart rate on admission was 140 beats per minute.' The doctor concluded that the patient was in the first stage of labor and admitted her to the ward.

The labor sheet was simply a matrix containing pertinent data on the progress of labor: cervical dilation, fetal heart rate, mother's blood pressure and pulse. According to the entries, Mrs. Hodson was in labor for almost sixteen hours. Everything appeared routine to Victor. He found no indication from the entries of any complications, except the unexpected and terse note at the end of the page — 'stillborn, 3 pounds, 13½ ounces, July 14, 1975, 5:00 A.M.'

The pathology report was even more confusing. 'Gross specimen: 3-pound-13½-ounce putrid male fetus; umbilical cord cut. Autolysis of tissue specimen.'

Next, Victor flipped to the nurses' notes. There, in Emmie-Lou's neat hand, he found Mrs. Hodson described as being 'in good spirits and fairly comfortable' when she went off duty at 3:00 P.M. He searched the page for the name of the nurse on the next shift: Eileen Adelman — 3:00 to 11:00 P.M. Her entry was in the same up-and-down school-girl handwriting: 'No change, patient doing well.'

At 4:00 A.M., the night nurse had made her only entry: 'Patient having severe pain; medication administered.' He looked down the page to find out the nurse's name, but her signature was so smudged that Victor couldn't read it. He wondered if someone had deliberately obscured the signature.

Exhausted, he leaned back in his chair and stretched. He didn't hear Judy come up behind him. When she touched his shoulder, Victor was so startled that he jumped.

'Are you all right?'

'My God, Judy, you scared me half to death.' He turned to the young clerk.

'Gee, I'm sorry. I thought maybe you'd like a sandwich or something. I'm going on my break.'

Victor checked his watch. It was nearly five o'clock. His plane was leaving at seven. 'No, thanks.'

'You know, you doctors work too hard. It's not healthy,' she commented on her way out, but Victor wasn't listening. Instead, he was staring at a chart entry that had caught his eye: '10:30 P.M., contractions still irregular, patient 2 centimeters dilated, chief resident Mark Van Patten advised.'

Van Patten . . . Victor was certain he'd heard that name before, but where? Then he remembered, Mark Van Patten had also been Mrs. Hill's doctor in Atlanta. Could the doctor somehow be involved in all this? Victor was too tired to think anymore. The more he discovered, the more confused he got.

Realizing that he would need to study the chart later when his head was clearer, Victor quickly carried the document to the copier in one corner of the record room. A few minutes later he slipped the copies into his pocket, shed the white coat, and ducked down the hall. Once outside the hospital, he reviewed his findings as he waited for a cab. The truth was that he was leaving with far more questions than answers.

Los Angeles
July 25, 1981
Saturday

A knock at the door startled Juanita as she lay sleeping on the sofa bed. Slowly she eased herself up, swaying slightly. Soft gray light filtered through the open window. It looked to be nearly dawn. Hands shaking, she looked through the peephole in the door. She was surprised to see Marie standing there, a black doctor's bag in her hand. Juanita quickly opened the door. 'Is something wrong?' she asked. 'I thought you were coming last night. I was so worried; I tried to call you.' From a nearby table she picked up the paper napkin on which Marie had written her telephone number.

Marie brushed past her, leaving the door wide open. 'Shut it.'

'What?'

'I said shut the door.'

Juanita watched in confused fascination as Marie put down her bag and closed the window.

302

'It's so hot. I wanted a little breeze . . . '

When Marie turned around, Juanita saw a strange look in her eyes — a look that somehow made her shiver in spite of the heat. Something *was* terribly wrong. It was then that she noticed the scalpel.

Juanita's scream died in her throat as the scalpel sliced it open. Her voice gurgled through the blood. For several seconds she struggled, her hands pulling at Marie's hair with almost superhuman strength.

But her efforts rapidly began to fail. Her eyes were wide, first with fear and then puzzlement. She didn't understand why Marie would want to kill her.

Marie had already dismissed the dead girl and was now concerned with the baby. Deftly, she thrust the tip of the scalpel into Juanita's belly and slid the blade all the way across her abdomen, separating the layers of skin until the entire peritoneal cavity was exposed. Then, slicing open the pregnant uterus, she jumped back to avoid the squirting liquid. Seconds later she removed a healthy-looking baby boy, howling with life.

'I told her it would be a boy.' She laughed quietly.

The child continued to scream.

'Shh, you don't want to give us away, do you?' she hissed, wrapping the dark-skinned infant in a blanket.

Halfway out of the apartment, Marie stopped, remembering the paper napkin with her phone number on it. She turned quickly and walked over to the dead girl.

'Damn, I'm getting careless.'

One by one, she pried Juanita's clenched fingers open and retrieved the only link to her identity in the apartment. Then, looking down at the mutilated body for the first time, she spotted Juanita's gold cross. 'There is no sanctuary from evil,' she murmured as she yanked it from her victim's throat. 'Don't you know that?'

23

July 26, 1981
Sunday

Anne dreamed she heard someone cry for help. She struggled out of the comforting void of sleep to find that no one was there. She opened her eyes and shook her head, feeling groggy and disoriented.

As her head began to clear, Anne realized it had been only a dream. But then why did she feel so afraid? What was out there to make her so scared?

Propping herself up on her elbows, she peered around the room. It was early morning, probably no later than six o'clock. Gray light seeped through the drapes, deepening the shadows. It was too dim for her to see the details of the furniture, but everything seemed familiar to her. As she continued to look around, the surrounding chaos jolted her memory back to reality. She had sort of known she was in her bedroom in her apartment, but it was almost unrecognizable after the destruction of the night before.

This was no dream. What in God's name

was happening? Anne hugged herself and shivered. Someone was after her; that had become overwhelmingly clear. She struggled against giving in to the terror that gripped her.

July 26, 1981
Sunday

Bleary-eyed and unshaven, Victor sat hunched over his kitchen table, sipping black coffee. He stared at his list of clues, trying to sort out what he knew. Three similar notes had been given to three women in three different cities. The first woman had given birth to a stillborn infant six years before; the other two women's babies had been stolen. EmmieLou had been murdered, and Victor still didn't know the identity of Amanda Hodson's night nurse or whether the nursing school yearbook had anything to do with EmmieLou's death. And now Victor had to add Dr. Mark Van Patten to the growing number of leads to be investigated and connected.

Somehow he had to fit all these fragments together. He blinked hard, trying to wake up. Damn, what did it all mean? He was trying to put the pieces of a puzzle together, but some just didn't seem to fit anywhere. Perhaps McFadden was right; he had one hell of an imagination and not one solid piece of evidence. Still, Victor's gut instinct told him his hunches so far had been correct.

He went over the facts again in his mind. First, Dr. Westbourne had said the kidnapper was probably a woman who desperately wanted babies. That was why she took Shannon Hill and Justine Evans. He also knew that both mothers had received notes, as had Amanda Hodson.

He opened his copies of Amanda Hodson's chart again, trying to find something to connect her with the other women. Several things still bothered him about the record. First, there was the fact that up until 5:00 A.M. everyone had seemed to expect a healthy 8½-pound baby. How, then, could she have given birth to a stillborn baby less than half that size? And why didn't the night nurse notify anyone when the baby was born? He reread the nurse's report: '4:00 A.M., patient having severe pain; medication administered.' Slowly, Victor thought of something that might explain everything. What if the night nurse had sedated Mrs. Hodson long enough to switch babies? The kidnapper wanted a baby so much, she might do anything — even replace a live baby with a dead fetus.

He shook his head in exhaustion. Larsen, you really have some imagination. Still, hadn't Dr. Westbourne said that *anything* was possible when dealing with insanity? This woman was not a normal person with normal motivations and behavior. No wonder he'd missed it. The answer had been there all along, right in the chart.

He ran his fingers through his hair, considering the implications of his new theory. It would be incredible if it was true, but it was also the only explanation that fit.

Leaning back in his chair, Victor realized that before he did anything else, he had to get some rest and clear his head. After a shower and some shut-eye, he'd track down Dr. Mark Van Patten, the one person, other than the kidnapper herself, who could confirm his suspicions.

July 26, 1981
Sunday Evening

Each evening around ten, Carmen Gonzales returned home after spending the day with her son Tony. She would arrive at the intensive care unit early, before the night nurses had left, and sit quietly at his bedside until long after visiting hours were over.

308

The doctors offered little hope for the boy's recovery, but she refused to give up. In fact, that very afternoon she was sure she had seen his eyes blink. It was a sign from God; she knew it.

Now, as she dragged herself up the stairs to her apartment, she wondered if she would ever stop being tired. Every muscle ached. And as if she didn't have enough weighing her down, Carmen's building was like a furnace, sweltering and airless.

At her door, she glanced down the dimly lit corridor. A nauseating stench filled the air. Someone must be piling up garbage, she thought. If they didn't get rid of it soon, it would attract more rats — just what they needed.

As she turned the key, a thought crossed her mind. The smell seemed to be coming from the apartment next door where that poor pregnant girl lived. Maybe she needed help. Should she go over and knock? No, it was too late. Besides, she had that friend — the woman with the blond hair who visited her almost every night. And Carmen didn't want to get involved in anything messy anyway. She had her share of trouble as it was.

Anne stood in front of Dr. Westbourne's desk.

'I understand that you're upset, Anne, but don't you think perhaps you're being a little hasty?'

'I'm sorry, Doctor. I . . . I'm just not suited to this kind of work.'

'On the contrary. I think you're a wonderful psychiatric nurse. You were really making progress with Janet Evans.'

'It doesn't matter now, does it?'

'That's just the point, my dear. Janet's accident had nothing to do with you. She was extremely depressed. It was just one of those tragic quirks of fate.'

Anne shook her head. 'If the door to the clinic had been locked . . . ' her voice faltered.

'It doesn't help to speculate now,' Olivia urged. 'You're doing very good work here, Anne. I'd like you to stay.'

'I can't, Doctor.'

'Please, Anne, don't make that decision right now. I'd like you to stay until the end of next week; see what you think then. Besides, it will take me at least that long to find a replacement for you.'

Anne nodded vaguely.

'Perhaps you'd like to skip today's session, since we're both upset by Janet's death. Let's meet again on Wednesday. Is that all right with you?'

'I guess so.'

'Good.'

Watching the nurse leave her office, Olivia Westbourne wondered if Janet Evans's death was the real reason for her decision to leave the Institute. Or was Anne afraid to reveal more about herself? Olivia would have liked to spend a little more of the afternoon considering Anne's case, but she had to meet with the hospital administrators to explain how a patient had managed to commit suicide right under everyone's nose.

24

July 28, 1981
Tuesday

Victor studied Mark Van Patten as he reached for the copies of Amanda Hodson's medical record. Once he had located the doctor in Los Angeles, it had taken him another two days to get an appointment. Van Patten was obviously a busy man.

'Where did you get these records, Mr. Larsen?' Although he had been trained in the South, the obstetrician's accent was distinctly north-eastern. Probably Boston, Victor guessed.

'From San Antonio General.'

'With the patient's permission?'

'No.'

'That's against the law, you know,' Van Patten said dryly.

'Yes, I know,' Victor replied, 'but it was a matter of life and death.'

The doctor wrinkled his brow. 'I'm afraid I don't understand.'

'A nurse in Atlanta was killed last week because she was going to identify someone whose name is in this chart.'

'Whoa. You've lost me already.'

'Maybe I'd better start at the beginning.' Victor took a deep breath and explained his investigation. 'For the past few weeks I've been tracking down the kidnapper of several infants.' Quickly he recounted how his search had led to Atlanta. He told how EmmieLou had recognized Mrs. Hill's note from the kidnapper and recalled a patient named Amanda Hodson who had received a similar note in San Antonio six years ago. 'EmmieLou was murdered before she could reveal the name of Amanda Hodson's nurse on the graveyard shift.'

'You're saying this mystery nurse is a kidnapper and possibly a murderer as well?' The doctor shook his head. 'You don't seem to have much to back that up.'

'I only said she *may* be the murderer,' Victor replied. 'If not, she might know something about the murderer.'

The doctor spoke impatiently. 'Look, I've really got a busy schedule today. What exactly do you want from me?'

Victor refused to be put off. He had already worked too hard. 'Do you remember this patient, Amanda Hodson?'

'That was six years ago. I've seen several thousand women since then.'

'I realize that, Doctor, but if you could just review the chart . . . '

Reluctantly, Van Patten thumbed through the record. 'All right. So this woman had a stillborn child, and the record shows that I was chief resident on the case, but I simply don't remember it. Stillbirths occur once in about eleven hundred births. That it happened in this instance is nothing to get terribly excited about.'

'But does anything seem unusual about this particular case, Doctor?'

'Unusual?'

'Out of the ordinary,' Victor suggested.

Again, Van Patten merely scanned the record. A second later, he shook his head. 'Everything seems perfectly routine.' He started to return the chart.

'What about the pathology report?' Victor persisted.

The doctor smirked indulgently. 'You *did* say you're a reporter and not a doctor?'

'Yes, but — '

'Well,' Van Patten cut him off, 'if you'll take a look at all these diplomas on the wall, you'll realize how long I trained to be able to tell you that everything looks routine.'

'I appreciate your expertise, Doctor. That's why I want your opinion,' Victor said in an effort to appease him.

Van Patten read the pathology report. His brow became furrowed in concentration.

'There must be some mistake,' he said finally.

'Mistake?' Victor prompted.

'This fetus had tissue autolysis; that means it must have been dead for two or three days. That's impossible.'

'I thought so, too,' Victor blurted. When Van Patten gave him another disapproving look, he added, 'I mean, that's not consistent with the intern's report of a normal fetal heart rate before delivery.'

Van Patten was pensive.

'Look at the mother's admission record,' Victor suggested. 'The intern estimated the birth at eight and a half pounds, but sixteen hours later she delivered a three-pound-thirteen-ounce stillborn infant.'

'Interns make mistakes. Especially when they're new. Remember, not long before this date, the guy was still a medical student. No, that's a plausible error in a huge teaching institution. It's the path report that interests me — the autolysis *and* the fact that the umbilical cord was cut, but no mention anywhere of a doctor being called.'

'That's another thing,' Victor interjected. 'The night nurse's note is awfully sketchy.'

'It's almost nonexistent,' Van Patten declared.

'Isn't that unusual?'

'Look, San Antonio General is a big place, as you know — more than two thousand beds. It's impossible to keep track of all the staff. Besides, my responsibilities as chief resident were to the physicians in training and the patients, not to the nurses.'

The telephone on Van Patten's desk rang.

'Yes, Mrs. Millstein, that kind of nausea is something you have to expect during pregnancy . . . '

While he talked, Victor looked around the room. It was a typical doctor's office: wooden shelves filled with medical books, an oak desk, an entire wall of certificates and diplomas behind the desk. Van Patten had spent many years studying, first at Harvard, and later at Johns Hopkins.

Victor's jaw dropped open as he read the names of the hospitals where the doctor had trained: San Antonio General, chief resident in Ob-Gyn, 1974 – 1975; Houston Memorial, research fellow Gyn oncology, 1978; Grady Memorial 1978 – 1981, staff physician. He hadn't been in L.A. very long, then, and each city where he had practiced was the scene of one of the kidnappings. Victor was now certain he was on the right track. He had only to confirm his suspicions.

The doctor was still reassuring his patient.

'Yes, Mrs. Millstein, I will. Good-bye.

'Her father's on the board of the hospital,' he told Victor, obviously embarrassed by the conversation.

'I understand. By the way, where were you from 1975 to 1978?'

'I beg your pardon?'

'Your diplomas.' Victor gestured toward the wall behind Van Patten. 'There's a three-year gap. I just wondered.'

'I had military obligations. I owed Uncle Sam time on what was called the Berry Plan — a deferment until I could complete my residency.'

'Three years is a long time to spend in the army.'

Van Patten shrugged. 'It wasn't too bad, really. I was stationed in Germany. Got to see a bit of the world.'

'Oh, so you were out of the country,' Victor said, as much to himself as to the doctor.

'Mr. Larsen, I have a clinic full of patients. Are you almost finished with your questions?'

'Just a couple more. Amanda Hodson was your patient, right?'

'Technically, yes. As chief resident I was responsible for every patient admitted to the ward.'

'So your name would have been on her identification bracelet, and anyone checking would assume that she was your patient?'

'Would you please get to the point?' Van Patten demanded.

'What would you say if I told you that I believe Mrs. Hodson did not deliver a stillborn child?'

'What do you mean?'

'That someone — I think probably the night nurse — switched Mrs. Hodson's live baby for a dead one. That would certainly explain the discrepancy in birth weights.'

'And exactly where did she get this dead baby?'

'From pathology. Didn't the report say the fetus probably had been dead several days? I'd guess the nurse was waiting for the right opportunity and the right patient.'

'The right patient? *What do you mean?*'

'*Your* patient.'

'*My* patient! I think you'd better explain.' Van Patten was clearly agitated now, the muscles in his chiseled jaw taut as he waited for Victor to go on.

'Laura Hill was your patient in Atlanta. So was Janet Evans when you were in Houston. I called her husband this weekend to check. Now we know Amanda Hodson was also under your care.'

'I told you I've had thousands of patients so far. I don't remember those women. You

318

say these women were patients of mine — okay. What's your point?'

'An infant was kidnapped from each of these women, and the only connection between them is you. Perhaps the person who took those children from your patients has something against you.'

Van Patten stared at Victor in amazement. 'I don't know what you're talking about. First, you come in here with a wild story about a nurse switching a live baby for a stillborn. Now, you're telling me that two women in Houston and Atlanta had their babies kidnapped and that somehow I'm responsible.'

'I didn't say you were responsible. I told you I haven't figured it all out yet, but somehow I think you are important to the kidnapper.'

'I won't give your theory credence by even discussing it further. I think you ought to leave. Now.'

Victor got up. 'Thank you for your help, Dr. Van Patten. I didn't mean to make you angry.' He left as the obstetrician received a second call.

'Yes, Mrs. Millstein. No, that's okay, you're not disturbing me . . . '

On the way out, the receptionist called after Victor, 'Mr. Larsen?'

319

'Yes.'

'There's a telephone call for you.' She held up the receiver on her desk. 'You can take it here, if you won't be too long.'

'Thanks.' He took the phone from her. 'Victor?'

'Yes, Sy. What's up?'

'The *Trib* said I'd find you there. Vic, there's been a murder down on Alvarado. They discovered the body this morning. It's horrible.'

'I don't get it. Why are you calling me?'

'I owe you a story, remember? I thought you'd be interested because it was so bizarre.'

'Who was killed?'

'Her name was Juanita Hernandez. She was the pregnant woman who lived next door to Carmen Gonzalez. We saw her a few times, but we never talked to her.'

'Oh, yeah, I remember. That's too bad.' Victor wasn't really listening; he had his own puzzle to solve. Then he heard Goldblatt say something about the baby.

'What did you just say?' Victor asked.

'I said, the killer cut her belly open and removed her baby.'

That got Victor's full attention. 'What happened to the baby? Where is it now?'

'That's what's so crazy. It's missing. Not a

trace. No one heard or saw anything. No witnesses, *nada*.'

'Was there a note?'

Goldblatt was silent for a moment. 'Yes. How did you know?'

Victor held his breath. 'What did it say?'

' 'Hand for hand,' in red lipstick no less. Bizarre, isn't it?'

Victor was eager to get moving. 'Sy, stay where you are. I'll be there in twenty minutes.'

'But — '

Victor rushed back to Van Patten and caught him as he was about to enter an examining room. 'Juanita Hernandez. Were you her doctor?'

'What the hell's going on? I thought I told you to leave.' He started to walk away.

'Juanita Hernandez — young, Mexican, and very pregnant. Were you taking care of her? It's important.'

Van Patten turned around. 'The name doesn't sound familiar, but then I told you I don't remember all my patients.' He disappeared inside the room, closing the door behind him.

'Mr. Larsen?' the receptionist called.

'Yes?'

'I remember her.' The receptionist apparently had a better memory for names than

321

Van Patten did. 'She was a clinic patient of Dr. Van Patten's. After a couple of visits we found out she didn't have insurance. I told her to straighten it out with the office and make another appointment, but she never did.'

'She's dead,' Victor said bluntly.

'Oh, my God.' The receptionist was shocked. 'What happened?'

'She was murdered.'

'Jesus, that's awful.'

'Yeah,' Victor replied curtly. He didn't really want to hang around and discuss the case now. 'I've got to go. Look, thanks. And thanks for the use of the phone, too.' He hurried down the corridor toward the exit.

Marie stepped out of the nurses' station and watched him leave the clinic.

'Hey, who was that good-looking guy?' Stacy asked, joining her.

Marie shrugged. 'How should I know?'

July 28, 1981
Tuesday

By the time Victor reached Alvarado Street, a crowd had gathered outside Juanita's building, and the police had cordoned off the area. He flashed his press pass, edged through the

322

crowd, and took the elevator to the fourth floor. Two uniformed police officers watched the entrance while anxious tenants lurked behind the half-opened doors of their own apartments.

Goldblatt was waiting in front of apartment 401, looking grim. 'Victor, prepare yourself. There's a lot of blood and it's been there awhile.'

Victor shrugged. 'I'll be all right. I'm getting used to it.'

Goldblatt didn't understand, but he followed his friend inside without asking any questions. The stench, which had been nauseating in the hallway, overwhelmed them once they entered the tiny apartment. It was the thin, acrid, cloying smell of something rotting.

In the back of the dingy efficiency, two evidence technicians were busy talking, obstructing any view of the victim. 'Could have been dead for a couple of days or as little as a few hours. It's so hot in here that the tissue is breaking down too fast for us to estimate the time of death accurately.'

Victor approached them, his stomach turning over.

One of the homicide men recognized a sergeant from the local precinct as he walked in the door. 'Hi, Sarge.'

'Hollace,' the sergeant greeted him, 'what's the story?'

'Very weird, Sam. This is gonna be a ball buster. There are no prints and no sign of forced entry. The killer probably wore gloves. There was also a note written in lipstick. The lab has it, but they say they can't use it for a handwriting analysis. And look at the stiff.'

The sergeant walked over to the sofa bed and lifted the sheet off the body.

'Nasty way to go,' the tech noted unnecessarily.

'Uh-huh. What did the note say?'

'Just three words: 'Hand for hand.' What the hell do you s'pose that means?'

The sergeant shrugged, his expression blank. 'Damned if I know. Who found her?'

'Neighbor finally called. She must have noticed the smell.'

'She see anything?'

'Nothin'.'

'Hmm.'

Victor, who had been listening to the conversation from a distance, took a step forward to get a look at Juanita. As soon as he saw her, he gasped. The corpse was grotesque; it was barely recognizable as a human female. Death had turned the body of the young pregnant girl into a swollen

324

monster. She lay on her back, her throat slit from ear to ear.

Only now did Victor notice the rest of her. His knees buckled, and he felt slightly dizzy. A gaping incision split her abdomen, leaving her insides exposed.

'Steady, my friend.' Goldblatt put one arm around Victor's shoulder.

'According to the neighbor, the girl was pregnant,' the tech said. 'The whole thing is pretty weird. This was no ordinary murderer, Sarge.'

'You're right, Hollace. But this is a gang neighborhood. The 'hand for hand' thing is probably some kind of warning. This could be some sort of retribution killing.'

'Or a cesarean section.' Victor spoke almost to himself.

'What did you say?' The sergeant was frowning. He'd had a rough day, and he didn't need any more complications.

'Maybe the killer was trying to deliver the baby,' Victor suggested.

'Oh, really?' The policeman's sarcastic tone made Victor think of McFadden. 'Must be some new kind of obstetric technique: cutting the mother's throat first.' The homicide technicians laughed, enjoying the chief's joke.

'But if she was pregnant,' Victor persisted, 'then where is the baby?'

'How the hell should I know? We're dealing with a wacko; that baby could be anywhere.' The sergeant threw Victor a cold stare, waiting for a challenge that never came. Victor had decided to keep quiet — at least for the moment. 'I wouldn't be surprised if we find the little bugger wrapped up in some newspaper and thrown out in the trash like yesterday's stew meat,' the sergeant said.

Goldblatt was angered and revolted at the thought of disposing of a baby in such a way. He turned to his friend. 'Let's get out of here. I think we've both seen enough.'

Victor nodded.

Two white-coated attendants carrying a stretcher passed them as they left the apartment.

'Please let me know if you come up with any new theories,' the sergeant called after him, chuckling.

In the hallway, Goldblatt asked rhetorically, 'Horrible, isn't it?'

Victor didn't answer, but kept walking stiffly down the hall.

'What kind of monster would do something like that?' the lawyer asked.

Victor stopped looking at him speculatively for a moment. 'Someone who wants babies.'

'What?'

'Someone wanted Juanita's baby, Sy. That's

why she was killed.'

'You're not serious, are you?'

Victor was trying to put it all together in his mind. 'Did you see her face?'

'Yeah.'

'Even in death she looked surprised, almost as though she knew her killer.' Just like EmmieLou, he thought. And the note, the note was the clincher.

'What are you talking about?' Goldblatt wanted to know.

Ignoring the question, Victor asked, 'Who was the neighbor?'

'What?'

'The neighbor who called the police.'

'Oh. Carmen Gonzalez. You know, Tony's mother.'

'Let's go talk to her,' Victor suggested.

'What about? The cop said she didn't see anything.'

'That's what she told them, but I want to ask her a few questions. She might know something that could help.'

Victor knocked on her door before Sy could protest further. There was no answer. 'She's got to be home.'

'Let me try,' Goldblatt offered. 'Señora Gonzalez, *por favor, somos amigos.*'

A few seconds later, Mrs. Gonzalez tentatively opened her door, but just a crack.

After eyeing Victor and Goldblatt through the chain lock, she smiled gratefully. '*Buenos dias*, Señor Goldblatt. I'm sorry. I was afraid . . . '

'It's okay. We understand. You remember Señor Larsen?'

'Of course.' She beamed at Victor. 'You know my Tony is doing much better.'

Victor returned the smile. 'Yes, I heard. I'm so glad. Mrs. Gonzalez, I know you called the police today . . . '

The Hispanic woman's face clouded over. 'I don't know nothing. Honest. I told the police.'

'You know that your neighbor was killed,' Victor said.

'*Si*. A terrible thing. She was a very nice young girl. Never bothered nobody. And the poor baby, too.'

'Did she live with anyone?'

'No. All alone.'

'Did anyone come to visit her?'

'There was one woman who came almost every night.'

'What did she look like?'

'Yellow hair, lots of lipstick.' Then she added, 'Pretty, though, with nice clothes.'

Something about Carmen Gonzalez's description seemed familiar to Victor, as though he'd seen this woman. It was like

328

glimpsing a fish below the surface of a dark pond. The harder he tried to see it, the more the vision seemed to elude him. But then it came to him: He'd seen her the day of the fire. Victor could see them now just as they'd been when the photographer had snapped their picture. The young Mexican girl, plain and pregnant, had been walking with a tall, blond woman. That must have been Juanita's friend, the woman he was looking for. He could barely control his excitement.

'Do you know her name?' he asked.

'I'm sorry. She never told me.'

Impulsively, he leaned over and gave Carmen a kiss. 'It doesn't matter. You've already helped more than you know.'

Mrs. Gonzalez smiled in embarrassment. 'I'm glad.'

Goldblatt stayed at Victor's heels as he hurried out of the tenement to his car. 'What's this all about?'

'I'm not sure yet, Sy, but as soon as I know, I'll let you in on the whole thing. I promise.' He stepped into his MG, leaving the lawyer standing on the curb, mystified.

Driving away, Victor smiled to himself, certain he was only a step away from cracking the case. If the picture of Juanita and her friend was still in the newspaper file room, he'd finally have evidence even the police would have to believe.

He checked his watch. It was after five. The *Trib* photographer would be gone. He'd never be able to find the picture by himself.

Well, Victor thought, I've waited this long, I guess I'll just have to wait another twelve hours. First thing in the morning he'd have his answer; he hoped that would be good enough.

July 28, 1981
Tuesday Evening

Anne answered the doorbell, her face pale and drawn.

'I was just looking for you at the Institute when I heard about Mrs. Evans. I'm sorry.' Victor stood outside waiting to be invited in, but Anne said nothing. 'I, uh, forgot you don't work on Tuesday,' he added.

'No.' She pulled her terry-cloth robe closer.

Victor noticed that her eyes were red and glistening. 'It's cold out here,' he joked. The temperature was in the nineties. 'You wouldn't want me to catch a chill, would you?'

Anne didn't return his smile. Her reply was only a whisper. 'I'm very tired, Victor.'

She looked so alone, so weary and sad. He

wanted to comfort her but wasn't sure how to do it. 'Hey, I didn't mean to tease. I know you're upset. It's just that . . . '

'That what?'

He shrugged. 'I don't know. You're afraid of letting go, of being hurt, I guess.' His violet eyes tried to draw her in, but she averted her gaze. Moving closer until they were nearly touching, he gently lifted up her chin. She looked back with sad eyes. 'Please Anne, let me love you.'

She was startled and confused. 'I — ' She started to speak, but he cut her off firmly.

'Come here,' he whispered, stepping into her apartment and closing the door. He drew her to him and enfolded her in his arms, cautiously, aware of her reticence. She leaned against him, crying softly. He pulled her closer, noticing the soft, fresh scent of her hair and at the same time planting tiny kisses first on her cool forehead, then on her pink earlobes, then on her smooth cheeks, and finally he tasted the sweet softness of her lips.

'Don't be afraid.' He took her hand and led her into the darkened bedroom. Bending over her, he kissed her again, this time with a searching passion.

Anne responded in spite of herself, frightened by the intensity of her desire, but

331

not wanting him to stop.

'I *am* afraid,' she whispered.

'It's all right. I won't hurt you.' Victor lifted her and placed her tenderly on the bed.

'Victor . . . '

'Shhh.' He brushed her lips, her nose, her cheeks, lazily following the contours of her face. 'You won't need these,' he said, pulling off her glasses, then kissing her closed eyelids. For a long time, he simply held her close, sensing her tense uncertainty. Gradually, her breathing relaxed. He loosened the sash on her robe, tentatively moving his hand over her smooth skin until he cupped one naked breast.

Anne shuddered at the newness of his touch. *Please, Mama, I'm so afraid . . .* The pain between her temples became blinding. *I'll be good, Mama . . .*

Slowly, Victor continued his exploration. 'Hmmm,' he murmured appreciatively, savoring her soft curves. Lingering over her abdomen, he noticed a white scar. Tenderly, he kissed it.

Anne stiffened at his caress. At the same time, the pain began to pierce her skull. *Don't let him hurt me. Please, Mama . . .*

Victor placed his hand gently between her thighs.

'Get away!' she suddenly screamed, pulling

332

back. 'You're just like all the others. You only want to use me.'

Victor was stunned. Anne was shrieking, her voice unfamiliar, shrill. He could only make out part of what she screamed. The change in her was so sudden that it caught him off balance; for the moment he was too confused to think clearly.

'You bastard!' she yelled.

Victor didn't understand what was happening. He reached over and switched on the light. Anne's glasses lay between them. He picked them up and before she could protest, placed them gently on her face. 'I'm sorry, Anne. I thought you wanted it, too.'

Anne looked at him blankly, in a kind of daze, her emotional outburst spent. 'It's no good,' she said with such despair in her voice that Victor wondered what had happened to her to cause such hopelessness. She turned away from him, burying her face in the pillow.

Then the sobbing started, quietly at first, then becoming louder.

'Anne.' He put a hand on her shoulder and pulled her toward him. Tears streaming down her face, she collapsed against him, holding on tightly. Warm tears fell on his chest. He held her close, stroking her hair. It was a long time before her crying ceased.

25

July 29, 1981
Wednesday
5:45 A.M.

Victor awoke before six the next morning after a restless night. He felt curiously unfulfilled, and not simply because they hadn't made love. That was only a very small part of it. No, it was Anne's inability to drop her mask of cool detachment for more than a few moments. Even while he held her last night, he could sense her separateness, as though she were afraid. What was she afraid of, damn it?

He had known Anne only a few weeks, but already their relationship was complicated. He'd wanted to spend the night, to be there to comfort her, but she had insisted that he leave. Hours after returning to his apartment, he had tossed and turned, reliving the evening.

Now, despite the early hour, he decided to call her. He wanted to hear her voice, to talk to her, to make sure she was all right. He wanted to break through the barrier she had

334

built around herself. Whoever said it was more painful to love than to be loved was no fool. He laughed ruefully.

Her phone rang seven times. Annoyed, he hung up and dialed again. Just like last weekend. She had said she was home, but he had not been able to reach her. He let it ring eight times, and still there was no answer.

Frustrated, he hung up and walked into the kitchen to make a cup of coffee. He tried to think of something else, but the image of her tear-stained face kept coming back to him. Where could she be? He knew it was too early for her to have left for work.

Then he was struck with another, more reasonable thought. Maybe she just didn't want to talk to him. Well, if she didn't want to answer her phone, that was her choice. He might as well read the paper and prepare himself for the day ahead.

Passing the telephone he couldn't help himself. He dialed Anne's number once again. This time, though, he gave up after only three rings. Shit.

July 29, 1981
Wednesday
6:30 A.M.

Anne woke up screaming. She'd had the dream again, and this time she remembered all of it.

Oh, Mama, I don't want to remember.

She got out of bed and moved around the room in a kind of daze. Her head ached; the pain burned between her temples, a fiery poker piercing her skull.

You beat me, Mama. I didn't know it was a sin. I wanted to be good like you . . . I was only playing under the house where I was safe . . . But you got sick, and Luke took me away. He said he wanted me . . . Oh, Mama, no! Why did you let him touch me? It hurt so much . . .

Anne suddenly stopped and looked into the mirror. She was aware of another presence in the room. She could see her — there in the mirror. It didn't matter now. She was too tired to run anymore. Besides, where could she hide? The woman always found her, wherever she ran. She had run to L.A. to get away from her, to be safe. But she realized now that there was no safety anywhere, only the temptation to try to find it.

336

Anne didn't care now. There would be no more running. The other woman was here now and that was that. She laughed at her — blond and red-lipped like a grotesque clown. *Mama says you're vain.*

The phone rang.

'Too late, Anne,' the woman said. 'It's too late. I told you to forget everything, but you insisted on dredging up the past, helping that reporter with important clues. You shouldn't have done that, you know.' The woman's voice was laced with angry laughter. 'I got you that job at the Institute to find out if Janet Evans had really seen me the night I took her kid. Who told you to get so friendly? It's your fault I had to kill her. Good thing I keep an eye on you or we'd have been caught a long time ago.'

The phone continued to ring. 'Don't answer that. Now hurry up. We've got another baby to deliver.'

July 29, 1981
Wednesday
7:00 A.M.

'Here they are, Larsen. The shots I took the night of the fire.' The Trib photographer dropped a stack of photos on Victor's desk.

'Thanks.'

'Mind if I ask you a question?'

'Sure.'

'Are you starting an album? Victor Larsen, local hero? I've heard of big egos, but *really*,' he chided.

'I'm trying to find someone. A woman. I think you got a picture of her that night.'

The photographer grinned. 'A woman. Well, lucky you! Anyone I know?'

'Do you remember a blonde in a short dress?'

'Can't say that I do, but if I got her picture that night, it should be there. I'm a terrible hoarder. Can't throw anything out.'

He left Victor to sift through the pile. One by one the young reporter looked at them, reliving the night of the fire — Angela smiling shyly into the camera, holding her grandfather's hand; the building engulfed in flames; tenants crying over lost possessions.

He was almost through the stack when he felt a tap on his shoulder. 'Call for you on line three.'

'Who is it?'

'How should I know? I'm not your goddamned secretary.'

'Thanks.'

'Don't mention it.'

He picked up the phone while studying the

last few pictures. 'Victor Larsen here.'

'Mr. Larsen, this is Stacy Gardner. You don't know me. I'm a nurse at L.A.U.'

'Yes?' Victor wasn't sure what the young woman wanted, but he felt the excitement of new possibilities, new leads.

'I just read the morning paper. About the pregnant woman who was killed on Alvarado Street. She was a patient at the Ob-Gyn clinic.'

'I already know that.' His soaring hopes were quickly dashed.

'But I know why she never returned to the clinic.'

'She didn't have medical insurance. The clerk told me.' Victor was getting impatient.

'No. One of our nurses took care of her at home.'

'I don't understand.'

Stacy repeated the conversation she had overheard between Marie and Juanita. 'The nurse told the pregnant girl not to come back to the clinic, that she would visit her at her apartment.'

'Is that common practice?'

Stacy laughed at the absurdity of the thought. 'House calls? By nurses? You must be kidding. It's never done, at least not since I've been working in obstetrics.'

As he listened, something caught Victor's

eye. He lifted the picture from the pile. *There it was.* Even in black and white he recognized them — the blond woman, her arm around the pregnant Mexican girl. The expression on the nurse's face was odd. It was not really a startled look. No, there was an icy fury in those eyes.

'Tell me, is this nurse a blonde?'

'Yes, she is.'

Victor breathed deeply. 'What's her name?'

'Marie Fontaine.'

Finally he had her name. He couldn't believe it. He had something definite, some cold, hard facts. 'Miss Gardner, I'd like you to identify a picture. I think it may be Marie Fontaine. Could we meet somewhere?'

'I'm on my way to work. Why don't I stop by your office? If it won't take too long, that is.'

'That'd be fine, and I won't keep you long. We're on Santa Monica Boulevard.'

'I know. It's not far from my apartment. I'll be there in about fifteen minutes.'

'Fine.'

As soon as he hung up, Victor placed a call to the San Antonio General Nursing School.

'Mrs. Holloway, registrar, speaking.'

'Yes, ma'am. I'm calling from Los Angeles; I'm a reporter for the *L.A. Trib.* I wonder if you could check your records from the class of 1975. I'm looking for a Marie Fontaine.'

'Hold on a moment, young man. I'll check it for you.'

Holding the line, Victor stared at the picture.

'Yes, I have the class list right here,' the registrar said a few minutes later. 'Class of 1975. What did you say the girl's name was?'

'Marie Fontaine,' he told her. Then he spelled the surname slowly into the phone.

'Are you sure of the last name?'

'Pretty sure. Why?'

'I'm afraid there's no such person in this class.'

'Did you try Fountaine or Fontan?'

'I'm looking at all the names, Mr. Larsen. There's no one with a name even close. Perhaps Fontaine is her married name, or perhaps she was in another class.'

Victor asked the registrar several more questions, but she couldn't find a Marie Fontaine in any of her records. After exhausting all of the possibilities, he thanked her and hung up, disappointed. Why wasn't Marie Fontaine listed in the school records? Had she changed her name? Victor rubbed his eyes. For a moment he'd thought he had the puzzle licked. But one large piece was still missing. Maybe Stacy Gardner could help him find it.

July 29, 1981
Wednesday
7:30 A.M.

The first contraction caught Glynnis as she scraped the rest of last night's uneaten dinner from the plate. She swayed for a moment, then relaxed.

'Hey, kid, you're packing a mean punch today,' she spoke to her belly.

The next contraction came about five minutes later as she hung up the dish towel. That one lasted longer, and the room seemed to turn slowly. She clung to the edge of the sink, but her legs buckled and she slid to the floor. When she tried to stand, she noticed a stain, faintly pink, where she had been sitting.

Oh, God, what was happening? She watched the pink turn to a bright red puddle and spread across the floor.

It's too early, she thought. Marie had said she was in the home stretch, but surely she hadn't meant that it could come this soon. No, Glynnis was sure it *was* too early.

But the pains were coming close together, and then there was the blood. Something was wrong. A dull ache pressed across her back, taking her breath away.

Maybe it wasn't time. Maybe this didn't mean anything. Maybe if she lay very still, not

342

moving, the contractions would stop.

Slowly, crawling on her hands and knees, she reached the couch in the living room. A cold sweat soaked her body. Lying there, she tried to think. If only she could make it to the phone and call Marie to help her. But she just didn't have the strength.

Glynnis raised her head far enough off the pillow to read the tiny clock on the mantel. It was only 7:30 A.M. Marie probably wouldn't arrive before six that night. She started to cry silent tears. Please, God, don't let anything happen to this baby. Don't get born yet, kid. Please don't get born yet.

With each new contraction, her strength ebbed, and she panted, trying not to push. She knew she had to hold on for a while longer, but she had already lost a lot of blood and was quickly slipping away.

As she drifted into semi-consciousness, the baby dropped low inside her, ready to be born.

July 29, 1981
Wednesday
7:32 A.M.

'Mr. Larsen?'

Stacy found Victor hunched over his desk,

343

nursing a cup of coffee, lost in thought.

'Yes. Miss Gardner?' Even in his present frame of mind, he could appreciate the young nurse's good looks. She had copper-colored hair, bright green eyes with almost invisible lashes, and a pert, freckled nose that gave her an elfin look.

'How about some coffee?' he offered. 'It's not very good, but it'll wake you up.'

'No thanks,' she politely declined. 'I'm late for work already.' Accepting his invitation to sit down in a chair beside his desk, she said, 'I hope I did the right thing by calling you instead of the police.'

'I'm glad you did.'

'You see, there's a chance that I'm wrong about Marie. I mean, I saw her with Juanita, but I'm not really sure she committed any crime, and I don't want to get her in trouble if I'm wrong.'

Victor took the picture from the pile on his desk. 'First, tell me if this is the person we're talking about.'

Stacy studied the photo for no more than a second before making a positive identification. 'That's Marie, and that's Juanita Hernandez with her.'

'Have you known Marie Fontaine long?'

Stacy shook her head. 'Only a few weeks; I met her the day she started. She only works part-time, Tuesdays and Thursdays.'

'Do you know where she's from?'

'Umm. Her last job was in Atlanta, I think.'

That would make sense, Victor thought. Shannon Hill was kidnapped in Atlanta.

'She told me she worked in Texas a few years ago, in delivery.'

He wondered if she had worked in Houston or San Antonio or both. If Marie Fontaine had been in all three cities, she could very possibly be the kidnapper. He started to ask a question, but Stacy Gardner began to talk.

'You know, Miss Baxter thinks the sun rises and sets on Marie. The woman can do no wrong. I mean — well, it's true she's a good nurse,' Stacy conceded, 'but, personally, I never liked the type who think they know everything. They're always showing off to the doctors. I realize a nurse isn't supposed to be a doctor's handmaiden anymore, but I don't think we're really qualified to do the doctor's job, either.'

Victor tried not to show his impatience as Stacy continued to ramble. He wished she'd get to the point, but he knew from experience that a reporter could sometimes learn a great deal simply by letting people talk themselves out. When she had worn herself down, he would have an opportunity to ask more questions.

Stacy looked at the picture again. 'The newspaper article said Juanita was killed with a sharp knife,' she said.

'Hmm.'

'I saw Marie with Dr. Van Patten's scalpel. It was in her locker.'

'Tell me exactly what you saw, Stacy, please.' Victor held his breath.

'Marie had a scalpel,' she repeated. 'She didn't know I was watching, and she took it from her locker and just stared at it. It was really weird.' Anticipating his next question, she said, 'I peeked into her locker last night. The scalpel was gone, but I did find this.' She handed Victor a crumpled paper napkin.

'It's a necklace,' Victor murmured as he unwrapped Juanita's gold cross. 'Does this belong to Marie Fontaine?'

'I doubt it. Marie told me once that she has no use for religion. She thinks it's a waste of time.'

Victor looked at the paper napkin the cross had been wrapped in; there was a number written on it. He examined the paper more closely. There, scribbled in red lipstick, was Anne's telephone number.

Alarm shot through him as the full implication of the note hit him. Marie must have started following him when she learned he was investigating the kidnappings. She'd followed him to Atlanta, and she'd killed EmmieLou after he talked with her. Later, she had seen him with Anne and was following her, too.

Anne was in trouble, and he had to get to her right away. Interrupting Stacy in midsentence, he jumped up and extended his hand. 'Miss Gardner, thanks very much. You've been a great help. I'll be in touch with you soon.'

Stacy stood up and straightened her white uniform. 'Well, I hope I did the right thing.'

'Oh, you did. Listen, I've got to run. Can I walk you out?'

Stacy smiled. 'Sure, thanks. A girl can't be too careful these days.'

July 29, 1981
Wednesday
7:45 A.M.

Victor parked in front of Anne's building and sprinted out of the MG, arriving breathless at her door. He knocked twice, but there was no answer. He turned the knob, and the door swung partly open. That was strange; finding the door unlocked once was understandable, but twice was more than a coincidence. His

347

heart thudded anxiously, and he hesitated for a second before pushing the door open.

The darkness struck him as soon as he entered. In one of her rare open moments, Anne had confided her fear of the dark. That was why she always kept the drapes open, day and night. He knew something was definitely wrong as he walked into the apartment and surveyed the scene. Everything seemed to be in order, unlike the other night. Anne had obviously cleaned up the mess.

Cautiously, he tiptoed into her bedroom, afraid of what he might find. There was no sign of her, and Victor breathed a sigh of relief.

Returning to the living room, he sat down on the sofa and tried to pull his thoughts together. He glanced down at the table beside the couch. The ashtray, normally empty, was piled high with butts. He knew Anne didn't smoke and wondered where they'd come from. Then he noticed they were imprinted with bright red lipstick.

He'd better call the police. Reaching for the telephone, however, his hand stopped in midair. The wire had been sliced through. As he bent over to examine the severed phone wire, his foot touched something. He fumbled with the light switch for a moment, finally turned on the lamp, and peered down to see what his foot had touched. It was a book. Across the cover in big block letters it read: San Antonio General Nursing School, 1975. It was EmmieLou Madison's yearbook! A piece of paper was folded and tucked inside, as if to mark a page.

He opened the book to that page, and all he could see was blood, spattered across the entire page. Victor shuddered. It was as though the earth had stopped and time had been frozen. Staring at the page, his mind was a series of chaotic, jumbled images. No, no . . . it can't be, he kept thinking, shouting to himself. This was all some terrible mistake.

26

July 29, 1981
Wednesday
8:30 A.M.

'Glynnis, open up.'

Half-conscious, Glynnis pulled herself up from the couch. 'Marie, is that you?' Another contraction almost took her breath away.

'Open up.'

'I'm . . . coming.' With the last bit of strength she possessed, Glynnis dragged herself to the door and turned the knob. 'Marie, thank goodness. I — the baby . . . I think it's coming,' she panted. 'The pains are two minutes apart now,' she gasped, lying back down.

Marie slammed the door shut and followed Glynnis to the couch. 'You're in labor. Why didn't you call me?' she snapped. 'I told you I'd help you.'

'Tried . . . No answer,' the girl gasped as another contraction grabbed her. 'It's getting worse.' Her face was chalk white from loss of blood. 'It hurts so much.'

'Well, I guess we'll just have to make a

350

slight change in plans, won't we?'

Glynnis watched, uncomprehending, as Marie dug into her black bag. When she turned around again, she was wearing surgical gloves. 'Lie back with your legs spread apart,' she ordered, pulling down the girl's underpants.

'What are you doing?'

'Examining you. Now lie down and relax.' Expertly, Marie inserted her index finger into Glynnis's vagina, trying to locate her cervix.

Glynnis cried out in pain at the height of another contraction.

'You're almost fully dilated.'

'It hurts so much!' Glynnis tried to grab Marie, her face twisted in agony.

'Shut up, you stupid bitch!' Marie snarled. 'I haven't got all day. Push!'

July 29, 1981
Wednesday
8:50 A.M.

After leaving Anne's apartment, Victor headed straight for L.A.U. He knew he would have to call in the police eventually, but he wanted to talk to Dr. Westbourne first. He was also hoping against hope that she knew

351

something that would implicate someone other than Anne.

He parked in front of the main entrance of the Institute and charged up to Dr. Westbourne's office. His hair was tangled, and his face was pale and unshaven. 'Dr. Westbourne, you've got to help, please,' he said breathlessly. 'It's Anne . . . She's — she's the — oh, God.'

Olivia Westbourne came forward, put an arm around Victor, and led him to a nearby chair. 'Sit down,' she said gently. 'Now, take a minute to calm yourself and catch your breath. Then you can tell me what this is all about.'

'It's Anne,' he repeated as soon as he was able to speak again. '*She's* the kidnapper.' He handed her the open year-book and pointed to the name beneath a photograph in the right-hand corner of the page: Anne-Marie Fontaine Midlands. 'Our kidnapper has a face now,' Victor sighed. His words brought a terrible aching pain. It was the sharp ache of loss.

Dr. Westbourne shook her head in stunned disbelief. 'I knew Anne was disturbed, but I had no idea it was anything like this.'

Victor looked at her in confusion.

The doctor explained. 'I've been seeing Anne a few times a week for her migraines.

We were just beginning to make some headway into her emotional problems. In addition to that, I received this letter from the psychiatric hospital in Laredo.'

'Her letter of reference,' Victor said, remembering the night Anne had found it on the floor of her apartment. 'I mailed the request.'

'But this isn't a letter of reference. It's her medical record. Anne was a patient there.'

Tension had been building in Victor, but upon hearing this final indictment, the tension dissipated. He could deny her involvement no longer, and the realization of that fact brought with it a feeling of relief. 'I don't really understand any of this, Doctor. Can you explain it to me? Please.'

Olivia looked at him sympathetically. 'Are you involved with Anne?'

'I thought I loved her, but she never let me get really close to her. She seemed . . . I don't know . . . afraid of something.'

'She was probably afraid you would discover who she really is.'

'Who *is* she?'

Dr. Westbourne sipped her coffee, studying the yearbook picture. 'After reading her medical report and now seeing this, I believe Anne is a victim of what is commonly termed the multiple personality syndrome. I've seen only one other case.'

After a long, stricken silence, Victor turned to the doctor. 'You mean like the woman in *The Three Faces of Eve*? Or like *Sybil*?'

'Precisely.'

'How? It doesn't seem possible.'

'Apparently she has been living at least two separate lives — as Anne Midlands and as Marie Fontaine.'

Victor found himself still more incredulous. 'Let me get this straight.' He shook his head. The pieces were just beginning to tumble together. 'Are you saying that the two personalities — Anne and Marie — are separate and unknown to each other?'

Dr. Westbourne sighed. 'Possibly. Multiple personalities are separate parts of the same person. The syndrome is very rare, but in some cases, one personality does know of the existence of the other.'

'Do you think Anne knows about Marie?' He couldn't bear to listen, and yet he had to know.

'I don't think Anne is aware of Marie, at least not on a conscious level. Often in this syndrome there is a devil-angel rivalry among various personalities. I think Marie Fontaine is the dark side of Anne Midlands. Marie probably exists only part of the time, and she may have been struggling all along to gain

354

total control by suppressing Anne entirely. That's probably why Anne has been having *such* severe headaches recently.'

'I still don't get it. You mean part of the time she's Anne Midlands, and part of the time she's Marie Fontaine? Wouldn't her friends figure it out?'

'You said yourself that Anne is very aloof. When she works at the Institute, she is Anne Midlands, soft-spoken and reserved. She seems to avoid making contacts.'

Victor shook his head. 'I just talked to an obstetrics nurse named Stacy Gardner. She told me that Marie Fontaine works part-time in the Ob-Gyn clinic. Tuesdays and Thursdays, I think. Anne works here all week, so they couldn't be the same person.'

'Anne was only here on Mondays, Wednesdays, and Fridays.'

Victor was grasping at straws now. He said, 'Anne can't stand cigarette smoke, yet I found cigarette butts in her apartment.'

'That's quite plausible,' Olivia explained. 'There have been several cases where one personality had an aversion that the other lacked.'

A sense of despair filled Victor. 'I suppose the cheap perfume I smelled in Anne's apartment the other night belonged to Marie?'

'Very possibly. The different personalities sometimes dress differently, speak differently, even speak different languages entirely.'

'But why would someone like Anne develop multiple personalities?'

Olivia spoke frankly. 'Ordinarily, I would never break a patient's confidence. But since you obviously care for Anne, I suppose I ought to help you to better understand her. She had an extremely traumatic childhood.'

'She told me her father died,' Victor commented.

'Her real father killed himself when she was born. Apparently, he couldn't make a living on his ranch in the desert.'

'His name must have been Fontaine,' Victor surmised.

The psychiatrist nodded. 'Anne's mother, Lucinda, blamed the child for her husband's death. Anne still carries that guilt. Lucinda survived by working at a roadside café near the ranch. The years when she lived as a young widow were very hard. She turned to her Baptist fundamentalist background for solace, becoming obsessed with the notion of sin. Whenever Anne misbehaved, Lucinda severely punished her. She beat the child unmercifully for the ordinary playfulness of a small child. She also locked Anne in the closet and submerged her in cold water.'

Victor cringed. 'That's horrible.'

'To Anne, at five years old, this was impossible to understand. Her mother called her a sinner, but Anne didn't really know why. She was terrorized into obedience, constantly trying to please Lucinda, but Lucinda was apparently schizophrenic and had no consistent idea of how she wanted Anne to behave. When her mother was finally hospitalized, Anne lived alone with Luke Midlands.'

'Her stepfather?'

'Yes. Luke also mistreated Anne, but in a different way.' Olivia hesitated.

'Please, Doctor, you don't have to spare me at this point.'

'Luke raped his stepdaughter.'

'Oh, my God. No wonder . . . '

'No wonder, what?'

'Anne and I . . . we . . . '

'You slept together?'

'Not really. Anne was afraid. She wouldn't let me make love to her, and I didn't understand why.'

'There's more to her sad story, I'm afraid.'

'I want to know everything, especially if it means I'll be more able to help her.'

'Her stepfather was an alcoholic. He used to bring his friends home to drink. When they were through with the bottle, they often took turns with Anne.'

'You mean they slept with her?' Victor was shocked, remembering how Anne had shunned his touch. 'How could she let them?'

Dr. Westbourne's look was piercing. 'Those men were a rotten lot. She was barely thirteen and living alone with that beast of a stepfather. She had no choice. There was nothing she could have done. They simply raped her.'

Victor regretted his outburst. 'I'm sorry, Doctor. I'm just upset.'

Upset for yourself, the psychiatrist thought bitterly. What about that poor girl? 'Years later Anne became quite sick.'

'What do you mean?'

'She developed chronic pelvic infections. Eventually, she had a hysterectomy.'

'Of course. That's what the scar was from.'

'I suspect that knowing she could never have babies of her own triggered or at least contributed to the emergence of her two distinct personalities. The split first began to develop while she was a nursing student at San Antonio General. According to her medical report, she was discharged from the Laredo psychiatric hospital in June 1975, in time to graduate with her class.'

'Just a few weeks before Amanda Hodson lost her baby,' Victor murmured.

'That's right. I think Anne desperately wanted children, but was incapable of kidnapping them. Marie gradually evolved and was able to steal the babies for her. Eventually she began to want complete control, as I said before.'

Victor recognized the irony even as he let the words sink in. The bizarre circle was closing. Until that moment, he had hoped Dr. Westbourne could explain away what he'd discovered. He had hoped to absolve Anne of these acts — the stolen babies, EmmieLou's murder, Juanita's murder. And she had probably killed Janet Evans as well; her death looked less and less like an accident.

Those were monstrous acts. Yet the Anne Midlands he knew was no monster. But Marie Fontaine was a different matter entirely. In a sense, Dr. Westbourne had vindicated Anne, the girl he loved. She was hardly responsible for any of this; Marie had committed the crimes. He couldn't bear to think that Anne and Marie resided in the same body, yet he could think of nothing else.

He had only to fit one last piece of the puzzle into place. Victor sat quietly for a few minutes, sipping his coffee. Finally, in a voice just above a whisper, he asked, 'Dr. Mark Van Patten performed the hysterectomy on Anne, didn't he?'

'How did you know?'

Victor shrugged, exhausted. 'Just a hunch. I talked with him yesterday.' Victor told her what he had learned in San Antonio. 'The medical record indicates that the stillborn infant was clearly not Amanda Hodson's baby. Anne — or rather Marie — somehow substituted a dead fetus for the Hodson baby. After I talked with Van Patten, things began to make sense to me. It seemed so bizarre at first, until I recalled what you said the other day.'

'What was that?'

'You explained that the need to have babies was the essence of the delusion. I was expecting another baby kidnapping, like the Evans and Hill cases. I didn't realize that the *way* Marie got the babies was not important. The link between the kidnappings was that all the mothers were patients of Dr. Van Patten.'

Olivia leaned forward. 'My God.'

'She followed Van Patten from city to city as he completed his medical training, and she stalked his patients.'

The psychiatrist interjected, 'In her own twisted way, Marie was trying to punish the gynecologist for leaving her incapable of ever having her own babies.'

'You certainly have helped me put everything together, Doctor.'

'I'm afraid I was very slow on this one. Perhaps I let my personal feelings for Anne interfere with my professional judgment. I seem to have missed a number of clues along the way.'

'We're both guilty of that.'

'I suppose so,' the psychiatrist agreed.

'I still don't understand why Marie didn't focus her hostility on the gynecologist himself.'

'You wonder why didn't she kill *him*?' Olivia asked pointedly.

'Yes.'

Dr. Westbourne sighed. 'The human mind is a strange and fascinating mystery. If you ever look at the naked brain, without the protective case of the skull, you would see its convolutions, like a meandering river, taking twists and turns here and there, following an unknown course. In the same way, the thoughts that travel those pathways may become twisted and confused. When you deal with the mind, you learn that nothing is very straightforward. That's what makes psychiatry so interesting and also so frustrating. For years, Anne probably tried to deal with complex feelings — for her mother, and father, her stepfather, and then Dr. Van Patten. At some point, her circuits probably became so overloaded that she could no longer handle these feelings in a normal way. Marie finally appeared to take up the slack, a new personality able to express all the pent-up hostility. As long as Anne had some control, there was never any real danger of violence. EmmieLou's murder suggests that Marie is now taking control. With her capacity for violence, she could also be responsible for Janet Evans's death, although we'll never know.'

'There's been another killing.'

Olivia paled. 'When?'

'Sometime last weekend.' Quickly, Victor told her about Juanita. 'Her baby is still missing. The police think it's probably dead. Naturally, I don't agree.' He spoke in dull tones, feeling emotionally drained. 'What can we do now?'

'I'll have Anne paged right now. I hope she'll agree to be hospitalized here. Then I'm afraid we'll have to notify the police.'

Victor nodded miserably.

Olivia dialed the operator. While she waited on the line, Victor looked at the crumpled paper that had been stuck between the pages of the yearbook.

'Operator, this is Dr. Westbourne. Will you please page Anne Midlands for me? Thank you.'

Hanging up, Olivia heard Victor cry out,

'Oh, my God.' His eyes were wide with disbelief. 'Look at this.'

Trembling, he handed her the paper. 'It's from the Bible, Deuteronomy, chapter 21, verse 24. Look at it, Doctor. Next to each phrase she wrote a name, an address, and a date.'

The psychiatrist studied the list carefully: 'Life for life — Amanda Hodson, July 14, 1975. Eye for eye — Janet Evans, July 24, 1978. Tooth for tooth — Laura Hill, June 28, 1981. Hand for hand — Juanita Hernandez, July 25, 1981. Foot for foot — Glynnis McCombie, July 29, 1981.'

Victor's voice cut in on her thoughts. 'That last date, Doctor — July twenty-ninth! That's today!'

The phone rang before Olivia could reply. She recognized the voice of Mrs. Milsap.

'I heard you paging Anne Midlands.'

'Yes.' Olivia was impatient. She wanted to keep the line clear.

'I thought you should know that Miss Midlands called in sick today. Or rather, her friend called in for her.'

'Her friend?'

'The woman only gave her first name. She sounded very nice. A real deep southern accent. You know, like Scarlett O'Hara.'

The psychiatrist was in no mood for a

friendly chat. 'Her name, Mrs. Milsap, what was it?'

'Marie.'

Olivia thanked her and replaced the receiver. She bit her lip in frustration, overwhelmed by a sense of helplessness.

'What is it, Doctor?'

'She's not here. Marie called in sick for her. She said that Anne was sick.'

Victor was frantic. 'We've got to find her. Before she hurts this Glynnis McCombie, that last name on that paper. She's Marie's next victim. We need that girl's address. We've got to get to her before it's too late.'

Olivia looked at Victor, her hazel eyes a blend of sadness and resignation. 'If it's not too late already.'

July 29, 1981
Wednesday
9:30 A.M.

'I said push!' Marie yelled.

Damp wisps of dark hair lay plastered against Glynnis's forehead. She panted with each new contraction. 'I can't.'

'You sure as hell can!'

Glynnis looked up to see Marie hovering over her. The strange look in Marie's icy eyes

364

terrified her. 'When are you going to call the hospital?'

Marie ignored the question. Instead, she went to the radio and turned it on full blast. A satisfied smile caressed her reddened lips. 'You can scream as loud as you like now, honey,' she purred.

July 29, 1981
Wednesday
9:35 A.M.

The slow pace was torture.

The drive downtown had taken Victor longer than usual. A summer drizzle had made the road so slick that the cars had to inch carefully from one congested street to another. The lazy, rhythmic sweep of the windshield wipers mocked the urgency of the situation. Victor beat his fist on the steering wheel impatiently as Dr. Westbourne looked helplessly at the snarls of traffic, trying to find a clearer route.

A jagged bolt of lightning flashed across the cloudy sky, followed almost instantaneously by the firecracker snap of thunder. Startled, Victor slammed his foot on the brake. Skidding on the slick surface, the MG swerved out of control, nearly spinning into

365

oncoming traffic. Quickly, Victor pulled back into his lane, then over to the curb.

'You okay?' he asked as the MG came to a full stop.

'Remind me to take the bus next time.' The psychiatrist managed a thin smile, though she was obviously shaken.

Victor got out of the car and looked at the street ahead. Traffic was backed up for several blocks.

'Damn it!' he cursed. 'We could be tied up here for hours.'

Olivia stuck her head out the window. 'We don't have time to sit here. Let's walk; it's only a couple of blocks.'

They abandoned the car, and Victor hurried down the street, the psychiatrist close at his heels.

As they neared Vermont Avenue, the rain began to fall harder. They quickened their pace. Victor glanced at Olivia. Her hair was plastered like a cap against her ears, its wet sleekness accentuating the roundness of her face. She was breathing heavily, trying to keep up with him.

'I'm okay,' she shouted, motioning him on.

At last, the apartment building loomed into view.

July 29, 1981
Wednesday
9:45 A.M.

Glynnis watched anxiously as Marie grabbed her right arm, rolled up the sleeve of her dress, and thrust the tip of the needle into her vein.

'Marie, what are you doing? Oh, don't, please ... '

It was too late. Glynnis's scream froze in her throat the instant the golden liquid entered her bloodstream. Her eyelids became heavy. In spite of her efforts, she couldn't fight the fog that rolled over her, pulling her under, into a vast nothingness.

July 29, 1981
Wednesday
9:46 A.M.

Breathless, Victor and Olivia climbed the stairs to the sixth floor of the building. They stopped in the hallway, their hearts racing furiously. 'Which apartment?' Olivia asked.

'Six-twelve.'

At the end of the darkened corridor, Victor motioned Olivia to one side of the door. He strained his ears to catch any possible sound, but he could only hear the music blasting from inside. Victor turned the knob and pushed the door open cautiously.

Stepping inside, he stopped short, horrified. The sight that confronted him was one he would never forget. Victor reeled backward and almost collided with Dr. Westbourne.

Blood was everywhere. Glynnis McCombie lay on the couch, her eyes closed, her face pale, almost devoid of life. Her legs were spread-eagled. Suddenly her huge bare abdomen quivered convulsively. Victor's eyes widened as he saw her entire pelvic area bulge. A reddish-pink liquid squirted from her vagina at the height of each contraction before running down her thighs to the floor.

A tall, blond woman, drenched in blood, bent over her, holding a scalpel in midair.

'No, Marie, don't!' Dr. Westbourne ordered.

The woman turned, staring strangely, almost wildly at them. 'You,' she screamed at Victor, 'it's your fault. You with your love shit. Because of you she turned against me. Me! I'm the one who gave her the babies she wanted. Not you!'

Victor gazed at her, incredulous. This was Marie Fontaine? He couldn't believe that this creature was also Anne Midlands. It wasn't just the blond hair — that was probably a wig

— or the exaggerated makeup — that could be washed off. It was her eyes. There was no trace of Anne's gentleness; he saw only madness blazing in those grayish blue eyes.

'Victor, grab Marie. Glynnis is crowning. The baby's coming!' Dr. Westbourne snapped.

A tiny black head appeared between Glynnis's legs, then rapidly receded. Startled, Victor grabbed Marie and pulled her away from the pregnant girl, wrenching the scalpel from her hand. He set the knife on a table and tightened his grip on Marie Fontaine. The woman in his arms was a complete stranger to him.

'Hey, you're hurting me,' she shrieked, struggling to break free of Victor's grasp.

Olivia tended to Glynnis, who was in active labor despite her deeply tranquilized state. Wishing she'd had more obstetrical training, she rolled up her sleeves and examined her patient.

Inserting two fingers into the girl's vagina, she spread the labia to ease the baby's passage. Beads of perspiration covered her forehead. After several tense moments, the head reappeared, sliding out into her hands, twisting sideways. Gently, she freed first one shoulder and then the other, until a tiny, pink-skinned male infant emerged.

'It's a boy.' Lifting the baby, she gave it the traditional smack on the buttocks, producing a spontaneous lusty squall. Then she milked the blood from the umbilical cord before severing the thick rope with a slash of the scalpel. Glynnis, still unresponsive as a result of Marie's injection, lay spread-eagled in a puddle of amniotic fluid, blood, and urine. The doctor carefully placed the infant on his mother's abdomen while she tried to deliver the placenta. Without Glynnis's cooperation, it would be difficult to coax the uterus into discharging the afterbirth.

Victor watched wide-eyed, still holding Marie, who had now become surprisingly quiet. As the placenta spurted forth, Olivia jumped back. Reflexively, Victor leaned over to help, easing his grip on Marie.

Quickly, Marie darted away. She ran over to Glynnis and grabbed the baby by the legs. 'If you want it back,' she hissed, breathing hard, 'come and get it. You'd better hurry.'

Dr. Westbourne and Victor were stunned. Marie glowered triumphantly, filled with a sense of power. She felt like laughing, like screaming, like dancing madly. Being in control of the situation was intoxicating. She raised the baby over her head. 'Come and get it,' she taunted, backing slowly toward the open window.

Victor's heart was in his throat. The distance to Marie was no more than fifteen feet. If only he could get a little closer, he could grab the child. He took an almost imperceptible step forward, but Marie saw him and climbed out on the window ledge. Somehow she managed to maintain her balance and still hold the baby.

'I'm too smart for all of you,' she mocked, obviously pleased with herself.

The psychiatrist realized that Marie was capable of anything while she was in this crazed state. Both she and the baby were in jeopardy. Olivia knew what she had to do; she had to try to coax Anne to appear. Maybe she could reason with her.

'Marie,' the doctor said calmly, 'I'm Dr. Westbourne. I'm Anne's friend.' She paused. Marie said nothing. 'I'd like to help you, too.'

Wild-eyed, Marie hissed, 'Any friend of that bitch is no friend of mine.'

The psychiatrist continued as though Marie had not spoken. 'I want to talk to Anne. Can you hear me, Anne?'

Marie's face was contorted into an ugly grimace. 'It's too late, Doctor. Anne's gone for good; she won't ever be back.'

'Anne, just listen to the sound of my voice. Remember how easily you relaxed in my office? I'm going to count slowly. When I get to ten, you'll be in a deep sleep.' The psychiatrist began to count in a slow, deliberate cadence, 'One . . . two . . . '

'No!' Marie screamed. 'I won't let her come out.'

'Five . . . six . . . '

Sweat poured down Marie's face. Electrified by the sound of Dr. Westbourne's voice, she stiffened, then jerked almost convulsively. Victor watched in awe. Finally, after several seconds, Marie's limbs relaxed, her eyelids closed, the pulse in her neck slowed perceptibly, and her breathing became more regular.

'Can you hear me, Anne?'

Don't let her in, the other voice warned. *She wants to come in. Keep her out, Anne. Hold on.*

Dr. Westbourne's voice softly carried her back through time. She was sitting in the psychiatrist's office, waiting for her interview. It was going to be all right.

'Yes, I can hear you,' she whispered.

'I want to talk to you, Anne. Okay?'

Marie opened her eyes. They had lost their icy cast, and even without the glasses, she was obviously Anne. The transformation was incredible. Victor wanted to rush to her, comfort her, but Olivia waved him back.

'Where am I?' Anne whimpered. She saw

372

the baby in her arms, and great sobs began to rack her body.

Victor watched, bewildered. Was it possible that Anne didn't know what was happening?

Closing her eyes, Anne winced as she put one hand to her temple, pressing hard. 'My head . . . everything is mixed up inside my head.'

'Will you talk with me, Anne?' the doctor asked again.

She nodded slowly. Her voice softened to a whisper, and a strange, blank look came into her eyes. Olivia worried that she might lose her balance on the ledge and fall; there was no time to lose.

A siren wailed a few blocks away. Someone must have called the fire department or an ambulance.

'Look at the baby, Anne. That's your baby. The one you've always wanted.'

'*My* baby?'

'Yes.'

Anne looked confused. 'But I can't have babies. The doctor cut me open. He said I could never have my own babies.'

'No, Anne. That was a dream. That *is* your baby. You don't want him to get sick out there, do you?'

Rain beat against the building furiously. Anne's face felt cold and wet as water caught in her eyebrows and lashes. She pressed herself against the brick wall. The baby wailed. 'My baby?' She ignored the curious glances from the people who had gathered on the sidewalk below.

'Yes,' the psychiatrist insisted. 'Now I want you to give him to Victor. Then we'll help you come inside where it's nice and warm.'

'No, no. Don't! Please stop.' Anne felt someone inside her head, fighting her.

'Give the baby to Victor, Anne.'

Olivia's voice sounded muffled, distant, as though it were reaching her through a kind of fog.

'I can't . . . She won't let me.'

'Yes, you can. Just hand the baby to Victor. He's right there.'

The psychiatrist motioned Victor over to the window. Anne looked at him, her expression a mixture of sadness and pain. Carefully, she placed the crying infant into Victor's outstretched arms.

Olivia took a deep breath. 'All right now, Anne. I want you to take my hand. I'm going to help you climb back inside.'

Turning her head toward the doctor's voice, Anne glimpsed her image reflected in the window. It was Marie in that window, staring back at her with that taunting smile.

'They tricked you.' Marie laughed. 'That's

not really your baby.'

'It is. Dr. Westbourne said so.' Anne addressed the reflection.

'She lied to you. They all lied to you. Including lover boy over there. Don't you remember what the Gypsy said? Life is an illusion; we see what we want to see.'

Anne stared intently at her reflection. Suddenly she recognized everything. Everything she had tried to push back into the recesses of her mind, all the memories Dr. Westbourne had begun to dredge up came rushing at her.

It was Marie. She had switched Amanda Hodson's baby for a dead one; she had sneaked into Janet Evans's home and taken her daughter; she had lifted Laura Hill's sleeping infant from the carriage in the park. She had murdered EmmieLou and Juanita and she had pushed Janet Evans down the stairs. Marie had even taken Juanita's baby, and now she wanted Glynnis's child. She would have killed that poor girl if they hadn't come. This illusion in the window was her tormentor. She had always been there with her, and now finally she wanted to kill Anne. A part of Anne's mind now knew this with utter clarity.

This fear weakened Anne's legs as she leaned against the ledge, lightheaded, her knees shaking. Rain blurred her vision, and she began to sway.

She knew it *all* now. Marie was poison. *She* was poison. 'No,' she said aloud, 'I won't let you take over.'

But it was too late. Neither of them could escape. Marie had only one choice now . . .

Victor stood mesmerized, watching in disbelief as Anne's body fell through space, landing with a thud, like a bag of wet sand, on the pavement six floors below. It had happened so quickly that he still had the hazy notion it was all an illusion.

Epilogue

July 29, 1984
Sunday
Somewhere near Laredo, Texas

The scorching sun beat down on the barren hills. Occasionally, a hot, dry wind swept down, blowing dust across hundreds of miles of brown, baked earth, and scattering clumps of sage and tumbleweed. Otherwise, the torpid air was still.

Under the house where the three-year-old child hid, it was cooler. She was too young to remember that her real name was Shannon Hill and that her six-year-old sister was once called Justine Evans.

She heard her sister's anguished pleas, 'No, Mama, not the closet. I'll be good . . . Don't make me.' She hated the broom closet behind the kitchen, too. It was dark and scary.

The other children started to cry. If they didn't stop, she knew they would be punished. After they'd been here awhile, they'd understand. 'Shh.' She willed them to silence.

A moment later, the back door swung

377

open. Mama had come out on the porch; the wood floor was creaking under her weight.

'Where are you, child? I know you're out there.' Lucinda Midlands scanned the horizon.

Footsteps approached, making crunching sounds on the crisp, dry earth as they came closer. A hand reached under the porch, snatching at empty space. The child crawled all the way back against the house, curling herself into a tiny ball, out of the woman's reach.

'The wickedness of the wicked will be upon himself.'

Mama's angry face appeared under the porch. Her eyes were tiny blue-gray chips of ice. 'Aha, I found you, you evil child. You must be punished.'

She screamed, the sound echoing off the distant hills. 'No, Mama. Please . . .'